BEAUTIFUL JAIL

Beautiful Jail

Janet H. Wolfe

Onion River Press
89 Church Street
Burlington, VT 05401
info@onionriverpress.com
www.onionriverpress.com

ISBN: 978-1-957184-95-1 Paperback
ISBN: 978-1-957184-96-8 eBook

Library of Congress Control Number: 2024924522

To my mother for her unwavering
love and support.

I want to be saved.
Saved from this beautiful jail.
Saved from this feeling that weighs heavy
        on my chest.
Saved from the nausea I push down anticipating
        another day of worry, fear and doubt.
I await my knight in shining armor
That emerges within me.

PROLOGUE

Curt Anderson was fuming. He didn't sign up for this, and he wasn't going back in there. He would let her rot in that chair. The last thing he wanted to do was to get stuck taking care of some invalid. She was supposed to take care of him. All the money in the world was not enough for this. He knew exactly what he needed to do.

There was a bit of chill in the air so he slipped on his coat while he walked along the edge of the canal. He pulled out his phone from his coat pocket and dialed her number. No answer. She was probably just ignoring him but he would not give up. He would leave a voice message knowing she could never resist his accent. Thinking perhaps a text might get faster results, he began typing: *Please Diana, pick up the phone. It's urgent.* He decided to call one more time and pressed dial again. Oddly enough, he heard the phone ring behind him getting progressively louder. He turned to see who was coming and quickly broke out into what had become his several million-dollar smile.

"Oh darling, it's you! I can't believe it!" He moved to embrace her. "I've made a terrible mistake."

"Fuck you, Curt!"

She pushed him with all her might, just enough to send him over the edge. His arms flailed as he fell backward, and his body contorted to try and catch himself but all he managed to do was bring himself closer to the concrete bulkhead. He took the brunt of the blow with his head and had a moment to realize the pain before he hit the water. Sinking deeper into the blackness, the current began to pull him under. His arms reached for the top, grasping for a chance to surface, for one more breath, but he didn't have the strength. The water streamed through his fingers and pushed him further down. The fight left his body, and any evidence of movement had ceased.

She turned to see an old man at the adjacent marina waving his arms, shouting "Hey, what's going on there?" He raised his cane to try and shake some action from her, but all he received in return was a spiteful smirk as she raised her hands and shrugged, then turned again to run back along the canal. The old man quickly limped back to his booth that overlooked the marina parking lot. Whipping off his "Disabled Veteran" cap, he picked up the phone in the booth.

"South Benton 9-1-1, what's your emergency?"

"Yeah, hi Darlene. This is Walt down at the marina."

"Oh hey, Walt. You alright? You sound like you're out of breath."

"Yeah, yeah, fine. So, listen, I just saw some broad push a guy into the canal, and it doesn't look like he's gettin' out anytime soon."

"Oh really, Walt? That doesn't sound good. I'll send the EMTs and a squad car right over. Just sit tight, Walt, okay?"

"Yup. I ain't goin' nowhere." He hung up the phone, put his cap back on, and checked to make sure the security cameras were all working before he left the booth.

The squad car showed up first. Detective Tom Kennedy and Officer Suarez pulled up to where they knew they would find Walt.

He was standing on the sidewalk, leaning on his cane, trying to catch his breath.

"Hey Walt, what's going on? Darlene said you saw something unusual." Kennedy walked up with his right hand resting near his holster. He had the rugged look of a Western cowboy with a stance ready to shoot, but his tattooed forearm told a softer story. Large angel wings spread across his muscular forearm, and the name of his daughter was proudly displayed across his bicep.

"Yeah, I did. I saw some gal push a guy into the canal. She looked pretty angry, and then she just took off." Walt wiped the sweat from his brow.

"Okay, can you tell us where it happened?" Detective Kennedy was suspicious of Walt, as he was pretty old and was known to be a heavy drinker. Walt had been telling people he was sober of late, but Kennedy knew not to trust the claims of an alcoholic.

He slowly lifted his cane up to point it down the canal. "Yeah, you see where that bench is about halfway down?" He lowered his cane to move into his standing position. "It was just beyond that. The guy was just walkin' along, and I think talkin' on his cell phone, when she came running up."

"I'm surprised you can see that far, Walt." Kennedy chuckled and gave Suarez a sideways glance to see if he got the softly-delivered joke.

"I just got new glasses, guys. I can see just fine."

"Okay, Walt. We'll check it out."

Although he jested, Kennedy had to take Walt seriously. Even though he was old, Walt had been faithfully watching the marina for years and had given them a few tips on things that didn't look right to him. If nothing else, Walt had good intuition; he was a decorated war hero after all. Kennedy figured this guy probably just climbed up the marina ladder and out of the canal.

Kennedy called over his shoulder to Walt, who was slowly following them. "Did you see the guy climb out, Walt?" He flashed his light around the ladder landing to look for wet footprints. Nothing.

"No, sir," Walt returned with conviction as he tried to measure his breath from the long walk.

"Was it right about here, Walt, where you saw him go in?" Kennedy shouted.

Yes, sir, that's the spot. She gave him a real good push, and then just stood there watching."

"What time was this, Walt?"

"It was 7:20 PM. I know because I had just finished heatin' up the mac and cheese the wife made me and marked the time on the microwave. I was just trying to figure out how much more time I had on my shift."

They were starting to lose daylight quickly. Kennedy pointed the beam of light into the water and caught something floating on the surface near the piling—it was a man's cap.

"Hey Suarez, make yourself useful and get something to fish that cap out." Suarez headed off towards the boats to borrow someone's boat hook. There wasn't anyone around since it was a Saturday night and most people went out for the happy-hour specials.

Kennedy looked along the sidewalk and flashed his light across two sets of partial footprints made by some red substance. It wasn't blood, but it was definitely something that had recently dried to the surface. He put on a pair of latex gloves and wiped his fingers across the surface then brought them to his nose. That was odd.

Suarez came back with the cap attached to the end of the boat hook. He handed it to Kennedy, who took it to put in a plastic bag. The cap was a lavender blue with an emblem of the local golf course on it; it looked pretty worn.

"Suarez, step back." He didn't want anyone messing up a potential crime scene if, in fact, this was one. Walt had finally caught up with them, so he repeated his warning as he took photos of the footprints and grabbed a sample of whatever had made the prints. He would have to get the lab to confirm his hypothesis.

"So, Walt, can you tell me anything more about what you saw?"

"Like what?"

"Like, what did they look like?"

"She had long blonde hair; I remember that. He had a baseball cap on, but that's all I noticed."

"What color was the cap, Walt?"

"Not sure. Maybe blue? Kinda blue, anyway."

"Like this one?" Kennedy held up the bag that contained the wet cap.

"Yeah, just like that one."

"Thanks, Walt, you've been great. I'll let you know if we have any more questions. We may want you to come to the station to file a report. Are you going to be home?"

"Yeah, you know me, I'm either here or there. I'll probably hang around awhile to see how it goes, anyway. If that's okay with you, Detective."

"It's okay, Walt. I'll just have to ask you to stay out of the way. There may be some divers coming in to see if we can find anything. We're going to be taping off the area soon."

He took his phone out of his belt to contact the desk sergeant. "Hey Sarge, how quickly can you get a few divers out to the marina?"

"I don't know, Tom. It's dinner time. How important is it?"

"It's urgent."

"Okay, give me a half hour."
"Thanks, man."

PART ONE

1

The floor was cold, but she wasn't going to sit on the bed. It was filthy and smelled of urine. Shivering and huddled in the corner, she held her knees bent to her chest in the yoga position she had often used to relax her back. The irony made her head spin—the countless times she had taken this position for relief on the safety of her mat in the peaceful studio in the woods. Rocking back and forth to comfort herself, she repeated her personal mantra: *I will take care of you. Everything will be alright. Don't worry.*

She jumped at the hard clank that reverberated down the hallway. Someone was coming. As the heavy footsteps got closer, she wondered, *Are they coming for her?* Closing her eyes, she hugged her knees tighter to her chest. *Just breathe - in, one, two, three; out, one, two, three.* The anxiety welled up again, and she thought she might be sick. *How am I going to get out of here?*

She opened her eyes, and it took a moment to register the cell door opening. She quickly stood up and fought back the urge to run through it. Her exit, however, would be blocked.

"Stand back from the door, ma'am." The female cop eye-balled her as if she was some hardened criminal. *As if, I'm gonna rush the door.*

Behind the cop, was a disheveled woman who would soon be Diana's cellmate. "Yeah, you don't wanna come near me. I'm dangerous," her new cellmate scoffed, expelling the scent of cheap whiskey from across the room.

"Keep quiet." The cop spun her around to remove the cuffs.

"Hey, be careful. You're hurtin' me."

"Oh, please forgive me," the cop said sarcastically. "By all means, make yourself comfortable." The cop waved her hand towards the filthy bed with a smirk.

"Thanks a lot." Cellmate plopped down on the urine-coated mattress and rubbed her wrists.

Diana hid her look of disgust from the thought of touching the stained mattress let alone sitting on it... *ugh.*

"What's your problem?" Cellmate jerked her head up, setting her pale, jiggling jowl in motion like a flounder just pulled from the water.

"No problem," stated Diana in a forced but even tone.

"Well, mind your own business then." Cellmate threw her body back, clashing with the suffering springs voicing their protest.

Sitting back down, Diana put her head in her hands. *Can this get any worse?* She briefly fell asleep in the corner leaning against the cell wall. The concrete felt cool to her skin as she tried to stir herself awake. She opened her eyes with that fuzzy thought: *Where am I?* Then reality set in. Slowly lifting her head to take in the scene, Diana observed her new roommate from across the cell strewn across the mattress in a snoring sleep; the type of snoring that is impossible for someone else to sleep through. This woman had obviously been to some type of party. A purple boa, the kind you would pick up at the party store, was draped around her neck, and a tiara announcing "Birthday Bitch" teetered on the mass of curly brown hair currently matted to the drool running down her reddened cheek. For some reason, she reminded her of Janis Joplin. Maybe it was the slightly-flared purple jeans she had on or the flower-child shirt to match them. It could be her drunken state, or perhaps it was the way she was taking up space like she didn't give a crap what anyone thought; she was going to do her thing. Diana decided to call her Janis until further notice.

Janis stirred and let out a loud, obnoxious yawn. She drew her hand across her mouth to wipe the drool that was caking down her chin. Sitting up and leaning on her hands, she began coughing and openly spewing last night's toxins across the room. Diana cringed and bowed her head to form some protective measure against the onslaught.

"What's your problem?" Janis was not letting up.

"I told you. I have no problem." Diana let out an impatient sigh.

"Then stop lookin' at me, bitch."

Diana sat up in a posture of readiness and thought it was best not to entertain this one.

"What, you some uppity bitch?"

"No!" Diana let it slip out in a gut reaction. She was not a snob; she never wanted anyone to think that. She regretted it as soon as she said it; Janis had baited her and was just waiting for some reaction. Diana didn't know how long she was going to be locked up with Janis, and there didn't seem to be anyone keeping an eye on them. "I'm sorry, did you have a bad night? Was it your birthday? Happy birthday, by the way."

"Bitch, you don't know me. Why you askin' me this shit?"

"Sorry," said Diana. Again, she cringed as soon as she said it. This was not coming from a position of strength; she was being too submissive. She decided to return to sitting in silence.

"Yeah, that's right. I do the talkin' here. I ask the questions." Janis got up and walked over to stand over Diana. She gave her a little kick. "Why you sittin' on the floor like that? Is that some Buddha shit?"

A switch flipped. Diana jumped up—she could get up from a sitting position in one quick motion—and rose up to her full height to tower over Janis, who was precariously balanced on purple platform heels. Diana moved into the defensive position she had learned in kickboxing, fists ready, mirroring the Robert DeNiro character from Taxi Driver. "Are you talking to me?" Tired of living in fear, Diana stood in her strength and stared Janis down. Their faces were inches apart. Diana swooned from the smell of Janis' breath, who thankfully started laughing.

"Alright, I'm just messin' with you." Janis moved away, laughing and shaking her head, to sit back down on the bed. "Alright, Kung Fu, you alright. You don't take no shit," she snorted. "So, why you in here anyway?" Janis held her head to coddle the throbbing and looked at Diana sideways. "I'm gonna guess you weren't giving BJs in the parking lot. Wait, hmmm, let's see, buying drugs, maybe, for you and your little friends?"

"I'm just in here for questioning," mumbled Diana. "They said my ex was found dead."

"Oh, I see. Interesting." Janis gave Diana a suspicious glance. "You don't seem to be that broken up about it."

"I—I don't believe it's true." Diana raised her head and looked to the ceiling to ward off tears. "This has to be some kind of mistake."

"Maybe it is, maybe it isn't, but whatever it is, what I wanna know is where were you when it happened, huh?" Janis chuckled as she mimicked her best detective voice.

* * *

Only hours earlier, Diana had returned home from one last trip to her family's beach house before it would change hands. It was bittersweet to say good-bye to the place. She loved it there despite its cruel reminder of when her life had been blown up by Curt. Those were painful memories, the power of which she fought hard to rid. She promised herself that one day she would find her own beach house and fulfill the dream she would not give up despite it all.

Not long after she pulled into the driveway, Diana got a call from her girlfriend asking her if she wanted to have dinner in SoBo that night and followed with, "And maybe we could go to one of the clubs afterward for some dancing." Even though she was tired, Diana was all in; she never turned down an opportunity to dance.

They had a blast and stayed out a little too late, actually closing the bar, or more accurately, the dance floor. It didn't matter; Diana had pushed the wrong button and purchased 24 hours of parking time. Since she wasn't drinking, she didn't have to worry about driving, so off she went, calculating how long the dog had been left without the bathroom. Diana arrived home to let a very excited Nutmeg out, who was extremely efficient at that time of night and just as anxious to settle back in. Diana dropped into bed without even brushing her teeth or washing her face; she just stripped out of her clothes and went right in. *Ah! There are some wonderful things about being alone—owning the bed is definitely one of them.* Given his heavy snoring, sweating, twitching, and tossing, rudely-interrupted sleep with Curt had been a way of life that she was happy to lose.

She wasn't asleep very long when there was a heavy thumping on the front door. It startled both Diana and Nutmeg awake. Looking at the clock through blurry eyes, it read 5:33 AM. *Who in the heck is at the door at this hour?* She pushed herself out of bed and grabbed her robe. She looked through the window and saw two cops standing at the front door. Panic rose to the surface as the pace of her heart quickened. She took a deep breath and opened the door.

Two uniformed officers stood at the doorway, one much younger than the other. In fact, the young one was rather cute, Diana quickly thought, and then she laughingly scolded herself: *No, Diana, no more young guys.* Actually, the older one wasn't so bad either with his rugged looks and a tattooed arm.

"Good morning, officers. Is everything alright?" Diana stepped aside to let them in the entryway, but they stayed on the front porch.

The older policeman spoke first. He had a calming voice and a nice manner about him, Diana thought, *kind of sexy in a cowboy sort of way.*

"Are you Diana Wall?" he asked.

"Yes, I'm Diana."

"I'm Detective Kennedy, and this is Officer Suarez."

The young cop looked up at the older one, silently asking permission to speak. The older one gave him a quick nod.

"Ms. Wall, we would like you to come down to the station with us."

With a furrowed brow and a quizzical look, Diana stepped back. "Why? What's going on? Is my daughter alright?" Possible scenarios quickly ran through her head.

"Your ex-husband Curt Anderson is missing, ma'am. The captain would like to talk to you down at the station."

"What? Curt missing?" Diana bent down to pick up Nutmeg, who was trying to greet the officers after she had scurried out to relieve herself in the front yard.

"I don't know anything about this." She paused. "But if I can help, I will certainly come down to the station. Would it be alright if I come, say, at 11 o-clock?" Diana was thinking about making her favorite morning dance class with her friends.

"No, Ms. Wall. We would really appreciate it if you came now." Officer Kennedy was more emphatic. "The Captain is anxious to see you."

"Well, of course. Let me get dressed." She turned and with measure began to walk up the stairs, holding tight to the banister, which was a welcome crutch while she attempted to breathe. Nutmeg faithfully followed her.

She turned to ask with as much composure as she could muster, "Can I get you gentlemen some coffee?"

"No, ma'am," they said in unison. "We will wait for you here."

"Okay then. I'll only be a minute." Rummaging around her room, she found jeans and a soft shirt to throw on. She quickly ran a toothbrush across her teeth and, as she spit out the paste, wondered, *Am I supposed to go with them? In the police car?*

She grabbed her shoes and started to make her way down the steps.

She opened the door and found the cops standing in the same spot she had left them. "Shall I just follow you to the station?" said Diana.

"Ms. Wall, why don't you just ride with us?"

"Oh, okay." She turned to make sure Nutmeg was okay and locked the door, the keys jingling in her shaky hands.

The younger officer opened the back door of the squad car to let her in. How strange to get into the back seat of a police car. *At least they didn't push my head down into the car like you see on TV.*

"Should I be concerned?" Diana shifted nervously in her seat.

"We don't really know anything, Ms. Wall, other than we were asked to pick you up and bring you in for questioning," explained Suarez.

"And that the Captain wants to see you," the older cop quickly added in an apparent attempt to stop Suarez from continuing.

As Diana entered the station she noticed there weren't a lot of people around. There was the officer working the desk and one old guy sitting alone in the first of a line of chairs that looked like they were borrowed from the local elementary school. He seemed to be sleeping under his veteran's cap. When Diana walked in, he lifted his head to study her with a look that suggested he knew her. He cocked his head, furrowed his brow, raised a finger to point at her, and opened his mouth to say something. It was strange. *Maybe he's drunk.* It was early Sunday morning, giving the sleepy town's station an extra dose of quiet. Nonetheless, Diana was not feeling very peaceful. The officers filed her past the desk sergeant, who gave them a quick nod, and guided her into the captain's office.

The captain stood as she entered the room and hoisted up his pants over his middle-aged girth. He was balding with a distended gut hanging over the belt line that was tighter than it should be. His manner was gruff, and he spoke as if it was with great effort, clearing his throat to force out the words.

"Good morning, Ms. Wall. I'm Captain Porter. Please have a seat." He gestured to a metal chair opposite him. He slowly sat back down and pulled his chair in tight, then proceeded to study her looking over reading glasses that were balanced at the tip of his crooked nose.

"Can I get you a cup of coffee, Ms. Wall? Officer Suarez would be happy to get that for you. Wouldn't you Suarez?" Nodding to the two officers that it was time for them to leave. "We have a Keurig here, so it's not too bad."

Considering Diana did not stop to make her usual espresso, she thought that might help to keep her alert. "Why, yes, thank you."

"How do you take it, Ms. Wall?" Suarez asked politely.

Diana turned and smiled at Suarez. "A little half-and-half if you have it. Thanks."

"No problem." The two officers left leaving Diana sitting opposite the captain. He just looked at her for a moment, and then pushed his glasses up to look down at his opened folder.

"So, I just need to ask you a few questions, Ms. Wall, about your ex-husband."

"Please, you can call me Diana." His formality was making her more uncomfortable. She decided she should try to be polite; she had no idea what was going on.

"Okay, Diana. So, can you tell me where you were last night?" He looked up over his glasses, awaiting her response.

"I was with friends in SoBo. We went out for dinner and then dancing."

"About what time was that?"

"I was a little late, so I got there about 7:30. We stayed out until the bar closed around 1 o'clock." Officer Suarez came in with her coffee and handed it to Diana with a smile.

The captain cleared his throat. "Where did you eat?"

"At the Japanese restaurant." Her eyes looked up to the right as she tilted her head to think of it. "I can't remember the name. The one along the canal."

"Kotubuki?"

"Yes, that's it. They have really good sushi there."

"So, were you drinking last night, Diana?"

"No, I don't drink."

"And when did you leave the restaurant?"

"Probably around nine?" She hesitated. "Can you please tell me what this is about? The officers said something about Curt?"

"Oh, is that what they told you?"

"Yes." She was starting to get frustrated on top of tired and hungry. The questioning was beginning to feel more accusatory than for purposes of assisting them.

The captain continued. "So, let me see if I have the picture. You were late to dinner. Why was that?"

Diana's eyes started darting around as she thought about the message from Curt. She didn't want to tell the captain how upsetting it was to hear Curt's voice apologizing after all this time, telling her how he had never stopped loving her and wanted her back. She'd been so flustered she'd had to pull over by the canal and pull herself together before going to dinner. She'd thought about how ironic it was to finally hear him declare his love before she went in to eat sushi at their favorite place. She had proclaimed she would never eat sushi again after finding those two sets of chopsticks in the bottom of that bag.

"Oh," she said quickly as it popped into her head. "The dog got into a mess just before I was leaving, so I had to clean her up."

"Made a mess?"

"No, she was a mess from rolling around in something awful in the yard, so I had to give her a quick bath."

"And how much time did that take?"

"Please, Captain, can you tell me what is going on?"

"Your ex-husband was found in the canal this morning." He hesitated for her reaction. "He was found dead."

"What! Curt is dead?" Her hand came up to her mouth to cover it; she thought she might be sick. This couldn't be. This was not the ending she had expected.

There was a soft knock on the door. "Come in," the captain yelled. "Excuse me, Ms. Wall."

The captain looked annoyed as he pushed himself away from his desk, hitching up his pants. Suarez had motioned him over and was whispering in his ear. He nodded his head in response to the piece of information Suarez was sharing. He slowly made his way back to his desk, and Suarez followed him into the room.

The captain pulled his chair in and looked over his glasses at Diana.

He cleared his voice. "I'm afraid, Ms. Wall, I'm going to have to take you into custody."

"What?" Diana moved forward in her chair to look the captain in the eye. "What are you talking about?" Diana started to get up out of her seat.

"Please sit down, Ms. Wall." The Captain stood and signaled to Suarez.

"This is ludicrous. I don't know what this is about, but I didn't have anything to do with it. I want to go home."

Officer Suarez started reciting the Miranda rights. "You have the right to remain silent. If you do or say anything, what you say can and will be used against you in a court of law. You have the right to consult with a lawyer…"

"I want to make a phone call," Diana interjected.

"…and have that lawyer present during any questioning. If you cannot afford a lawyer, one will be appointed for you if you so desire. If you choose to talk to a police officer, you have the right to stop the interview at any time."

"Of course, we will grant you a phone call." The captain nodded to Suarez. "Before you go, is there anything else you want to tell us?"

"I have nothing more to say to you." She glared at him as her chest heaved from the adrenaline coursing through her veins.

"Well, I'm sorry to hear that, Ms. Wall. Nevertheless, you will have to stay here." He signaled to Suarez to remove her from his office. "Make sure Ms. Wall gets her phone call, Suarez."

2

Diana was trying hard not to panic; she had to stay in control. As she walked down the corridor, she focused on her phone call. She knew exactly who she was going to call; he was the guy that she thought of when she was in trouble. He had been her hero when she needed one the most. He was her hero because he shed light on what she needed to know to give her strength. He was her hero because he saved her from a life of lies, deceit, and manipulation. She was hoping he would be her hero once again.

"Abbott here." He cleared his throat from the cigarette smoke.

"Robert, it's Diana."

"Hey kid, how's it goin'?"

"Robert, I'm in jail, and I need your help." Her eyes began to tear up as she started to emotionally unfold the severity of the situation.

"Jesus. Where are you?"

She started to break up. "They have me locked up downtown."

"I'm coming." He hung up the phone before she could say anything else.

She wasn't worried; she knew he would come.

They had her wait in what she thought was probably the interrogation room for what seemed to be hours. She sat with her hands folded in her lap, ignoring the cuffs to the best of her ability, her feet planted firmly on the ground in a position of strength.

She looked around the room and up at the ceiling. She noticed the cameras in the corner and thought perhaps they were watching her. *But why? I didn't do anything wrong.* She wondered if she should have called a lawyer. No, calling Robert was the right thing to do; he knew these guys, and he would know what to do.

The door to the room opened, and two cops walked in, one male, one female. They both seemed very unfriendly. Behind them was a familiar face.

"Robert!" She wanted to throw her arms around him, but the cuffs held her back.

"Diana. How ya doin' kid?" He pulled out the chair so he could sit opposite her. The two cops stood against the wall with their arms crossed.

"Robert, what's going on? Why am I here?" Diana did not like the look of concern on his face. She could tell when he was troubled.

He cleared his throat. "Where were you last night, Diana?"

"I was with some friends; we went out to dinner, and then we went dancing."

"Okay, but where did you go?"

"To SoBo," Diana explained.

"Did you see Curt?"

"Yes, I saw him walking along the canal."

"I was afraid you might say that."

"Why, Robert? What's going on? I didn't understand what they were saying when they brought me in. They said something about Curt being dead. Why am I being held, Robert, why?" The panic in her voice started to rise.

"Okay, here's the deal. They found Curt dead in the canal outside his apartment. They have an eyewitness that someone pushed him in, and you, my dear, are the prime suspect. We need to get you a lawyer. Do not talk to them without one. They are just holding you on fuzzy evidence. I'm not sure exactly what they have, but it was enough to arrest you. I know these guys, but they're not telling me everything. Normally, I wouldn't be allowed to come in here, but they owe me." He spared her the details of how he helped out the captain, especially since it was not a flattering story.

Diana sat in stone silence as her head started spinning. This couldn't be happening. She didn't know what to react to first. *Curt is dead?* Oh God, she would never see him again. After what he did to her and Abby, she didn't really want to see him again, but this was final. The end. After so many years of having him in her life, it seemed impossible. *Wait, forget that. What about me?*

"I didn't do anything, Robert, I swear to you." She looked deep into his eyes to make sure he knew she was telling the truth.

"I know, kid. The guy is a scumbag, and he's not worth going to jail for. However, there is a long list of people who wouldn't mind seeing him suffer."

"Robert, I have to get out of here." She was beginning to panic. "Nutmeg… my daughter. I'm supposed to move."

"I know, I know. I'll take care of it. My guess is that you will have to stay in here for a few days until you can get in front of the judge for arraignment. This will be a high-profile case for them; they are not going to mess around."

"Oh, Robert, I can't believe this." She held her head in her hands, trying to fight off the headache that was threatening to come.

"Try not to worry, kid. I will get you out of here. Remember, what do I always tell you?"

"You have my back." She briefly remembered how Shelly used to tell her that, but she knew Robert meant it.

"Right." He stood up and signaled to the cop that he was done.

They allowed Robert to walk Diana back down to her cell so she would somehow feel less like a hardened criminal. Innocent until proven guilty, right? She now looked at the walls differently. *This just got real.* There was a possibility of being trapped here indefinitely. She knew she was innocent, but how could they prove it? As they opened the door to the cell, she turned to face him.

"Robert, I'm scared."

"I know, kid, you're going to be all right. I promise. I won't let anything happen to you."

She took a deep breath, entered the cell, and moved back to the corner. The hard clank of the door reverberated and sent a cold vibration through her as ice-cold fear ran through her veins.

Janis had woken up from her slumber and was sitting up watching them.

"Who was that?" she asked enthusiastically. "Is he your man? Hmm, he is fine."

"We're just friends." Diana sat on her make-shift cushion; she was just going to try to meditate through this whole thing. *I will sit here and just think positive thoughts. I have to believe that evidence will be found; there has to be something to clear me. I wonder who did it?*

"Seem more than that to me," she shot back. "What's wrong with you, Kung Fu? You one of those lesbians? I know what you rich white girls are like. Always bored and pissed off at your man." Janis wrinkled her nose and then rubbed it with her hand as if to remove something lodged deep inside.

"No, it's nothing like that." Diana rolled her eyes and shook her head. "He's just a really good friend, and he's always there for me." The pillow seemed welcoming but still hard underneath.

"Well, then, what's your problem? Isn't that what a good man does? Be there for you? Trust me, I never had nothin' like that." Janis waved her hand and shook her head. "All I got is boozin', lyin', and cheatin'. You crazy, Kung Fu. You dunno a good thing when you see it."

"Maybe you're right. I've never had much luck with men."

"I hear ya on that one. It's like some bad magnet. Always going for the wrong guy." She paused to shake her head. "Was your ex the wrong guy?"

"He turned out to be. He wasn't always." A tear slowly rolled down her cheek. "I still do not know what happened to him. I thought he was the love of my life when I met him and that we would be happy together forever." She wiped the tears away and thought about when she first fell in love with Curt. She had known every inch of him, and loved every centimeter.

3

Janis could not handle this display of emotion.""Uh come back to me, Kung Fu. Let's not get too weepy." There was an awkward silence in the room while the weight of past wounds surfaced and settled. "So, how did you meet this love of your life, anyway?" Janis used air quotes to communicate her sarcasm but sat up a little taller to listen to Diana's story.

Diana thought back to all those years ago. How many had passed since she stepped onto that plane? Almost twenty? She would never forget the sense of freedom and relief she had felt.

* * *

Diana was flying direct to Spain from France after an exhausting family vacation—ten days of gastronomic indulgences, staying at places chosen for their Michelin-rated chefs. Diana found her seat, dumped her bag, and let out a deep sigh. She would miss her little girl, Abby, with her curly hair and happy disposition; Diana had held her close as she said good-bye. Her husband had stood by with his usual disapproving expression. She closed her eyes and played the parting conversation over.

"When are you coming back? I don't know why you have to be gone for so long."

"This is a business trip, Dave. It's only four days. Don't forget, you wanted me to work and make money. Remember?" She rolled her eyes and sighed.

"Well, I didn't know you'd have to travel and leave me with Abby." He looked down at their two-year old in a manner that suggested she was merely an inconvenience.

"I arranged for the nanny to be available to you whenever you need. She is literally across the street. I don't know what else you want me to do."

"Fine. Go. But I would change your outfit before you see anybody you know." He grabbed Abby's hand and turned to leave.

"Bye-bye." Abby waved her little hand as Dave pulled her away.

Dave was slowly sucking the life out of Diana with his perfectionist, obsessive-compulsive behavior and never-ending demands. She was excited to be going to Marbella even though she would be running a three-day meeting with the sales team from Europe. This would be her first European meeting where she was expected to present something of value to the top salespeople from the region—not an easy feat under the stern gaze of this multinational conglomerate. It would take all her energy to wow and entertain them while she provided training on how to sell the new products corporate was pushing.

Diana wiped down the tray in front of her with an ever-ready baby wipe and stretched out her long legs to settle in, shifting her identity from loving mother and exhausted wife to corporate consultant whose career counted on the success of this meeting. Crossing her arms, she wiggled in her seat and closed her eyes to relax; a small smile crossed her lips as she rejoiced in the idea of getting away from her husband. Four days of peace, and she would enjoy every one of them, even with the work she had in front of her.

The meeting was to begin with lunch at the hotel, where attendees could gather for a meal and social networking with their colleagues from around Europe. Diana eye-balled the room; it looked as if all eighty had shown up, leaving only one empty seat directly across the round table from her. Dressed simply in a white blouse and black pants chosen for their stretchy waistband, she hoped her elegant attire would mask how harried she was feeling after jumping from a family vacation directly to a business meeting.

"So, are you ready?" Her client had the seat next to hers and leaned in to press his arm against hers.

Diana shifted in her seat to face him. "Of course, William. It's all under control." Moving to break contact with the discomfort of his familiarity, she was reminded that he had her financial future in his hands, so she needed to tread carefully.

The door to the room opened, and the last guest strolled in. He was about six feet tall with curly brown hair and a rugged build, indicating strength and masculinity with a confident but casual manner that suggested he was comfortable in his own skin. Despite her forced composure, Diana couldn't help but give him the once over. *Boy, this meeting is looking up!* She held herself a little straighter as he sat down in the empty seat, casting his baby blues upon her and flashing his winning smile. The small but smarter voice in her head had some advice: *Stay away from him. He's trouble.*

On stage, Diana took a deep breath before she moved up to the podium to officially open the meeting and welcome her guests. She gave a quick introduction to the three-day agenda and the keynote speaker, knowing the audience would be anxious for the hotel bar afterward. She had been forewarned by her colleague Cathy that this group "really liked to party" - there were tales of late-night, drunken food fights that had gotten the group kicked out of some very posh places. Fortunately, Cathy didn't scare easily and would be a strong comrade for Diana in a sea of men with various accents and cultural norms.

With the first step completed, Diana smiled in part relief, part anticipation as she approached the bar, recognizing a few of the men standing with Cathy who had previously traveled to the U.S. for their global sales meetings. The guy who had strolled in late was leaning against the bar and returned Diana's smile, at the same time scanning her body like a robotic assessor.

"Diana, this is Curt." Cathy introduced them with a bit of a smirk; she noticed Diana's reaction and the renewed vibrancy in her eyes that had a habit of changing color with her mood. Cathy gave her a little nudge with her elbow to wake her from her trance.

While everyone else was tucking into the martinis and Rioja, Curt was drinking Diet Coke. He explained in a serious tone that he was "in training."

"For what?" Diana asked as she absently spun her wedding ring around her finger.

"An 8-K run," he replied, delivering the message with a clear sense of pride and bravado.

Diana teased, "Oh, I thought maybe it was a marathon."

After some initial resistance, Curt's colleagues easily talked him into adding vodka to the Diet Coke. Diana feigned disgust about his choice of beverage. Curt moved closer, they chatted some more. She noticed his crooked nose, which gave him a rugged look—not too polished or pretty. He also smelled good, like the freshest rain on earth. He was sexy, Diana had to admit. Of course, the accent didn't hurt.

"Australian?" she asked.

"No, a Brit," he confessed. "I don't often tell people where I grew up. It's quite a shoddy little town in the North of England."

"Oh." Diana didn't want to pry, but he went on without prompting.

"I was pretty anxious to leave and attend Uni in the South. I never looked back. I just visit Mum once in a while." This may have explained the smoother, more polished accent.

"I did the same thing," Diana said, feeling the need to validate his story for some reason. He was charming, with a nice manner about him and an easy smile. He gave her his full and complete attention. "I feel like I've met you before," said Diana with a small tilt of her head.

"I have the same feeling." He paused and raised his eyebrows. "Have you ever been to one of these meetings in the past?"

"No, this is my first one in Europe." Diana twisted her mouth and looked sideways as she tried to conjure up where she had met this man before. It was such a powerful feeling. "Maybe you've been to the States… to a corporate sales function, perhaps?"

"No, I try to avoid corporate meetings." He laughed softly. "I wasn't going to come to this one, but something told me it was important." He turned to her. "Perhaps it was to meet you."

Diana smiled to hide the heat rushing to her face. He was flirting with her shamelessly, but she liked it. Usually, she grew uncomfortable with a man's attention, but Curt's blue eyes were penetrating, and they were not moving away from Diana's. She was flustered by his attention, but he left her feeling exhilarated with a hint of trepidation. One by one, they all said their slightly tipsy good-byes for the evening.

When Diana opened the meeting the next day, she energetically moved around the stage to engage her audience. Curt kept his eyes trained on her. He seemed very interested in what she was saying. His stare came with a knowing smile; he was putting her on edge, and he obviously knew it. Diana felt as if she were being slowly undressed by those piercing blue eyes. It was thrilling, she had to admit, but she needed to be careful with this one. *You're married, remember, with a beautiful baby girl. Behave yourself.*

She took extra care getting dressed for the evening's events, choosing a blue and white flowered dress that, according to her mom, "flattered her figure." Diana was the last to get on the bus that would take them to an estate in the outskirts of the region. When she boarded, she noticed the empty seat next to Curt. He smiled broadly as a subtle invitation to sit next to him. She decided at that moment that it would be better to avoid him and picked another, less dangerous seat with Cathy.

"How are you doing, Diana? You seemed a bit frazzled" Cathy had a look of mild concern as she knew Diana could get anxious even though she came across as super confident.

"I'm good, Cathy, thanks. Just a bit nervous about the meeting… and that guy over there is putting me on edge." Diana nodded in the direction of Curt, who was sitting a few rows ahead and turned to smile in Cathy and Diana's direction.

"Oh, Curt. Yeah, he is kinda cute." She giggled. "I wouldn't mind…"

"Don't even say it, Cathy. Bad girl."

"Just kidding. He's harmless." Cathy smiled back at Curt and waved.

"Stop," she whispered.

"Listen, Diana, the meeting is going to be great. You've got this. You always do."

As soon as they walked into the entryway, Diana loved the vibe of the estate chosen for the evening's entertainment. It had a colorful history as a playground for the rich and a hangout for famous artists and writers. Covered with exquisite artwork, its yellow patina and dark woodwork were warm and comforting, which was good because her nerves were rattled when William insisted he sit next to her at the long table. Diana hid her disgust from his stale breath, and she felt her face turn bright red when he complimented her on how lovely she looked. Curt had made sure he got the seat on her right side, she felt herself absent-mindedly sidling up to him. For some reason, she felt safe with him, as if he would somehow protect her. Plus, he was making her laugh, and Diana loved to laugh.

The waiters, dressed in white to complement their beautiful Mediterranean looks, served trays of cured meats to begin the meal. Always one to try something new, Diana chose what looked like hard salami. As soon as she put it in her mouth, she knew she had made a mistake. Curt had been watching her, and there was laughter in his eyes as she squirmed to either discard or swallow the unsavory substance.

"Here, put it in here." Curt grabbed the ashtray from the middle of the table and opened the cover. She tossed in her mouthful and laughed as he placed the ashtray back in front of him. That small gesture told her everything she needed to know. He wasn't prim and proper like her husband, who had way too many rules about how she should behave. And he was paying close attention to her and responding to her needs. It was a delightful first.

After dinner, the group went to a local dance club. She felt like the belle of the ball, even with William clinging to her. Finding Cathy, she instructed, "Whatever you do, don't leave my side tonight."

Curt seemed to sense her discomfort and stood protectively behind her; everywhere Diana went, he was right there. "Hey, why don't we dance?" Curt led Diana onto the dance floor, and they began to move to the Latin rhythms. The sexual energy between them was palpable. As Diana swayed to the music, Curt got closer.

He put his hand on her hip, and she felt a shockwave running through her body. She hadn't been this turned on since...forever.

"Let's get out of here," said Curt, taking her hand.

Diana's eyes widened; warning bells went off in her head. This was fun, but she knew that no matter how bad her marriage was, she couldn't cheat on her husband. She had to prove to herself that she could be faithful despite Dave's torturous treatment; promiscuity was not a character trait she wanted to possess. "I have to stay with my client, Curt."

He shrugged his shoulders. "Okay. Let's keep dancing, shall we?"

With the club soon to close, William, Cathy, and Diana, with Curt by her side, decided to head to the Golden Mile and hit the small tapas bars lined up in a row along the water. Each bar was filled with late-night dancers looking for a last chance at romance. Diana could not believe she had stayed up all night since seeing midnight was a rare event. She got up in the wee hours of the morning only to answer Abby's cries. This seemed crazy, but she was incredibly happy, and her defenses were way down. It was going to be a beautiful morning.

The four of them walked to the beach that ran along the edge of the main street. Diana and Curt stopped to sit on the concrete jetty to watch the sunrise as William and Cathy unknowingly continued down the beach. Suddenly, Curt took her in his arms and pulled her to him. His smell was intoxicating. Diana sucked the breath back into her body as he kissed her, more and more intensely. *So, this is what they mean when your foot goes up in the air and all?* She was blown away; she wanted to be locked in that kiss forever.

"Let's go back to the hotel," Curt said. He started to get up and held out his hand to her. She waved it away and instead lifted her arm to signal Cathy that it was time to go. She didn't dare look back into Curt's eyes for fear of caving to his advances.

They all taxied back to the hotel together. Diana stepped out of the cab and realized that in just a few hours she would need to be back up on stage, opening the meeting. As they rode up in the elevator together, Diana panicked. *Will Curt follow me off?*

Bing.

This was her stop. The doors opened, and she stepped through. She quickly turned to look at Curt to deliver a casual warning: "See you guys tomorrow." She wanted him desperately, but she knew it wasn't the right thing to do; she needed to get her act together.

As she undressed to flop into bed and catch a few hours of sleep, she heard a soft rap on the door. She grabbed her robe, looked through the peephole, and saw Curt. She hesitated and then opened the door a crack.

"Are you okay?" he asked. He pushed the door open to walk in.

"I would be better if you kissed me."

He quickly crossed over the threshold to take her into his arms. He picked her up and laid her down on the bed. As their lips parted, Diana resisted for a second longer. "Please, I can't." But it was too late; Curt was not going to take no for an answer, and as he pulled her robe away, Diana succumbed to his advances. *Oh God, what am I doing?* She tried one more time to pull away. Curt was busy tracing his lips down her neck, kissing her stomach, and as he made his way down, Diana arched her back in response. This was not usual for her. Unlike her husband, who, on the rare occasion when he performed this maneuver, acted as if he were carefully licking the back of a large envelope with a fear of cutting his tongue, Curt was not holding back. She gripped the sheets and bit her bottom lip before releasing a long-suppressed orgasm. He quickly wiped his mouth and moved to enter her, claiming his prize with a powerful kiss and a forceful thrust that made its way deep inside her. This wasn't the alcohol, or just the heat of the moment; this was something much more. She had never in all her thirty-five years experienced such intensity; he was playing her like a finely-tuned instrument and hitting chords she didn't know existed. He was unlocking something in her, and she knew that once discovered, it would not easily be put back. Every part of her body was awakened, and he knew exactly what he was doing to her.

They drifted off to sleep, Diana in Curt's arms. *What have I done?*

* * *

Diana cried during the entire plane ride home, all eight hours of it. She cried because she was weak. She cried because she had put everything on the line—her job, her family, her peace of mind—all for a night of passion. She cried because she had never felt so alive, so wanted, and she thought that she might actually be in love. She cried because she would never see him again and was headed back to an emotionally abusive relationship. She had been temporarily released from her prison, and now she would be pushed back into her beautiful jail.

She was tired and overwrought, and the heaviness she felt as she approached her home could not be soothed by the easy banter of the limo driver, who was happily sharing cooking tips. "Yeah, I used to cook for a real famous guy." He dropped the name of someone Diana had never heard of and explained in what Diana presumed was a Brooklyn accent. "I was sort of his right-hand man... driver, cook, and all-around confidante, and then all of sudden, he dropped me like a hot potato. I did everything for that guy, and then one day..." He snapped his fingers to accentuate the speed of the termination.

"Oh, I'm sorry. That must have been really hard on you." Diana tried to listen to his story as she pushed away thoughts of how she had given herself to a man she didn't know. *Why did I open that door? How did he get my room number, anyway?*

Finally at home, she slipped into bed next to her husband, who was in a deep sleep and didn't even notice her return, let alone welcome her with an embrace. In the morning, she would slip back into her suburban routine, just as she had slipped back into her marital bed—with no one noticing.

When she woke up, she was relieved to find Dave already out of bed. Laying there for a moment, she tried to gather her thoughts and gain her grounding before facing into the day. *Life is never going to be the same.* Moving into the bathroom, she glanced in the mirror to see the dark rings under her puffy-eyes that told the tale of her exhaustion and hours of crying. Splashing cold water on her face, she thought, *how am I going to get through this? Stay focused on the routine,* she told herself. *Stick to the routine.*

Shuffling into her daughter's room, Abby was just waking up from her innocent sleep. The little curls were wet with sweat, her eyes, blurry from sleep, opened wide when they registered her mommy and brightened with her usual broad smile, her arms outstretched to be lifted from her crib. Diana picked her up and held her close to breathe in her sweet baby smell, delighting in their reunion. She carried Abby downstairs cooing in her ear, talking about what they would have for breakfast. Abby was all smiles, so happy to have her mommy home.

Dave came rushing into the kitchen to rattle off the list of things she needed to do now that she was back home. "And the lawn service is coming today," he finished. "Make sure they cut the lawn to an inch and a quarter. I measured it last time; it was off at the top of the hill."

She rolled her eyes. "Uh-uh."

"Don't pay them if they do it again."

The image of Dave walking around the yard with a ruler to check the landscaper's work stuck in her mind. There was no way in hell she was doing his bidding.

"Okay, I'm off to Chicago." Dave pecked her on the cheek, grabbed his suitcase, and kissed Abby on the forehead. "Don't you forget, Diana. You know how you can be."

At least it would be peaceful with him gone, without the daily demands and criticisms of her personal failures. She was often reminded that the pillows were not fluffed properly, his socks were not organized correctly by color, the white-wire hangers were not facing the right direction. The empty toilet paper roll he left in her sink was a warning not to repeat the oversight. These complaints, though maddening, were not nearly as hurtful as the constant attacks on her appearance and behavior, which were never quite up to par. "Why can't you lose that last five pounds, Diana?" "Sit up at the table, Diana." "Don't chew gum in the car. Someone might see you." "Nice hairdo. Can't you at least run a comb through it?" "Do you need to wear those earrings with that outfit?" It went on and on, leaving her unloved, unsupported, and unhappy.

After breakfast and hours of play, Diana put Abby down for a nap then stepped into the light of her little office, which overlooked the backyard and dense forest behind her house. Should she do her laundry or her work—always the challenge, since her office was also the laundry room. As she settled on beginning the task of post-meeting follow-up, she received a fax. It was a handwritten note on the cover of the sales kit she had written and then presented at the meeting. "I am very interested in your tools. Contact me. Curt.Anderson@bd.com."

Her heart leapt into her throat and then down to her stomach and back up again. *Oh my, it's him!* He was not going to make this easy after all. She had half-hoped he would leave her alone so that she could forget what she had done and try to tamp down her feelings. *What should I do?*

She would email him, but keep it on a professional level. "I have received your note about my tools. I would be happy to share more information with you. What exactly are you looking for?" She pushed the send button and then reread her message. *Might that be interpreted as suggestive?*

He immediately responded. "What I am looking for is better conveyed in person. I am planning a trip to the U.S. in a few weeks and would like to meet with you to discuss it."

He's coming for me! She wanted to see him, but could she really carry on an affair? Every fiber in her body responded, "Yes! Yes, you can!" He was going to save her from her repressed, dull, and tortured life. Her heart pounded with the excitement and anticipation of seeing him again, smelling him, hearing his deep voice in her ear. She couldn't deny him if she tried.

4

Janis sat on the edge of the bed, her hands pressed against the edge, always ready to spring, while Diana waited for her judgment. It didn't take Janis long, and Diana was prepared with a practiced answer, the rationalization that fell short of completely removing any sense of her long-standing guilt. Even after all these years, she had not completely forgiven herself.

"So, you saw him again? What were you thinking, Kung Fu?"

"I don't know. I was so tortured in my marriage."

"Really? How so?"

"My husband—he was emotionally abusive. I was walking around on eggshells, an empty shell of myself. I couldn't do anything right. I don't know how to explain it."

"Sounds like he was sucking the life out of you—joy suckers, that's what I call them. So, you had an affair? Bad girl."

"It wasn't like that. I was falling in love with him." She hesitated as she realized she didn't have to explain herself to some random woman she happened to be stuck in this cell with. "It's a long and complicated story," snapped Diana, "and I'm not sure I want to share it."

"It's not like we're goin' anywhere," quipped Janis. "Not for a while, looks like."

"I won't be here for long. This is a mistake." Diana crossed her arms and sighed.

"Whatever you say, Kung Fu, but I'm ready for a bedtime story." Janis flopped down on the bed and feigned indifference.

"It just brings up a lot that I have worked hard to let go of."

"Oh, so then it shouldn't be that hard. It's not your story; it's just a story."

"I suppose." Diana so resolved that this was a means to keep her mind off the current situation.

* * *

On her way over to London, Diana upset a few people on the plane by taking a little longer than she should to freshen up—after sleeping in a twisted position for six hours next to a man who needed a seat and a half. Exiting the plane quickly, her mind was filled with the prospect of seeing Curt again. They had been trying to see each other every six weeks, the most they could stand apart. Luckily, they both had jobs in the company that required travel: Curt in sales, and Diana in sales training.

When Diana entered the arrival hall at Heathrow, she scanned the long line of people waiting and spotted him immediately, standing just beyond the barrier, awkwardly holding flowers that paled in their beauty next to his beaming smile. She raced towards him, and he picked her up in a twirling embrace. They kissed with abandon, not caring who was watching. This truly was a dream. She breathed him in as they left the terminal holding hands.

Spending hours emailing each other after reuniting during Curt's business trip to the U.S., it was apparent that they were falling deeply in love. They asked revealing questions, searching for intimate details, wrote sappy love poems, made plans to see each other again. She could not believe how intense her feelings for him had become. After Curt had come to America to see her, Diana started to find excuses to travel to London on business. She didn't enjoy lying to her husband or leaving their two-year-old in the care of the nanny, but she knew Abby would be fine since Dave was so fussy.

Now she watched him as he drove, studying the strong jawline and neck she loved to nuzzle and the cute little ear she liked to tease with her tongue. She loved everything about this man; she wanted to eat him up.

"Are you okay, darling?" He constantly asked her that, studying her face as if to read her mind.

"Yes, I'm fine. Just anxious to get to the hotel."

"Are you a bit hungry from the flight? Perhaps we should order in." He smiled his devilish grin and winked.

Oh, I'm hungry, thought Diana as she smiled back, knowing that as soon as they entered the hotel room, they would be tearing each other's clothes off. The prospect would usually make Diana self-conscious, but with Curt, she felt at ease, even proud, in her skin. He made her feel sexy and wanted. What a departure from what she usually got from her whining husband who didn't question or complain about the fact that they hadn't had sex for over six months.

She checked in at the front desk and was eagerly greeted by the manager of the hotel. She had to remember that she was there on business. She shook the manager's hand with a firm grip and exchanged the usual business pleasantries.

"I'd like to take you to lunch," he said. "This will give you a chance to check out the property for your sales meeting and the quality of our food."

Diana looked over her shoulder at Curt and threw him a quick frown, knowing that he was not going to be happy about this change in plans. *I guess he can wait in the room; it will just make him more hot-to-trot.* Curt tried to hide his displeasure with a shake of his head, then let out a little smile to show he understood. They got the keys for the room and headed over to drop off the luggage.

"I'm sorry, Curt. It shouldn't take too long."

"It's okay; I'll just be waiting in bed. Maybe that will hurry you."

She gave him a long kiss to hold him.

Despite the beauty of the resort, which was nestled outside the suburbs of London, they rarely left the bed. They ordered room service while they frolicked. Diana tied Curt to the headboard, and when the knock on the door came, she threw on her robe but did not release Curt. He sat in the middle of the bed, somewhat covered, with his muscular arms raised outstretched to meet the bed posts. She gestured for the attendant to come in; he blushed red as he quickly passed the bed to place the tray on the table. Diana gave him a large tip, let him out, and then jumped back on the bed, hysterically laughing. Curt took it in good humor.

These were the moments that Diana enjoyed the most. She had never experienced such freedom, acceptance, and joy. She had fallen hard and was finally able to be herself—passionate, expressive, fun-loving—with her clothes both off and on. Diana was also discovering how competent Curt was at many things—another turn-on, since she herself was a jack-of-all-trades. They would go to play pool, and he would run the table in no time. They went swimming, and his butterfly stroke was impressive. When they took a side trip to Belgium, he ordered their food in fluent French. There was much more to him than he had initially revealed.

* * *

It was very hard to leave him this time. She knew she couldn't live without him much longer. Of course, her guilt and dread grew as she got closer to America. She felt terrible about what was happening, and she wrestled with herself: *should I give up my one chance at happiness?* She had always been responsible, doing the "right" thing, trying to please her husband, which was impossible, and being a good mother to Abby. Her affair with Curt went against all of that. She struggled with her feelings and so wrote to sort through what she would say to her daughter after she had grown to explain her difficult decision.

My darling Abby,

You may never understand what I am about to do. Believe me, I want only what is best for you. Someday, you may ask me why I left your father, and that will be the day I give this to you.

I know that in your little heart you want your father and me to be happy together. I'm discovering that this is impossible. You have brought us so much joy, and you should always know that we both love you dearly—more than you will ever know or, perhaps, believe. But this love for you will be stronger and healthier if your father and I are apart from each other.

I was never very good with matters of the heart. I married for the wrong reasons; I didn't know how to recognize true love. Always asking, "How do you know when your love is real?" No one seems able to answer this question. They say, "Oh, you'll know." But you may think you have it before you really have it.

I will tell you how I knew...

The person you love won't be perfect, and you'll love every imperfection.

The person you love will bring you the greatest joy, and you them, simply by being yourself.

The person you love will open their heart and share what's important, tell you what you need or want to hear, because that's how they feel.

The person you love will make you laugh, inspire great passion, be your friend.

The person you love will help you through your difficulties and give you support.

The person you love will admire you - their eyes will sparkle as they relish in the person you are.

But this does not come without being open and honest and true to yourself. And believe me, if love is real, you will want the person to know everything about you, to understand you, to accept you for your greatest qualities and your greatest faults.

When you love someone truly, and that love is returned, you're not afraid. You can be yourself and enjoy that experience. The key thing is communicating. I can't tell you how important this is. I used to be afraid to tell people how I felt (and still am sometimes), afraid that they wouldn't understand or would belittle my feelings, run away from me, not return my expression.

I must tell you, I have found someone very, very special who I want to share the rest of my life with. He knows everything about me. He thinks I'm funny, although he takes me seriously. He admires me for who I am, how I behave—there is no judgment. His eyes see right through me, right into my soul. His love is powerful, so intense that I feel nothing can ever harm me. He's kind, tender, warm, caring, intelligent, happy, confident. He has character, honor, and love to give, and he gives it 100%—no holding back.

I sometimes think I'm in a dream, that this cannot be real. It's so wonderful—how can it possibly be of this earth? He has the greatest capacity to love me, but he could also break my heart if he took his love away. This is my biggest fear—that I am going to disappoint many people for a love that doesn't last. But does that mean that I shouldn't try? When you have something special before you, can you deny it? I just want to do the right thing—but from whose perspective? If I put myself first, I would leave your father tomorrow. I hold on because I don't want to hurt you.

My hope is that you will grow up to love my love so we can all be happy together. I know we could, and I want that more than anything else.

But what of your father?

I would never deny you or him the pleasure of your love for each other, and he does love you very much. But I can't be the best mother to you if I am with him. I'm too unhappy. He makes me feel too inferior. I can't go on living with him when I'm deeply in love with another.

You will know someday, when you're in love. I just hope it comes more quickly and more easily than it did for me. Recognize love when you have it; don't try to force it. If you question it, it is not love. Wait for it.

I don't know if this will help you, but please never feel that you had any role in the demise of my relationship with your father. If you need to blame someone, let it be me, but please don't hate me—that would destroy me.

I want us to be happy, Abby, and I'm afraid that if I stay with your father, we will not be. I'm afraid that you will be exposed to an unhealthy relationship that I would never want you to model. I want you to see what real love is like, what wonders love can present, how it feels when it's working, and when two people are committed to it forever.

After reading her own words, she tucked the letter away and wondered how she was ever going to tell Dave how she felt. Would she ever have the guts to do it? *Should I?*

* * *

It was a beautiful summer day, the kind you wanted to jar and take out in February. Diana pulled back the curtain to look for Dave, who had decided to do some yard work after breakfast. He was dressed in his usual work-in-the-yard attire, his lanky 6'2" body in old jeans, flannel shirt, and work boots. His thick, salt and pepper hair pushed out of his baseball cap, which tried to do its work to contain it. They had agreed to take Abby to the playground, just the three of them, since they had both been so busy as of late. Their love for Abby was the one thing they still had in common. The more she looked at this man, the less she liked him. She couldn't help but compare him to Curt, who, in her eyes, was perfect for her. Diana was finding it more and more difficult to be around Dave; she felt like an empty shell with nothing to give. Her precious moments were those spent with Abby and when she made contact with Curt. Each morning, she would rush to her office and turn on her password-protected computer to see what message would be there to greet her, and he never disappointed her. On the screen, there were words of encouragement, desire, support—he seemed to know exactly what she needed, when she needed it.

Diana took another look out the front bay window to see if she could spot Dave. She went to the windows on the side of the house, then to the back sliders, and she opened them to step onto the deck overlooking the backyard. Dave was nowhere to be seen. Her frustration began to mount as she counted the hours that she and Abby had been waiting. She returned to Abby to continue playing; they were working on counting. At just over two years old, she could talk in full sentences, and now she was learning her numbers.

The front doorbell rang, and she thought that was probably Dave looking for something to eat or drink since it was nearly lunchtime now. Diana let out an audible growl. She opened the front door; it was her neighbor. Diana's frown quickly turned into a friendly smile.

"Oh hey, Gigi. What's up?" Diana liked Gigi a lot; they had gotten very close over the past couple of years. Diana was pregnant with Abby and Gigi was pushing a stroller past the house while Diana waddled up the steep, stone driveway to get the mail. Gigi had just given birth to a beautiful baby boy. Soon after they met, Gigi told Diana that her little boy had been a twin, and she had lost the twin girl in the delivery. It was devastating, and Gigi had to carry that pain around with her every day.

"Hey, Diana. What's up with Dave?" She looked concerned and a bit perplexed.

"What do you mean?"

"He was just out by the garage picking Japanese beetles off the birch trees with tweezers."

"What?"

"Yeah, he was picking them off one by one, and putting them in a plastic bag."

"Oh God, Gigi, what is wrong with him? Abby and I have been waiting for hours to go to the playground, and he... ugh."

"Do you guys want to come with us? I came over to tell you—we're going to the merry-go-round at the mall."

Diana couldn't think of anything worse. It was such a beautiful day, and even on a rainy day, she didn't like the crowded mall. Plus, she tended to get dizzy on the merry-go-round. She was hoping Abby didn't hear the offer; she loved the merry-go-round.

"No thanks, Gigi. I should wait for Dave."

"Okay, well if you change your mind, you know where we'll be." She gave Diana a quick embrace and turned to head down the stairs.

"I'll talk to you later, Gigi." Diana hesitated. Maybe she should just go with her. She walked back into the kitchen and thought, *what am I waiting for anyway?*

***

Another business trip, and another opportunity to see Curt. It started with a thrill. Her flight had been canceled, but she managed to talk her way onto the Concorde to get the last two seats for herself and her client. As they hurried through the gate, a couple called out in a German accent, "Wait! We are here, we are here!" Too late. She felt a bit guilty, especially since the couple sounded so innocent reciting a line she remembered from Dr. Seuss' book, *Horton Hears a Who,* but her desire to see Curt far outweighed any remorse as she scurried onto the plane. She would never forget the sensation as the plane went into Mach 2, the speed even more enhanced by the fine Champagne served on board and the anticipation of being reunited with Curt.

After landing, Diana made excuses to her client when he asked to take her to dinner; she was just too exhausted from the flight. Once out of his grasp, she rushed to the hotel to call Curt and let him know that she had arrived early. Every hour was a gift, and every moment cherished. After spreading red rose petals on the crisp white sheets, she changed into the golden negligee Curt had sent to the post office box she had opened for their private communication. The note read, "Gorgeous in Gold. Can't wait to see you in this. x Curt"

The knock on the door was a soft rap; she knew it was him. Without a word, he picked her up and kissed her deeply as he carried her to the bed and hurried his clothes off. Diana's heart was beating wildly with the anticipation of feeling him inside her once more. There was no other place she wanted him to be.

"You are so beautiful, Diana. I love you and want you with me always."

He kissed her with such a bittersweet intensity that it brought tears to her eyes.

"I am yours, Curt, always."

They fell asleep in each other's arms, smiling and drenched in the sweet perfume of their love-making.

The morning had them both up early. Curt made coffee for them with the room's caffeinated offerings, drinking it as they hustled around each other to dress like a carefully choreographed dance. After work, they would have the entire weekend together. A special gift of quality time.

"I think you should check out of the hotel, luv, and stay with me over the weekend. I want to show you the new flat."

Much to her dismay, Curt had explained that even though he was divorced, as he had told her when they first met, for a long time he had continued living with his ex-wife and children so that he could be in their lives. He had purchased the flat when he told Candy he was leaving. He hadn't told Diana right away, and now it was too late to debate the consequences of his decision.

"Well, I would, but don't you have your children for part of the weekend?" Diana thought it might be too soon for her to meet his children, since he had just moved out, but he was adamant.

"They will have to meet you sometime, Diana. It might as well be now."

"Well, couldn't Candy take them this weekend so that we can work on the flat?" Diana had been sending suggestions for paint colors over the past few weeks and had purchased new fabric for him. She was looking forward to helping him decorate.

"No, that cow has already made plans with Charles."

"Who's Charles?" Diana found it hard to believe that Candy had already found someone to replace Curt. *How could anyone ever replace him?*

Curt turned to her with a look of disgust. "Charles is my best mate and next-door neighbor. Apparently, he and Candy were having an affair, and now they're together."

Diana was confused. *So, Curt and Candy were living together, but had an agreement? Then it wouldn't be an affair.* But it was still a betrayal, especially since it was his best friend. "I'm sorry, Curt." She couldn't help thinking how twisted and complicated his life seemed, even before they had met. Now, she was adding to the complexity and challenge of it all.

She took a deep breath and exhaled slowly. She turned her attention to the harder subject at hand—meeting his children. Nervous about how his kids would respond to her, she wondered how they might be feeling. *They are so young, and this is not an easy situation.* They would not understand the intricacies or justifications for their relationship, but it was important to Curt that she meet them.

"Okay, Curt. I'll check out around noon. Can you get out of work early and pick me up in the lobby?"

"Yes, that is not a problem, darling. I'll be here for you."

* * *

When they pulled into the parking lot of Curt's apartment, the building looked a bit outdated and not very well cared for. Curt explained that the flat needed some work, but this was all he could afford right now, since Candy was taking him to court.

"But I thought you were already divorced, Curt."

"I am, and I have been for years. Candy is being difficult and suing me for child support. I told her I would help out, but I guess she is angry and jealous and doesn't trust me."

"Oh, I see." Diana tucked the thought away that there should be no question that he would help support their children.

They walked up to the doorway of a brick building and past a small flower bed that had been haphazardly planted. No matter; everything seemed to grow so beautifully in England. Curt inserted the key to open the door. You could smell the mustiness through the fresh paint he had recently applied to the long hallway that connected the two bedrooms, small kitchen, and cozy lounge. The kitchen was not very clean, and Curt explained that he would be installing new cabinets soon. Diana didn't care, for she was just excited to be there with him in a space that wasn't a hotel.

"I know it's not much, Diana. I did buy a new bed and fresh linens for the en suite." He winked at her and kissed her hand. "Shall we try them out?"

"Aren't your children expected?" Diana fidgeted away; she didn't want to fall prey to his advances, as vulnerable as she was to them.

"They should be here shortly. I suppose I can wait." As he drew her to him, a loud knock on the door abruptly interrupted their embrace. Curt rushed to the door. The doorbell chime that was now sounded repeatedly played on Diana's stressed nerves. She stood behind Curt so she wouldn't be spotted by Candy, but apparently, the children had just been dropped off at the curbside. They ran in, wrapped their arms around their father's waist and legs, and eyed Diana. She knelt down so that she would be eye level with them.

"Hello," she said softly.

"Sammy, Rose, this is my friend Diana."

Sammy, who was eight years old, ran past her without a word. "Can I turn on the telly, Dad?"

Rose just looked at Diana with big, violet eyes, pushing her long golden hair away from her face. She was a beautiful little girl. She smiled and quietly said, "Hello." Diana took her hand and asked if she would like to watch TV, too. She quietly nodded and sat next to her brother, already entranced by the cartoons.

The next morning, Curt drove them all to the soccer pitch to watch Sammy play. He ran onto the field to greet his mates; his lanky body weighed down by the hordes of candy he had tucked into his track pants pockets. After some time, Rose got tired. It was a bit cold, so Diana said she would take her to the car for the remainder of the game. Rose was only a year or so older than Abby, and Diana already had a soft spot for her. Rose sat in the back, and Diana got into the passenger seat, how strange it was to sit on the left-hand side without the steering wheel in front of her. After a few minutes, she looked back at Rose, who was being quiet as a mouse, to see if she was still awake.

"Your earrings are very pretty," Rose said in her small, sweet voice.

"Well, thank you," said Diana.

"May I see them?"

"Sure." Diana leaned over, swept back her hair, and held out her ear so that Rose could see the earring up close.

"No, I mean, can I hold them?"

Diana hesitated; these were her good earrings, and she didn't want them to get lost.

"Pleeease," Rose begged, drawing out a desperate request.

"Well, okay, but please be careful." Diana removed one of the earrings and handed it to Rose.

Rose looked at it and smiled. She cupped it in her hand and then drew her arm under her leg.

Diana sat up in surprise. "May I have my earring back, Rose?"

Rose just sat there, looking up with her big violet eyes and a tiny smile on her face. She said nothing and did not move.

"May I have my earring back, please?" Diana repeated, more sternly this time.

Again, Rose just stared at her with no shift in expression.

"Rose, give me my earring back now."

No response. This was calculated. Rose had acted like such a sweet, shy little girl with her long lashes and blonde tresses, but now she was deliberately being naughty. Diana was amazed at the intent of her behavior.

Curt was heading for the car with Sammy. Rose spotted him, and suddenly she sat up and threw the earring at Diana. It fell in between the seats. Diana tried to compose herself, but her flustered reaction was plain to see as she rummaged around to reach the earring.

Curt opened the front door. "Is everything alright?"

Diana glanced at Rose and said, "Yes. Everything is fine. My earring just fell out."

Rose sat quietly in the back seat with a satisfied smile on her lips.

* * *

As Curt was getting the kids ready for the day and feeding them breakfast, Diana went out for an early morning run around the park near Curt's flat. She wanted to give him some time alone with his kids, and she needed time to think. It was just too much, too soon. She ran harder and faster than she had in a while, and although the track was lined with lush plantings that had benefited from the moisture of the morning air, her mind found no peace racing around what the two of them were contemplating long-term. *Can he really leave his children to come to America?* She wasn't sure if she could live with that. In fact, seeing him with his children made it unbearable. As she rounded the corner a final time, she had made the toughest decision of her life.

She burst through the door of his apartment, passed the kids in the lounge affixed to some strange British children's show, and found him in the bedroom.

"Curt," she began. She was almost hyperventilating as she eked out the words, "I can't do this."

"Do what, Diana?"

"I can't let you leave your children. I don't want to be the one who makes you leave them." She crumpled to the ground in tears. The thought of never seeing him again was horrifically painful, but she knew it was the right thing to do—to let him go.

He gently picked her up off the ground and held her close as she cried into his shoulder. Then he tenderly cupped his strong hands under her face and looked into her eyes. "First of all, Diana, it's not your decision. It is mine." He didn't take his eyes off of her as he gingerly wiped the tears away. "Secondly, I'm telling you, it's going to be alright. Candy won't want to take care of those kids on her own. She is miserable and selfish. And that means she'll send them to me once I'm settled. I promise you."

"But..."

"There are no buts. I am coming to America once I find a job, and that is how it's going to be."

At last, Diana nodded. She knew there was no arguing with him once he had made up his mind. It was better to communicate with him in writing so that he would have time to process and respond. She tucked a note under his pillow before she left for the airport.

Dear Curt,

I'm leaving you now in the safe and loving arms of your children. I wouldn't have traded it for the world—to see you in the role of father, a role that seems to come very naturally to you. So tender, so loving and caring—I can clearly see that you love your children deeply and that they love you very much as well. They need you... I could sense their need to be close to you, to touch you, to calm their fears that you would leave them. Do you think they know what you're thinking? They may be wondering whether or not you will follow me back to America—Sammy for sure, and perhaps Rose, too.

There is so much I want to say to you—so many thoughts swimming around in my head. While I was jogging today, I realized that I love you too much to let you leave your children. I know you say you would leave them anyway... but do I want to be the cause of it? Do I want Sammy and Rose to think, "You're the woman who took my Daddy away—the Daddy I needed so much?"

Then, what of us? You have to know that I want to be with you more than anything in the world, but at what price—and how many lives will be affected? Can we be that selfish?

I know we could be happy, and perhaps all this will work out. But how? I can't figure it out. I look at it up and down, inside and out, sideways, and still no answers. Our choice is either to deal with the pain we will inflict on others or the pain of losing each other. Is there some compromise?

My biggest concern is the children, yours and mine. No matter what we do, we will hurt them somehow and perhaps cause irrevocable damage that will be on our consciences for the rest of our lives. Can we live with this?

I tell you, we'd better be damned sure that we will indeed be extremely happy for the rest of our lives if we choose the path of hurting others. I certainly could not live with myself if I were to fail at our relationship after inflicting so much pain. Could you?

I guess I'm afraid. I'm afraid you're going to wake up one day and want to go home, and I won't be able to go with you. I'm afraid you'll wake up and decide it wasn't worth jeopardizing your relationship with your children. I'm afraid you'll wake up and want someone else. I'm afraid I'll fail again and lose you. Or lose you because I've lost all respect for myself in the process.

I know I'm pouring everything out here, but I think you should understand what goes through my head. I always want to be honest with you, and I want you to understand my struggles with this.

Oh God, Curt, I don't know. I don't know what is right. Four pages, and I haven't mentioned how I feel with you, and without you (perhaps the most important in all this). Let me try. I love you more than I believed was possible. I truly did not realize what it could be like—the intensity, the fulfillment, the absolute joy and wonder. I want to spend every minute with you, wake up to you every day, hold you, help you through life, lean on you for support, share our happiness with our families, our friends—share our laughter. There's still so much that I feel I need to do with you—I feel an intense pressure just to live life with you. I need you, and I would be crushed, devastated, badly hurt without you. I would be a shell, incapable of loving again, trusting again, sharing my feelings and thoughts as they come. This is as scary as it is wonderful because I leave myself vulnerable with you. If I walk now, maybe I can still redeem something of my life. Maybe I'll shrivel up and die. Even if I survived, I don't think I could look at life in the same way with such great joy and happiness.

You are incredible. You are everything I've ever dreamed of. How can I best protect it, nurture it, allow it to flourish? By being with you, allowing in all these possible forces that will potentially destroy it? Or by holding it up as a memory—a beautiful dream that will always remain in my heart? I can't bear the thought of it, one way or the other, so tell me there's an alternative. Tell me we'll be together, we'll be happy forever, everything will work out; Sammy, Rose, and Abby will all be fine. They'll work through it and come out confident, sure of themselves, loving—able to give and receive. Tell me that Candy and Dave will survive too – that they'll even find people to fall in love with as powerfully as we have and be happier in the long run. Tell me our families will respect us for it, accept our decisions as the right ones.

Tell me we'll have a family of our own, and that we'll look back at this one day, and you'll say to me, "See? You shouldn't have worried so much. You had faith in us, in our love, and it all worked out."

Can you please tell me all this? I know that in life there are no guarantees, but if you say this, I will believe you. I do believe in you. With all my insecurities and need for reassurance, I know that you love me.

* * *

When Diana arrived home, she moved quietly to her office to check for messages from Curt. She had to be careful, but using the excuse of work came in handy since Dave was focused on her ability to make money while she cared for Abby. And she did, a considerable amount, but it never seemed to be enough. She turned on the computer, entered her password, and sifted through the messages that had come in since she left London. As anticipated, Curt had sent a response to the letter she had left for him.

Dear Diana,

My preference would normally be to write to you by hand, but in trying to respond to your letter, which was everything to me, from wonderful to incisive to breathtaking even, I don't know where to start and so apologise for using the PC. I will try to address what I can, for the rest we need more time to see what lies around the corner.

Firstly, I feel tremendous respect for the fact that you have consistently put my children ahead of us as consideration, and I could never suggest that you have been "instrumental" in the physical separation between me and my children. Yes, you have been a "catalyst" (my father's words, as he draws parity with his own separation from mum when I was just 17) in accelerating my decision to leave home. Yes, a big reason for coming to the US is to be with you. And I agree, you have to be concerned about loving someone who is capable of leaving his children. I love Sammy and Rose dearly, and I can't explain to myself how I'm capable of it, but I know I will. I will try to manage quality contact, and I will come to terms with the pain such a separation will inflict on them. Only I know how much I love my children. The other thing to remember is, as much as we try to protect our children, they are extremely resilient and adaptable, and they, too, can benefit. They love me as I am now; in the future, they can love me as a much happier person.

I am massively independent, which is something that was forced on me from childhood. I lack confidence but, at the same time, believe in myself. I know if resolute, I can get what I want. This scares me because it doesn't help me share decision-making, and it is why I'm stubborn.

Thinking about Candy, as days go by, I care less about her and even some resentment is creeping in. I'm seeing her more and more in her true colours, and the idea of trying to be friends has completely gone. I don't trust her, she is materialistic to the point where it will destroy her, she is lazy, and it would not surprise me one bit if one day she walked away and abandoned Sammy and Rose. In short, she has chosen the life she wants and can get on with it. I guarantee she'll be married before long, living in a bigger house and with more money to spend (not that this will make her happy, as ultimately, I don't think she can be).

Diana, you are a dream, you are my inspiration, you are my savior to be loved, and you are everything I could ever wish for. You talk about being vulnerable, well, let me tell you, I have no idea what to do if you fail me. I know I will never believe in love again. I will never be truly happy because I don't believe anyone can match you or even come close—I would be forever making comparisons and be disappointed. I am selfish, and that's how I can focus more on myself in all of this. I want what's right for me because I've been disappointed thus far, and I don't intend to spend the rest of my life frustrated in a search for something better. Nothing in life is ever perfect, but it can be close, and the rest is up to you. You have to believe in yourself and not make every decision in the context of "doing what's right" for others. Being selfish is OK!

Finally, I would like to have a child with you for lots of reasons. You also know how much more I want... I hadn't thought about returning to Europe in the context of Dave, and if he'd allow it, and I apologise for not thinking about this. Returning to Europe is not on my agenda but was more a message to you that circumstances can change, and who knows where you can end up? Of course, I would never return without you. I'm only interested in a commitment for life, and yes, this means we have to be "damned sure," and yes, we'll have to work through the difficult stuff, of which there will undoubtedly be plenty. I'm damned sure we can be happy if we harness and nurture what we have.

The best word I can find today to capture what we have is strength. I feel a great strength or synergy in what we have. With strength, we can work through this as we continue to feed off each other. We still have bridges to cross, but think about those we've crossed already. Despite the huge distance between us, we've been able to grow our love in a short space of time. Then getting through leaving my home to buying a flat, and again in no time at all. My life has changed significantly already, and I can't wait for what's next. The excitement is electrifying. I gain confidence daily. Confidence about making the right decision, confidence about myself (which you are helping me with), confidence about us (with no doubts anymore about the love we have for each other). And all this is because I feel strong with you—it's tangible, and it's what we have, and it's what will get us through. Things will work out just fine! Trust me! Curt xx

5

So many red flags; she ignored them all. Blinded by her love for Curt and the loveless marriage she was in, Diana fell prey to his promises. It was impossible to say no to him, to someone who loved her the way she had always hoped to be loved, so completely and passionately.

"So, you ended up with some guy who would leave his children?" Janis wagged a finger at her. "Tsk, tsk, Kung Fu. What were you thinking?"

"What was I supposed to do? I was miserable, and there were no right answers. I thought I was doing the right thing for the chance of happiness, mine and Abby's, too." She mumbled under her breath, "And Curt promised he would get the children."

"How did that work out for you?"

"Not good. Despite making every attempt, it never happened. His children hated me for taking him away. My dream of having a big, happy family never came true."

"Well, I hate to tell ya, Kung Fu, I don't know of many big, happy families, especially blended ones."

"We were so happy when we were together. I really thought our love could conquer anything."

Janis scoffed, "You were reading too many romance novels."

"Well, it was romantic. I'd never felt so loved in my life."

"Yeah, those types are really good at that love-bombing thing. Did you fall prey, Kung Fu?"

No response from Diana, who just rolled her eyes.

Janis tried a different tact. "So, what happened after you met his children? I assumed you ended up with him, or you wouldn't be here."

* * *

Diana arrived home from another trip to London that afternoon and walked up the stairs to the kitchen. Dave wasn't home from work yet, so Abby would be across the street at the nanny's house. It was quiet, but something didn't seem right. She stepped into her office and noticed her cabinet door was open. Her eyes drew wide, and her heart started racing; it was missing. The blue binder was missing.

Her stomach lurched into her throat. She checked the cabinet again. It was gone. *Did Dave find it? This is no joke. What a fool! Why did I keep copies of those messages?* Was it to remind her that she was loved? Was it to relive the romance and sentiment that she thought she may never experience again?

She called Curt. She didn't care what time it was; she needed his support.

"Hello, Diana, is everything alright?" he said sleepily.

"Curt, the binder is gone." The alarm in Diana's voice was distinctive.

"What binder?"

"I made copies of our messages and now they're gone. He knows." There was silence on the other end of the line. "Curt, are you there?"

"Yes, I'm here." He sighed. "Why did you make copies, Diana?"

"I don't know. I just wanted to save our messages to each other... the poetry, the love."

She heard footsteps coming up the stairs from the garage. "He's here! I have to go."

"Call me later," Curt said hastily and hung up.

Dave walked into the kitchen and didn't say a word. Diana looked at him imploringly. She didn't know what to do; this was not a situation she ever thought she would find herself in. Dave couldn't look at her. He slowly walked across the kitchen and opened the cabinet door to reach for a glass.

Diana broke the silence. "Aren't you going to say anything to me?"

He spun around and glared at her, then abruptly turned and threw the glass into the cabinet, smashing the rows of neatly-arranged glassware, spraying sharp pieces across the room. Diana shielded her eyes and braced herself for another blow.

"You slut." His voice shook the remaining glasses left standing in the cabinet. "How could you? We have a daughter. I wish you were dead." He stormed across the room and left Diana standing amidst the remnants of her shattered life. It was done, she knew. Part of her felt relief; she did not want to continue to live the lie. It was tearing her apart, and she would now have to face it once and for all. She bent down to pick up the pieces of glass. She had no idea what would happen next. She was afraid, alone, and unsure of what Dave was capable of doing.

She couldn't call Curt just yet. Dave would hear her. She decided to go across the street to get Abby, plus, she could think over there for a few minutes. She opened the door to go out through the garage, and Dave was instantly standing there. He didn't say a word as he blocked her exit.

"Where do you think you're going?" he asked in a calm but eerie tone.

"I have to get Abby."

"No, you don't. You're going to sit down and tell me everything, you bitch."

"Dave, I..."

"Shut up!" He grabbed her by the arm and moved her towards the couch. He pushed her down to sit. "You better tell me what's going on, Diana. What have you done?"

"I love him" Her eyes were downcast, her tone hushed.

"Don't say that, it's not true," he shouted. "You love me. Who is this guy? Some Limey boy? I swear, Diana, I'm going to kill him if you don't tell me what's going on."

"I didn't mean for it to happen." She lowered her head and spoke under her breath.

"Sit up and speak up, Diana, I can't hear you."

"I said, I didn't mean for it to happen. It just did."

"Wow, really? That is the lamest thing I've ever heard. Did you fuck him while you were fucking me?"

"We haven't had sex for months."

"I've been busy with work." He glared at her and waited for a response. "Sorry, I wasn't meeting your needs."

"That's not all of it. You've been driving me crazy. I can't do anything right. You always criticize me and make outrageous demands. The only time you're nice is when other people are around. I can't take it anymore."

He took a step back as if someone had punched him in the gut. His eyes drew down to the ground as he softened his voice, "I'm sorry, Diana. I didn't know you were so unhappy. I thought you were just upset that I was working so hard."

"No, that's not it."

"What can we do to fix this?"

"I don't know, Dave. I really don't."

* * *

The therapist sat across from them in a soft chair with her notepad on the ready. She was buttoned-up, dressed professionally in a camel-haired, stiff skirt and jacket. Her hair was blond and short, and she looked as if she had just stepped out of the salon. Diana knew the type—wound up and ready to go toe-to-toe.

Dave was lying to her. He was pretending to be such a nice guy, a guy who really loved Diana. He was charming the therapist, and she was falling for it. She told Diana she had low self-esteem—the crux of the problem. She had no idea how much Diana suffered with Dave. She had no idea how strongly Diana felt about Curt. Diana tried to tell her that she could not live without him, that her feelings were too strong.

"Do the two of you love each other?" the therapist challenged.

They sat side-by-side on the small, leather couch like schoolchildren in the principal's office. Dave responded first.

"I love her." He shifted on the couch uncomfortably.

"Well, then look at her and tell her," the therapist commanded.

Dave awkwardly turned to Diana to recite the words as if they were scripted. "I love you, Diana."

Diana softened in response, thinking there was a glitter of authenticity in his proclamation, and then she remembered the list Dave had handed her well before she had met Curt. It was a bulleted list of all the things that were wrong with her—all things that needed to be fixed—everything from her body and hair down to her beliefs and values. She remembered how once he told her he had married her because he "took a look around and realized there probably wasn't much better out there."

"Well, Diana," the therapist challenged. "What about you? Do you love Dave?"

Diana hesitated, trying to compartmentalize the hurt feelings that Dave had generated over the years. "Well, I guess I care about him," she shrugged. "He is the father of my child." She looked up, sighed, and said more emphatically, "But the love I felt for him has been destroyed."

"How so, Diana?" the therapist questioned.

"Why don't you ask him?" She shook her head to fight back the tears of frustration. She thought this marriage would be so perfect. She thought about how Dave pressured her every day for perfection. She hated the word, the concept. And now, there was a man who adored her just as she was, warts and all. How could she pass up the opportunity to have the love she always craved? The love she never thought was possible for her?

The therapist ended the session by declaring that if they had any chance of reconciliation, the third person in the relationship must be omitted. She told Diana that she had to cut all ties with Curt, and there could be no communication with him for at least six weeks to give the marriage a chance. With a sick feeling in her stomach, Diana agreed. If nothing else, she had to do it for the sake of Abby, and she had to admit, although he was wonderful, she had some serious reservations about the realistic possibilities with Curt.

The phone was ringing in her office when they got home. Diana couldn't answer; Dave flew into her office whenever the phone rang. He now had access to her computer, he had taken her credit cards and checkbook, and he was threatening to take Abby. She felt like a prisoner in her own home. Diana knew he would never forgive her, and if she thought she was repressed before, she hadn't seen anything yet. She was suffocating as if she had been buried alive, and she couldn't quite reach the bell. Curt represented freedom, passion, and happiness. The phone continued to ring. He wasn't giving up.

"Answer it, Diana, and tell him you're never speaking to him again."

Diana rushed into her office and picked up the phone, "Hello, this is Diana." She answered professionally on the off-chance that it was her client or a colleague.

"Diana, are you okay, my love?"

She began to sob; she didn't know how she was going to do this. "I can't speak to you," she sputtered.

"Why, what's going on…? Is he around?"

"They told me I can't speak to you for six weeks." She started hyperventilating as she delivered the brutal message.

"What? Diana…"

"I have to go, Curt" She moved to hang up the phone.

"Wait, Diana!" His plea registered before she slammed the phone into its cradle.

She dropped to the floor and curled into a ball; Dave moved to help her up. Her heart was being ripped out; she couldn't take it. She was having trouble breathing. Dave picked her up and held her firmly; he smiled as he watched Diana suffer. He would continue to watch her very closely, keeping her on an extremely short leash.

A little over a week later, a package came to Diana's post office box, which was the only connection to Curt that Dave didn't know existed. She kept it open as the last form of possible communication she had with Curt. The package contained a letter written in Curt's hand and a CD.

Dear Diana,

This is not fair. I cannot go on without you in my life. I feel that you have freed me from a life of pain but have only taken me out to play with, and now I am supposed to go back into the box. I can't do it. I am coming for you; you cannot keep me away. No one has the right to tear us apart—we have a right to be happy. I will be there at Christmas time, and I am sending you the flight details. I hope that you will be there to greet me when I get off the plane.

Forever yours,

Curt xx

P.S. Please listen to the fourth song of the enclosed CD.

Diana read the note over and over. It did not solve the confusion she felt. On the one hand, she wanted Curt desperately. She wanted him to save her, to be her knight in shining armor. What she felt for Curt was extremely powerful. She could not deny it; it had to be true love. *What else could it possibly be?* How could she deny herself? Curt was right; they deserved to be happy.

On the other hand, there was her family. No one would understand if she left Dave. He appeared to have it all—good looks, good job, good family upbringing, and money. He could be so charming and affable with others, but what people didn't understand was the emotional torture she experienced every day.

But most importantly, there was Abby to consider. This was not fair to her. Didn't she deserve to have a normal upbringing with both parents intact? That's what she had, and that's what she wanted to provide Abby. *But how intact could we ever be?* Diana continued to argue with herself. She could somehow validate her desire to leave Dave by suggesting that with Curt, she could show

Abby what a loving relationship looked like—a relationship that would last a lifetime.

She placed the CD in her car stereo and forwarded to the fourth song, "The Drugs Don't Work" by The Verve. The words cut through Diana's heart like a knife as she thought about the intimate moments when Curt would whisper and sing in her ear. She couldn't take it. She had to have him and wanted to see his face again. Diana listened to the words over and over.

She buckled Abby into her car seat and drove to the nearest phone booth at the commuter lot at the entrance to the interstate. Curt picked up the phone immediately, and Diana said the four words that would change her life forever, "I will be there."

6

When Diana looked back at the time, she realized how emotionally squeezed she was by want and desire for Curt, her sense of responsibility for Abby, and the guilt she felt around Dave. She could assuage the latter with the remembrance of Dave's treatment of her and the sense of abandonment she felt every day, physically, emotionally, mentally. Any way she looked at it, she knew she could not survive the marriage. It would eventually destroy her, and in doing so, destroy whatever strength she had to be a good mother to Abby.

"So, let me guess, you decided to divorce your husband?"

"Yes, I did. I'm not saying it wasn't a difficult decision, it was, but Dave was making it easier for me with his behavior."

"Well, the dude must have been pretty upset."

"Yes, he was, but he kept threatening me, and with each threat, he pushed me further and further into Curt's arms."

"I betcha he didn't waste any time." Janis shook her head. "Man, he played you good, Kung Fu, when you were down."

"It wasn't like that. He saved me from the hell I was living in."

"I'm not sure why you taking his side, but I betcha he didn't wait too long before he was putting a ring on it."

* * *

It was a beautiful day; bitter cold, but clear and lovely with a blanket of fresh pure snow. Diana zipped her coat a little higher and jumped up and down to get the blood flowing. She was in her favorite place, and she beamed at the prospect of sharing it with Curt. She had been visiting this picturesque Vermont town since she was a child and always felt like she was stepping into a Christmas card each time she came. The narrow streets lined with pristine piles of snow accentuated the beauty of the interspersed white clapboard and brick homes, the majestic church steeples, and at its centerpiece, the elegantly preserved inn that had notably accommodated various revolutionary figures and presidents of the day. The smell of pine and burning firewood permeated the air. Every memory of this place was a fond one. In fact, she would cry as a child when it was time to leave. She can remember the first time her parents took her to this wonderland. She'd jumped out of the car but could go no further, as she'd been stuck in the snow that measured up to her hips. For Diana, this place equated to purity, peace, and joy.

The plan was to hike up Pineview Hill, a romantic venue with its pine-laden sides and deep woodland trails. After a leisurely, passionate morning hibernating in bed, followed by a good hearty breakfast complete with Vermont maple syrup, Diana and Curt made their way over to the head of the trail. Curt carried all the necessities for the day in his bright yellow backpack, including bottled water, a Swiss Army knife, chocolate for the journey, and even a small Johnson & Johnson first aid kit, which tickled Diana and made her smile. He was so proud to tell her, "I was in the Scouts, after all!" Diana felt protected and cared for, and she happily submitted to his directives to ensure a safe and comfortable hike.

They followed the red blazes that would take them directly to the top. Curt removed every obstacle in Diana's way, quickly chucking logs that blocked the path, holding branches back for her to pass. As they climbed further and further up, Diana's body warmed, and her heart once again melted from his tenderness. Huffing and puffing, they made it to the top in record time to catch the sun at the top of the pines. Curt opened his backpack for a refreshment, and out came a bottle of Champagne and a small black box.

Oh my God, he's going to propose!

They stood on top of the summit's rock pile in the light of the sun, he faced her to nervously recite the poem he had written:

Diana, you are my one true love.
    I know I can be the man you deserve,
    Caring and kind, loving, and supportive.
    You are my best friend and lover, and I want to share
the rest of my life with you.
    Say yes, and make me the happiest man on Earth.

As they embraced, tears rolled down Diana's face. This was a dream come true, finally true love, a love that would last a lifetime. She pulled away from him. "I'm not sure, Curt. I'm scared." She tried to lighten her response up a bit with a broad smile and a nervous chuckle. "I'm afraid marriage will ruin our relationship."

"It's going to be fine, Diana." He gently cupped her face in his hands. "Look at me. You are the love of my life, and I would do anything to make you happy."

He placed the ring on her finger and kissed her passionately.

Her head was spinning. *Is this too soon for me? I just divorced Dave, and Curt has only been here for six months. Am I doing the right thing?*

She wouldn't debate it now. It was too cold. They downed the first glass of champagne and headed back to continue the celebration in the room at the inn. As they descended, her thoughts went from elation to concern at the thought of marriage again. She shrugged off her misgivings; she just wanted a chance at happiness, and Curt was everything she had always dreamed.

* * *

It had been nearly two years, and Diana was still dragging her feet on the wedding plans. In the back of her mind, she was still worried that marriage might ruin the relationship. Everything was going so well. She had found a lovely home for them nestled in the woods of Connecticut but not too far from the coast. The house had a natural feel with floor-to-ceiling windows, interesting architectural details, and warm wood tones throughout.

Abby seemed to be adapting to her new life fairly well; Dave had found a place nearby to make it easier on her. Curt wasn't really happy about his proximity, but he managed to distance himself from the decision-making on behalf of Abby, opting to be the fun stepfather instead. This was good for Abby since her father was such a stickler about everything. Diana's parents and the nanny were helping in the transition, Diana would be forever grateful for the love and support they consistently showered on Abby.

But Curt's patience had begun to run dry. One morning, before heading to work, he made his proclamation on the way out the door. "If we don't get married by year-end, I am going back to England." Curt turned away from her without waiting for a response and walked out.

Diana stood in the middle of the kitchen, shocked at his behavior. *How could he say something like that and then just leave me stand-*

ing here, wounded? She understood that she had been stalling, but she just wasn't in a hurry to get married again.

The nanny walked through the front door, came into the kitchen to greet Diana, and immediately knew there was something wrong. Diana's usual cheery demeanor and welcoming smile was replaced by a look of fear and dismay. "What's wrong, honey?" She walked over to Diana to place her arm around her shoulders.

Diana burst into tears, as she always did when she was upset and someone showed her kindness. "Curt just threatened to go back to England if I didn't marry him by the end of the year. And then he just left the house."

The nanny looked deep into her eyes and said matter-of-factly, "Well, maybe he should go then."

She froze. *What? No. Wait.* The thoughts went flying through her head like rapid fire from an assault rifle. *I can't lose him. I love him too much.* She had divorced Dave to be with him, upsetting Abby's world, taking her back and forth from her house to his in the shared-custody arrangement. Curt had left England and his kids to be with her. There was just too much at stake. This relationship had to work. Plus, they had been talking about having a baby together, and she always wanted a big family. *I can't let him go back.*

"But I love him. I don't want to lose him." Her voice began to quiver. "I can't go to England with him. I can't leave Abby, and I can't take her from Dave. He would never allow that—it's in our agreement."

"But Diana, honey, what kind of man threatens to leave you if you don't marry him?" The nanny was not one to mince words. She had grown close to Diana and had watched Abby since she was a baby. She was an honorary grandmother to them. Diana respected her honesty and wisdom, and she listened. She needed to think about what she was saying.

Diana had her misgivings. When Curt moved to the U.S., he had to leave his children behind, Sammy and Rose. He promised that his ex-wife, Candy, wouldn't want to take care of them by herself and would be happy to give them up. This was a relief to Diana, and she was happy to accept his children as her own. But it didn't work out that way. Sammy and Rose stayed with Candy until their summer school break, when she would let them come to the US for the duration. This weighed heavily on Diana's conscience, but she could not admit defeat.

They decided to move forward with the wedding and would be married on one of the islands friendly to such matters. She thought it would be good to include the kids to solidify the blended family. When she mentioned this to Curt, he was absolutely against it and said he would handle how he told the children. "They're still hoping I will come back, Diana. Probably best not to let them give up all hope on that."

Diana disagreed, but she knew that ultimately it was his decision, since they were his kids. It just didn't feel right. Even at five years old, Abby was angry that she could not go and would stay with Grandma and Grandpa for the week.

They decided to go at the end of November just before high season. Diana planned the entire trip and arranged for the local minister to perform the ceremony. Diana's good friends would join them and act as witnesses. There would be no family. It would take place along the cliff's edge, and, as Diana would later joke, there was only one other way to go if she didn't go through with it: "Over the edge."

* * *

It was a beautiful day as the wind whipped through the grasses atop the cliff. The Atlantic was showing its spectacular strength with waves pounding and spraying against the craggy rocks. They walked up the bluff overlooking the ocean and stood before the minister to read the vows they had prepared. Curt went first.

This ring is for you, Diana.
   My best friend and partner in all things important.
   A symbol of my love
   And a symbol of my commitment to us both.
   Together we are focused and can achieve great things.
   Together we are strong and can get through the tough times.
   Together we have the power to remove fear and focus on what
   really matters.
   My commitment is:
   To openly communicate, good or bad
   To make time for each other, our family and our friends
   To listen carefully and respect your views
   To protect your vulnerability through counsel
   To experiment and try new things
   To make sure there's always room for laughter
   And not least, to always love you and remind you often why you're
   so special.

Curt slipped the wedding band onto her finger and smiled. He looked deep into her eyes as Diana recited the vows she had prepared.

Curt, with this ring, I vow to you:
   my unconditional love
   a trust that will not be compromised
   respect for what we have

acceptance of who you are
laughter in our home
care for our children
a friendship to last the years
a life full of passion and warmth
memories to inspire

It was done. They were officially married. They descended down the bluff, hand-in-hand, to commence with the celebrations. Diana's concerns briefly disappeared as she felt the love and security in Curt's vows, expressing what had escaped her in the past. This marriage was cause for great celebration as she anticipated many years of happiness with the man she could not live without, and who adored her to no end.

PART TWO

7

Diana sat silently remembering the climb up that grassy hill overlooking the ocean. How happy she had been; she had finally met the man she would spend the rest of her life with. Everything about him was perfect for her, and she could not believe that they had found each other and were able to overcome the obstacles to be together. At the time, it seemed it was meant to be.

"So, congratulations, you married the dude. Then everything was picture perfect." Janis was clearly being sarcastic.

"Well, it was for a while." Diana looked down at her feet. Still in a meditation pose, she could sit like that for hours. "I had Abby to worry about, and trying to co-parent with Dave was not easy. And it was really hard with Curt's kids; they were never happy about us being together."

"Well, you can't really blame them. They couldn't be mad at their father for leaving even though it was his choice. You had to be the bad guy. I'm sure they were angry and needed to take it out on someone. You were it, Kung Fu."

"I realize that. Honestly, I do. But it didn't make it any easier for me. I was on high alert every time they came over to stay, and it was usually for the entire summer. My stomach would be in knots the whole time. I started hating summers. I had that feeling that you do on a Sunday before you have to go back to work."

"I wouldn't know about that. I pretty much had to work every day to keep food on the table. It's kind of hard to feel sorry for you, Kung Fu."

"Despite all that, I was convinced we would grow old together. That is what I witnessed with my parents, and that is what I expected for myself."

"Oh yeah, I know that fairy tale."

* * *

Diana was in awe of her parents' 50th wedding anniversary. The plan was to take the entire family to Grand Caymen, the location of their honeymoon. Imagine, half a century with the same person. She was desperate to have history with Curt, to build a life and a family. They had been married for five years now, and she wondered whether they could ever make it to that golden moment. It was possible; they would only be in their late 80s on that day! There was still a lot of time to grow and make things right with the blended family they had.

Life together had been going relatively well but not without its challenges. Curt had quit his job and had been out of work for a year. This had put stress on the relationship that was already constantly and subversively under attack. Sammy and Rose were understandably not happy with the circumstances, and as much as Diana tried, they were not happy with her. It was awful to be hated by his children, especially for Diana, who wanted them to be part of a happy family. The attempt to get custody of the children had failed; she was frustrated that Curt didn't seem to try very hard. His promise that Candy would gladly give them up never came to fruition.

Perhaps, she thought, if she and Curt had a baby of their own, then it would help to solidify their family and provide Abby, Rose, and Sammy with a little sister or brother to care for. Abby was ex-cited about the prospect, but it was hard to tell with the other two. Despite their lack of enthusiasm, she wanted another baby desper-ately. She had gone to a fertility specialist after two miscarriages and was hopeful this last time would work.

She remembered laying on the bed, her legs propped up against the wall. This was the silly position the doctor had recommended "following intercourse". A smile came across her face as Curt left the bed to clean himself up; she always loved the view of his broad back and naked ass. Curt didn't care for sex on demand—he liked to be in control—but he accommodated Diana and her timing; he knew how much she wanted this baby. He did his part.

"I have to keep my legs up for ten minutes," Diana shouted. No reply from the bathroom. She waited.

"Can I get you anything?" he asked as he walked out of the bath-room past the bed.

"Can't you sit with me, keep me company?" Diana reached for him as he walked by.

"I have things to do, Diana. Just relax."

"Okay, then." As Diana lay there looking up at the ceiling, she was positive it would work this time, and they would have a beau-tiful baby to complete their dream.

Now, a year later, it was hard to admit that she was not going to have the big family she had always dreamed of. But at 40, she realized that it was probably best if it did not happen. Although she was in good health, Curt reminded her more than once what the risks would be. But more importantly, she couldn't take the pain of another lost baby. It was always two months into the preg-nancy. There would be a heartbeat and lots of hope one week, and then the next visit, nothing. No rhythm. It was gut-wrenching, and Diana would never forget the sting of the tears. Curt didn't seem that upset, but he was one to take things in stride, which was one of the things that Diana had first admired about him. She was emotional; he was steady, like a rock, and didn't reveal his emotions.

As they stepped onto the ship, she was content to be with her family and happy that his kids could come along. She wanted to be a good stepmother to them, and she was grateful to her parents for being so generous and including them on their big anniversary trip. Maybe this would be a good opportunity to get closer as one blended family.

They weren't on the beach for five minutes before Diana heard the screams. Her stepdaughter was swimming towards her with panic on her face. "Diana, Abby hurt herself. She's bleeding." Heart racing, adrenaline coursing through her veins, she started swimming to Abby and locked on the growing pool of bloodied water that surrounded her. Diana heard the theme music from *Jaws* in her head, grabbed Abby, and held her under her arm so she could swim on her side. She swam past Curt and Rose; they just stared at Diana while she struggled to get Abby on to shore. She accepted the help of strangers to carry Abby onto the beach; they wrapped her ankle that had been cut open by coral in a cheerful beach towel. Diana turned to see Curt, who hadn't moved an inch, standing waist high in the water only twenty feet away from the scene on the beach. She looked at him imploringly; she wanted to scream, "Why aren't you helping me?"

They had to get Abby up a long flight of steps to get her to the road, where a taxi could be hailed to take them back to the ship's doctor. She needed stitches for sure, as her ankle was gashed wide open. Abby continued to scream as her uncle, complete with rod and pins in his hip, scooped her up and painfully carried her up the steep concrete staircase and placed her in the cab. Curt never left the water, just sat back to watch the scene unfold before him. Diana felt alone in that moment and realized she was on her own when it came to parenting Abby.

Things got worse. It was bad enough that Abby had to be stitched up and couldn't swim all week, but Sammy and Rose were not being nice to Abby or to Diana at all. Diana felt as if they were plotting behind her back. She didn't want to be paranoid, but there was something sneaky about Curt's kids, and Diana was a bit freaked out by it. She could understand that they were excited about the trip, but she was still upset about the circumstances by which they were seeing their father. Diana tried as hard as she could to be good to them, but it was difficult.

She tried to kick back and relax while she watched Curt and his kids play in the pool. Abby was sitting next to her, happily coloring, but she knew she was missing out. With the fresh stitches in her ankle, she was confined to land for the remainder of the trip. Curt was throwing Sammy around in the water while Rose stood by and watched. For some reason, it was making Diana nervous. He was playing a little too rough with Sammy, and Rose was watching the exchange with a mischievous smile on her face. She knew it wouldn't be too long before Sammy would end up in tears. Curt did not know how to play nice.

"Curt, aren't you being a little rough?"

"No, he likes it. Don't you, son?"

Sammy wiped the water from his eyes. "No, I don't." Sammy pushed Rose under the water as he swam past her and quickly got out of the pool. He picked up his towel and plopped down on the chair next to Diana and Abby. Rose began to cry uncontrollably.

With the force of his large body pulling through the water, Curt followed Sammy out of the pool and picked him up by the towel that was wrapped around him, "Don't you ever lay a hand on your sister again," he shouted in his face.

"Curt, please. Calm down." Diana's eyes darted around to see some of the other guests looking over at them.

"Stay out of it, Diana."

Emboldened by what she had just witnessed, Diana got up from her chair, walked over to him, and said in a quiet, measured voice, "If you ever talk to me that way in front of the children again, you are on your own."

* * *

Diana's biggest concern about the children was realized on the last evening of the trip. It was the formal evening, and the whole family was dressed up in their finest. Diana was full of excitement and energy; she chose her purple dress to bring out the vivid green in her eyes. She always loved the formal evenings—getting dressed up, meeting the captain, dancing all night, and probably eating and drinking way too much.

Of course, on this evening, Curt didn't make it past nine, which was starting to become a regular habit. He decided to go back to the cabin after consuming incredible amounts of alcohol. Diana wanted to go to the casino to have some more fun; she was just getting started. She joined a table of tuxedo-wearing strangers to play blackjack and was having a bit of luck. She looked up from her cards to spot Curt storming down the hall in his underwear. She could see the image of his now-pudgy outline as he raced past the glass partitions. She couldn't imagine what he was doing. She watched him out of the corner of her eye as he silently stormed through the casino in nothing but his white boxers. She was going to pretend she didn't know him, then realized he was making a bee-line for her. He came up to her, silently poured a glass of ice-cold water down her back, and then walked out. Diana sat up with a look of shock.

"Did you see that?" Diana said to the guy next to her.

"Yes, everyone did."

Diana tried to compose herself. *How dare he.* She cashed out her chips and stormed out of the casino, wet from his assault. *What in God's name has gotten into him?* She quickly made her way down the gangway to the back of the ship, where their cabin was conveniently situated right next to her parents. She went to open the door, and it was bolted closed so she couldn't get in. She knocked but there was no answer.

Her teenage nephew, Drew, saw her in the hall and came running up to her. He seemed distraught and was breathing heavily.

"Hey, Aunt Di, are you okay?"

Diana blurted out, "Curt just poured a glass of water down my back and..." She started sobbing. "And now I can't get into the room. I'm locked out. I don't know what's going on!"

"It's okay, Aunt Di. Don't cry." He gave her a loving hug to let her know he was there to support her. He hesitated. "I think I should tell you that I saw Sammy and Rose go to your room, and I was walking down the hallway, and I heard them talking to Uncle Curt."

"What happened, Drew? Tell me, it's okay."

"I heard Sammy say, 'yeah, she was flirtin' with 'em a lot.' Then Rose said, 'Yes, it's true, Daddy. I saw them." He mimicked their English accents masterfully, infusing the odd differences between the two as if Rose was trained to speak in a more polished, polite manner.

"Really?" Diana was crest-fallen; they had purposefully tried to get her in trouble.

"Then Uncle Curt came storming out of the room in his underwear," Drew explained, "with Sammy and Rose following him all excited and giggling."

"C'mon, then. Let's go get security." Diana enlisted Drew to come with her so that she would not lose control.

The security staff eyeballed her as she tried to explain. "Yes, I'm very worried about him. He's not in the best shape, and he drank quite a lot."

"Don't worry, ma'am. We will open it for you."

"Thank you." She watched as the two men proceeded to open the door.

"You're all set. Have a good night, ma'am."

She turned to give Drew another hug. "Be safe, Aunt Di. You call us if you need anything."

"Thanks, honey. Good-night."

She wasn't in the room for two minutes when Curt started yelling at her. "What were you doing, you stupid cow?"

"What?" Diana cried. "What are you talking about? I've done nothing. I was just playing cards!"

"You're a liar. You were flirting with those guys. YOU ARE A CUNT!"

Diana was aghast. "I'm not Candy, Curt. Stop calling me those names. That's awful."

"If you keep this up, Diana, I am going back to England."

"Keep what up? I did nothing, Curt. You're out of your mind."

He rolled over and, without a word, went back to sleep.

Now I have to get into bed with this man? Who is he?

She couldn't sleep and decided to write him a letter. He would be up early to find it.

Dear Curt,

We need a better way of communicating.

Last night you acted outrageously and then threatened me with the idea that you will leave and go back to England. Do you really have one foot out the door? Are you committed enough to our love, our relationship, to try and make it work? Or will you just take off?

It seems I have been living with this threat for some time. If it wasn't the situation with your children, it was the lack of a green card, or unemployment, or now... my behavior. If I make one false move... you're out of here! That does not sound like a committed relationship with a solid foundation.

Remember how you felt about not knowing if you had a job? You can imagine how I feel not knowing what you're thinking and how close to leaving you might be.

As for me, I love you very much. You are the person I want to share my life with, but I cannot continue with this threat hanging squarely over my head. You have placed it there; it needs to be removed, or we cannot survive.

I am willing to do whatever it takes to get on track, but I can't do it alone. We need to talk, we need to commit to each other, we need to make a plan. If we need marriage counseling, I'll do that, too. I cannot let go that easily. I still believe what we have is very special, and I do not want to destroy it. But I need to know where you are with this—are you willing to do the work it takes to make this, and any good relationship, work?

We should be nurturing our love to make sure we stay strong and enjoy this beautiful life we've been given.

Love, Me xo

She woke up thinking: *Oh God, here we go again.* Curt was not in the room. The last thing she wanted was to go through another divorce, but this was just unacceptable. She didn't deserve this treatment, and she wouldn't stand for it. She spotted the letter and saw that it had been read and folded over. She got up and read Curt's scribble on top of it.

Diana,

I agree, but it's not ok to talk to me like dirt or humiliate me. I love you very much, and I'm very committed to you and our future, but NOT at any price!

Love,

Curt xx

She contemplated the meaning of the short message, and the interpretation was less than satisfying. The way he talked to her, and within earshot of her parents—that was inexcusable. He was not going to take responsibility for his actions, let alone apologize for them. Worse yet, he was making the choice to not believe her and instead perpetuate his children's pronouncement of her flirtatious behavior, and branding in the process. *This does not bode well.*

8

Replaying that scene in her head made Diana realize that that was the moment she should have woken up. She let her desire to stay in a marriage for the long haul outweigh the potential consequences of what that would do to her health, her spirit, her soul. More importantly, she was worried about the children. Even though Sammy and Rose were clearly not in favor of their marriage, she did not want Abby to experience another breakup.

"So you just took that from him? You're not as tough as I thought, Kung Fu."

"Well, I'm tougher than I look, now anyway." Diana took a moment to reflect on those beginning years of marriage. "You know, looking back, I really needed the marriage to work. I couldn't put my daughter through another breakup. She had learned to trust Curt, and I think it would have done a lot of damage if she lost another father figure. I had to make it work, if no other reason but for her."

"What can I say? Kids can really set you straight or screw things up, depending on how you look at it." Janis reached into her shirt-front and pulled out a locket. "This is my baby girl." Janis carefully opened the locket and pointed it towards Diana.

"Oh, she is beautiful." Diana was touched at how Janis proudly shared the small photo she held next to her heart.

"I would die for her, Kung Fu." She kissed the locket and tucked it back inside her shirt beside her heart. "So, stayin' in a bad marriage for the sake of children seems like a small price to pay."

"You're right. It should have been enough to know that he could leave his children behind, but I believed him when he said everything would work out." Diana's face twisted as she spoke. "I guess he was a liar from the beginning."

"Look, Kung Fu, sometimes you make the best decisions you can with the information you have at the time."

Diana closed her eyes while Janis' pearl of wisdom sank in. She let out a heavy sigh. "Yes, but I still haven't told you all of it."

"I'm all ears. Like I said before, it's not like we're goin' anywhere anytime soon."

* * *

Curt sauntered into their newly renovated kitchen. It was the final project they needed to complete in their home of seven years. Diana loved to cook, so she'd designed the space with everything she ever wanted. The Viking six-burner gas stove and the Sub-Zero French-door refrigerator gleamed in their stainless steel glory. The wooden cabinets were custom-designed to sit in their space for ultimate efficiency, crowned with hand-signed, copper-finished handles and pulls. It was beautiful; it inspired Diana to cook every day and entertain with fervor and vigor. The kitchen was always the heart of the home for Diana, so this project represented rebuilding a home for the family. She sat at the new counter, feeling pleased with the new space, and watched Curt as he began to make a cup of tea. Now they could relax; this had been a big, expensive project. It would be nice to spend money on something other than the house—maybe even a nice trip for the two of them.

"Diana, I am getting tired of this house. It's too small." He flicked on the kettle and held his back to her, not wanting to face her.

"What? I love this house," she said cheerily, "and we've done so much work on it." She moved towards him to place a hand on his shoulder so he would look at her. He shrugged her hand away and turned towards the kettle to wait for the water to come up to the perfect temperature.

"I am done working on this house."

Diana could feel the heat rising in her face. "Exactly," she said stiffly, then hesitated. "I was hoping that we might just kick back and enjoy it. Maybe now we can use our money to buy a boat or something fun." She smiled but could feel the dread building in her gut. She hated these conversations with Curt, when he would claim a decision had been made without any real discussion or consideration.

"Oh, please," he said sarcastically, as he dunked his teabag five times exactly. "Be real, Diana. This house is just too small and you know it."

Her voice started to speed up and rise in tone as she repeated, "I love this house just as it is. We've worked so hard to finish it. Why would you want to leave it now?"

"It's far from done. The windows are failing, the roof is leaking, and I hate that there's no basement."

"I didn't know a basement was that important to you." She calmed down and started to feel badly that he might be unhappy, that there was something he always wanted but didn't get, adding to the long list of disappointments from his childhood. She decided to try a more rational response. "Well, we just refinanced, and we're in a great financial position now. I don't want to spend the money to move just for a basement." She rolled her eyes at the thought. She hated basements anyway; she remembered many terrifying moments when her sister would run up the basement stairs, turn off the lights, and bar the door, leaving her alone in pitch darkness, crying at the top of stairs to be let out.

"It's always about what you want, isn't it?" He flung the teabag in the sink and stormed out of the kitchen.

Diana held her head in her hands; she didn't understand why he seemed so unhappy. They worked so hard to make a beautiful home, and there had been so much love between them. *Why is he behaving this way?*

She knew he wouldn't give it up. Once he made a decision, it was all over. He was like a dog with a bone; if you even got near to try and take it away, there would be growling and snapping. Diana could not take that. Later, after Curt calmed down, Diana tried a different approach. "How about an addition?" She would call a friend whose husband was a builder and invite them over for brunch. He could take a look around and discuss the possibilities with them. Curt showed some interest at the thought, while Diana held onto hope that they would stay in her home.

She really loved everything about the house in all seasons. The dramatic rock outcroppings that lit up at night, their crevices casting shadows across the native Mountain Laurel, which would proudly bloom over the hillside on Curt's birthday each year. In the winter, the sledding run cut though the birch trees to whisk the kids down in tubes for a gentle and safe ride into the yard. Nature surrounded the house and could be viewed from every room through the floor-to-ceiling windows. At night, they made love in front of the dancing flames of the concrete-rendered fireplace embedded with antique tiles depicting various scenes of Dutch life. The house had been lovingly built, and it showed. Diana did not want to go.

Weeks later Curt voiced his discontent more profoundly. "If we don't move from this house, I am leaving," in another jaw-dropping point of realization for Diana. For a moment, he wondered whether or not she could buy Curt out; she was so tired of the threat, "If you don't do this or that, I'll go back to England." She just wanted to say, "Go, already." But once again, Diana was faced with a no-win situation. Did she want to end their relationship over a house? Was it that important? Another dilemma, another letter.

Dear Curt,

It is my dream to maintain a loving, lasting relationship that does not waver in the wind but stands strong against time. I feel like I will never be able to do anything right in this relationship because I am ultimately the cause of so much of your pain. I knew that there would always be a possibility that you would need to go back to your family, but do you have to undermine anything that was ever good that we had and trash me as a person to substantiate your actions? I give you my support and blessing to go. I still love you despite your attempts to kill it. But I make this sacrifice so that we can save some good.

I feel like you are looking for any reason to leave and go back to England. I'm not perfect, but I'm not the selfish person you think I am. I am willing to give you up if it would mean your happiness. We can end things very peacefully. As I say, I'm not Candy. I can't handle a lifetime of threats from you every time I do something that upsets you or don't do something you want. If you can give up this relationship, like everything else in your life, then I don't think it will be worth the pain to hold on. I want peace in my life, love and friendship, a place of sanctity and understanding, trust, and respect. Instead, I get humiliated every time you treat me nastily in front of my family, every time you play the "us vs. them" game with your children, every time you drink yourself into oblivion. You selfishly harbor your pain and don't try to understand others, then you throw away what is good for the sake of your pride.

You destroy what we have for a reason to change your life...you throw it away so easily.

She re-read the letter, then tucked it away. Defeated and depleted, Diana begrudgingly agreed to list the house, hoping the universe was on her side, and the home that she loved so much wouldn't sell. Unfortunately, the universe had other plans. It wasn't even officially on the market, and they had two offers over asking. Now, they would be moving farther away from the quaint coastal town with its tree-lined main street, shops and restaurants that allowed for some entertainment, the coastal path where she enjoyed her walks on the sound, the train station that would take her into the city, and the dance studio where she had made most of her good friends. It was unsettling to think she was being dragged further away from it all.

* * *

Perhaps it wasn't the house she wanted. It was quite isolating, but Diana had to admit there were some nice features of this new lifestyle tucked away in the deep woods that she could embrace. The morning skinny dip was one of them; it was the best way to start the day. Because the house was surrounded by a nature preserve, it was unlikely that someone would see her disrobe and jump in to start her day. The person would have to be really creepy to be watching her from the woods. The house wasn't even on the main trail, and only she and Curt knew the path they had personally blazed to get to the trail system.

She enjoyed those hikes with Curt. It reminded her of when he first moved to America, when he was a willing playmate on the weekends they didn't have Abby. They would venture off and discover new places, once having the goal of hiking every peak on the Appalachian Trail. Now they had everything at their fingertips, and their new lifestyle came with a pool, a boat, and a house that was large enough for his kids to have their own room, even though they were only with him for a few weeks out of the year. Abby was making friends in the new neighborhood, and now she had a place for them to gather. A great place for large parties—Curt loved showing off his skills on the stainless Weber grill that sat on the deck. He was so happy, riding around on his John Deere to prepare the yard for guests, riding shirtless with a full beer jostling in the cup-holder. *It is good to see him smile again.*

Floating on the surface, trying to shake the latest hangover, Diana started thinking about what was next for her. She had been through a lot with her mother's disease; it was soul crushing to watch her fade away both physically and mentally. The new house was a safe place for her parents to visit; her mother would sit in the chair overlooking the yard that backed up to the sanctuary. Nutmeg would sit by her side for hours, continually licking her as if she sensed the disease. It was gut-wrenching to watch, and despite the trappings that would suggest marital bliss, Diana could not shake her sadness.

She opened her eyes to see Curt at the side of the pool looking down at her, freshly shaven and dressed for work. His swim came much earlier in the morning, and she had prepared breakfast for them to have at the round table under the turquoise umbrella beside the pool. She stood up and lifted herself out to join him.

"So, what are you doing today?" he queried, as if it was an interrogation.

"I'm going to dance this morning. Not sure after that."

"Diana, why don't you think about getting a job? You haven't worked for a while now. You need a purpose."

"I've been taking care of my mother, remember? Plus, I have a job."

"You mean that class you're teaching? Right. Listen, don't you want to make more money?"

"I am making some money."

"Diana, that's a joke, and you know it."

Actually, she didn't know it. She was really enjoying teaching at the local college, and she was thinking that maybe she would like to do more of it. She was tired of the corporate rat race and chasing clients. Maybe she could go back to school and get her advanced degree so she could teach in the program full-time. They liked her and would probably hire her.

"I don't know, Curt. I'll figure it out."

"Well, I'm off to work. You enjoy your day." He gave her a peck on the cheek, and she could feel the resentment oozing out of his pores like a boil's pus making its way to the surface.

9

Diana was thinking about the choices she had made, always accommodating Curt when he threatened her. And when she needed the support from him, he seemed to disappear, both emotionally and physically. She realized that fear of abandonment was her Achilles' heel. Curt used the threat of leaving to get what he wanted time and again. Anger lurked under the surface for the treatment she withstood over the years.

"It's still hard for me to feel sorry for you, Kung Fu. Sounds like you had it pretty cushy."

"Yeah, you're right. I liked to refer to it as my beautiful jail. You know, when you're all locked into something, and it looks great from the outside, but reality tells another story."

"That's where you and I part ways. My situation looked awful from the outside, and it was. No sugar coating like you had."

"I'm sorry." Diana hesitated to go on. "Is your daughter's father still in the picture?"

"Are you kiddin'? That scumbag." Janis' voice reached a new crescendo. "He left me when I was pregnant. Just up and took off without a word."

"Oh, I'm really sorry." Diana immediately regretted that she had uncovered what was probably a deep wound.

"Listen, I really don't like answerin' questions, so let's just stick with your story."

"Why? Aren't we sharing here to pass the time?"

"I don't trust people. No offense, Kung Fu, but my shit was real."

"Well, my shit was real, too. At least it was for me."

* * *

"I didn't know where you were." That was Curt's answer when Diana asked, "Why didn't you come get me?" They were on the 18th hole playing golf while on a visit to England, and she had been knocked off her feet by a golf ball hit off the adjacent first tee. It was like being shot. She didn't know what had happened at first. The impact seared through her body as if she were an innocent calf being branded. Sammy, now a young man, was the only one who came over to see if Diana was all right. He tried to help her, which was kind considering he had always blamed Diana for the rocky relationship he had with his father. Instead of helping Diana, Curt chose to climb the hill that the ball had come over to yell at the person who'd drove it.

"Hey, did you hit a ball over here?" he shouted.

"Yeah," the guy shouted back, "but don't worry, I can take another."

"Well, you hit my wife." Curt turned to make his way back down the hill and walked right past Diana.

"Get up, you're okay," he said over his shoulder as he approached his ball.

Diana watched him as he lined up his shot to play out the hole. *What an asshole.* She pulled herself up off the ground and felt the pain seer into the fleshy part of her back. She didn't seem to have any broken bones. Thank goodness the guy didn't shout "Fore." She would have ducked. That line drive could have hit her in the back of the head. It could have killed her.

As she watched the outline of Curt's body fade away down the fairway, Diana slowly put one foot in front of the other, struggling to pull the cart behind her. The clubhouse was in sight, and she was hopeful that someone there might be able to help her. She wasn't familiar with this course in England and wasn't sure where to go. Diana abandoned her clubs, walked into the clubhouse, and went up to the bar to get some ice. The heat was expanding from the point of contact, which was squarely on her left hip. Diana made her way to the bathroom with the cup of ice from the barkeep. She opened the door, and the tears came. Tears from the fresh wound on her back and the bigger wound in her heart, as she thought in rapid succession: *he didn't come over to see if I was okay; he didn't walk me off the course; he isn't coming to check on me; he's never there when I need him; you would treat a stranger better; he's treating me like he treated Abby when she was hurt. He just doesn't care about.*

The ice melted quickly, but the lump in her throat would not budge. She gathered herself up to go back into the bar for more ice. The manager had been alerted and came running over with a clipboard full of forms for her to sign. She looked out the patio doors, and there Curt sat, in the sun drinking a beer, chatting, laughing, and enjoying the moment with his brother and son. The ache in her chest grew tenfold and far exceeded anything she was feeling in her back. After calming the manager's fear of a lawsuit, she slowly limped over to their table on the patio. Curt didn't even look up or take a break from the conversation. Is this what betrayal feels like: a heaviness in your chest like someone has laid a cement block squarely in the middle of it? The nausea grew; she decided she needed a drink. She went back to the bar to get herself one, as no one was making a move to help her. Clearly Curt was not getting up. At least the barkeep had enough heart to give her one on the house.

The pain was intense and persistent all night long. She could not find a comfortable position; the bruise on her hip had grown into the size of a football. It was dark black in color; it frightened her. She didn't know if she broke a bone or maybe had internal bleeding; she had no idea. When she had asked Curt to take her to the clinic after it happened—after all, didn't they have free health care in England?—he just said in a nasty and direct tone, "You're fine," as if she was being a drama queen. When they got to his mum's home hours later, he asked his mother to use her nursing skills to "take her blood pressure," as if that would suffice as a means to assess the situation and show of concern. Rose sat silently with a smug look on her face, as if she had the winning hand in a long game of cards.

Diana couldn't sleep that night. She picked up her iPad from its place on the floor slowly and carefully so she wouldn't disturb Curt's sleep. Although he had consumed so much booze with his brothers—he absolutely reeked of whiskey—she couldn't imagine how he could even wake up. She navigated to WebMD to study the anatomy of the back and figure out what bones might be under the point of impact marked by the angry-pink oval centered in a growing field of purple and black. She could have caught a tip of the bone that the hip was wrapped around. Although there was a sizable imprint where the ball had struck her, it looked like she might be okay. But in her heart, she knew she was not. She began to sob and could not sleep. She thought about how close she came to losing her life, her ability to walk, or any number of awful scenarios. She realized how lucky she was, and then she realized how undoubtedly Curt no longer cared about what happened to her. She was dispensable.

The next evening, Curt's family sat around the farmhouse table after dinner—his mum, his children, three of his brothers and their patchwork families, and their newly-returned father after a 30-year absence—and had a good laugh at Diana's expense. They went on about how she was hit in the "arse." Diana had suffered years of their low-brow behavior, but watching grown men lift a cheek to fart and then laugh uncontrollably at the dinner table was nothing compared to this. As her anger hit a crescendo, she stood up to her full height, turned around, and pulled her pants down far enough to display the blackened, football-sized bruise.

"Does this look like my ass to you?" she shouted. She had no idea what came over her. This was not her style; she practically mooned the entire family. Although it felt good for a moment, she was not proud of herself for stooping to their level. To add insult to injury, what she received in return was more laughter. No sympathy whatsoever from anyone. No comments of shock or concern at the size of the bruise. She felt herself spiraling downward. Finally, after all these years standing strong, she had lost, they had won. She grabbed for the bottle in front of her.

Diana would later think about the timing of that trip, the last one to England for her. Curt had uncharacteristically paid for her airfare and made it a point to schedule it on her break from work. He had even agreed to a side trip to Wales, just the two of them, which was definitely unusual. At the time, Diana had read it as a sign that things between them might be taking a positive turn. In retrospect, it was more like a swan song.

10

Maybe she had more in common with Janis than she first realized. They both seemed to have gone through a lot with the men in their lives. At least Janis had some common sense, which was more than she could say for herself. But that had been changing, and Diana was learning to take care of herself again, and now here she was, pushed back into a literal jail this time, not just suffocating from toxic relationships that jailed her emotions. Somehow, she had to find the beauty in this. Could this somehow be freeing? If she could stay calm in a situation beyond her control, if she could keep faith that all will be well, maybe she could find a way to live her life free of the anxiety and fear that she had suffered all those years.

"Man, that's pretty rough. I can't believe you took that from him, Kung Fu. Here I was thinkin' you take no shit." Janis shook her head. "Was I wrong about you?"

"I don't know. I was confused and always hoping it would get better. It's like that frog story."

"The kissing one? That creep was no prince."

"No, the one where if you put the frog in boiling water, it jumps out, but if you slowly heat the water up, it sits there and boils to death."

"So, you the frog. Okay, I get it."

"Yeah, sometimes he seemed really happy, and I was always waiting for those moments."

"Yeah, but what about you? Were you happy? Sounds like you were depressed, maybe drinking too much? Maybe we do have somethin' in common." Janis chuckled.

"Maybe we do, maybe not." Diana smiled to show Janis she was kidding with her parroting. "I was happy at times, I guess. I had my dance and my friends there. I think that saved me. But you're right, I was definitely drinking too much to dull the pain. It wasn't long after that I hit my all-time low and stopped."

"I've stopped, too, plenty of times." Janis chuckled.

"No, this time it was bad. I had to quit."

* * *

The moment they walked out onto the stone patio that ran the length of the house, Curt took off to the makeshift bar set up for the night. Margaritas, bottles of red and white, and Diana's favorite, Patron, were lined up in an invitation to forget about your troubles for the evening. Once Diana caught up with Curt, she poured herself a tall one as he slithered off. She turned to get more ice for her tumbler of tequila, but not too much; she wouldn't want to dilute it. She looked around to find Curt. Since they had gotten back from their last trip to England six months ago, this is how it had been. He was always leaving her side and wandering off.

They had been spending a lot of time with the couple hosting the party, Shelly and Alden, who had been on the fringe of her group of friends. Shelly kept inviting them out, and then she hosted these lavish parties that "they absolutely had to attend," according to Curt. Diana liked Shelly; they had been taking walks with the dogs and playing tennis during the day. She seemed to be so interested in Diana, always asking lots of questions about her life and relationships, and she was always bringing over little gifts and whatnot. They must have made quite the pair—Diana tall, blonde, and lean; Shelly about a half-foot shorter, stocky with large breasts and flaming red hair. Diana had to admit, she was a good catalyst for organized entertainment.

Diana finally spotted Curt as he entered the house and thought he must be going to the bathroom. She shrugged. *Just let him be; he's been such an ass lately, anyway.* He was never around, always running or going out for drinks. The only time he seemed to be at home was when Diana was not. She moved to the other side of the patio to chat with her friends Elizabeth and Ted. It occurred to Diana that this party was mainly intended to show off the new house and all its accouterments. She settled on one of the many outdoor couches that surrounded the massive fire pit to try and relax. She had never been a fan of big parties, always a bit shy, but the tequila was helping. She looked around, still no Curt. *What is he up to?*

Diana didn't remember much of that night. She remembered getting into Abby's Jeep, which was "hired" to bring them home from the party. She remembered that she didn't have her shoes, and someone found them for her. She remembered being mad at Curt, which seemed to be a consistent feeling of late. She remembered trying to get out of the Jeep by herself, missing the step, and tripping over her long skirt. She remembered waking up face down on the asphalt driveway of their beautiful home in the middle of nowhere.

It was very dark. She came to and rolled over, face up, and she realized the shadow of her teenage daughter was standing over her yelling, "Mom, Mom, wake up!" She moaned as she tried to lift herself up from the pavement. Not good. Abby and someone else (her daughter's friend, maybe?) helped her up and carefully moved her through the house into the bedroom.

"Mom, are you okay? Abby was removing some of her clothes to get her into bed. "Where's Curt, Mom?"

Diana immediately fell asleep. She didn't know how long she had been out when she was awakened by her daughter putting a cold compress on her head. She could sense Abby's worry and heard the panic in her voice.

"Mom, are you okay? I'm worried about you!"

"I'm okay, don't worry." She moved to sit on the edge of the bed. "Where's Curt?"

"I don't know, Mom, don't get up. What do you need? I'll get it for you."

"Just some water, sweetie." As Abby moved out of the bedroom to take care of the request, Diana settled back down and thought, *what happened, what have I done?*

The next morning Diana awakened to find Curt standing over the bed.

"Well, I hope you're proud of yourself," he sneered. "I want you to call everyone and tell them my birthday party is off."

Her head felt like there was an anvil resting on it, a depth of pain she had never felt before. There was a lump over her left eye the size of a golf ball. She couldn't move; the slightest turn would send her into a wave of nausea. Curt did not seem concerned as he charged in and out of the bedroom with a disapproving look on his face; he was just interested in making her feel worse. This had to be her all-time low. She shuffled to the bathroom and looked into the mirror. Shit, her teeth were chipped! That would explain the strong taste of iron that pervaded her mouth. She moved to splash water on her face, and her diamond ring caught on her skin. Her setting was mangled! She must have hit the ground really hard. *Should I go to the hospital?*

She started to sway and grabbed for the counter's edge. She groped the walls as she carefully headed back to the bed, squinting against the sunlight coming through the patio doors. She placed a cool washcloth over her eyes and fell back to sleep.

Everyone, which consisted of Elizabeth and Ted, Shelly and Alden, was supposed to come at 6 PM. *I have time. Time to think about what to do.* She knew two things for sure: she had concussed herself, and she was officially quitting alcohol. Cold turkey. It had been getting out of control with these people. It was hard enough keeping up with Curt, who claimed being English entitled him to drink a lot. *Why, in all these years, did I think drinking brought us closer together?* When she questioned whether they should quit, he always said, "I like to drink."

Well, this was it for her. She was done. No more. It was destructive and embarrassing. She couldn't do it anymore, and clearly, she was out of control. The final straw. She swore it off as she laid in bed and tried to find the strength to call Elizabeth.

"Helloooo," Elizabeth's cheery voice called out from the phone.

Diana cringed. "Hey," she managed to get out.

"Are you okay, Diana?"

"No, I'm not. I think I concussed myself. I fell out of the Jeep last night, and it's not good."

"Oh Geez," Elizabeth said with a twang, which must have been a carryover from her Midwestern upbringing. "Is there anything I can do for ya?"

"No, it's okay, but I'm afraid the party is off." Diana closed her eyes from the bright light and listened for Elizabeth's reaction.

"Of course. Don't worry, Diana, just take care of yourself. Get some rest. Bye-bye."

Curt stormed into the room. "So, are you just going to lay there all day?"

"Curt, I'm sorry. I think I really hurt myself. And I chipped my tooth." She stuck out her upper teeth to show him.

"That's great, Diana," he shot back sarcastically.

"I called Elizabeth, like you asked. They're not coming."

"Well, Alden and Shelly still are; I asked them to. If you're just going to sit here in bed, I want someone to party with. So, they're coming." He walked out of the room and slammed the door. She didn't have the energy to get upset. This was just another example of how horrible he had been of late. *I don't care what he does.*

She stirred to hear Alden and Shelly arriving, but she wasn't going anywhere. This was ridiculous. How many times had Curt passed out at parties, embarrassing her with his drinking, year after year? She could never understand why he never got sick and only sometimes hungover. He could drink multiple types of alcohol, and lots of it, and then just pass out. And she wondered why he always said he didn't remember anything. And look at the judgment she was getting with this one episode. *Screw him and his fucking birthday party.*

About an hour later, she woke up again to hear them laughing and splashing in the pool. They were having so much fun without her. She decided to rally to say hello at least. Slowly making her way outside, she covered her eyes from the afternoon sun. Very bright. Finding the nearest chair, she sat down while Shelly came bounding up to her and cupped her hands around her face.

"Poor baby. Let me see your tooth." Clearly Curt had filled them in on all the gory and embarrassing details.

"Hey, are you okay, Di?" Alden followed suit to give her a quick hug and a pat. "Thanks for coming out. We were worried about you."

She glanced over Alden's shoulder to see Curt boring his eyes into her with so much disdain, she could feel the blaze of the heat penetrating through her.

"I'm fine," she said. "But I'm telling you now, I am done with drinking."

"Oh, come on, Diana." Shelly scrunched her face up and mocked, "You know you want a drink."

"No, thank you, really. I just came out to say hello." She gently lifted herself up. "Have fun, see you guys later." Diana slowly made her way back to the bedroom. *Oh yeah, I am done.*

* * *

Diana stayed true to her word. She stopped drinking, and she sat back and watched the show. She watched as Curt carried on acting like a complete imbecile, out of control, laughing like a hyena, flirting with her friends, paying way too much attention to Shelly. She watched as he drank too much, danced with everyone but her, and stumbled to the car she would shuffle him into on the many summer evenings she was designated driver. Diana started to seriously wonder what was up; she was getting frustrated and angry. She asked Curt point blank one day while they were on the boat with Alden and Shelly. It was odd that they seemed to be invited almost every weekend on that boat; Curt said it was probably because Alden wasn't comfortable going out alone yet.

It was a beautiful day, one of those warm August days that made you lament the end of summer before it had arrived. The sound was choppy; the afternoon wind had kicked up, which made navigating through the outcroppings of rocks that dotted the entry of the cove that much more tenuous. But Alden handled it well, and Curt was primed and ready to hook a mooring to settle in for their afternoon outing. Diana watched with narrowed eyes as they bobbed around, drinking in the middle of the day; Shelly poking Curt in the ribs, tickling him, which she knew Curt hated but seemed to endure. Curt jumped into the water.

"Why don't you go swimming, Diana?" Shelly seemed to pose it as a provocative challenge.

Diana pulled off her long, orange dress, and she could feel Shelly's eyes assessing the back of her legs to witness all the imperfections of her aging body; she had almost ten years on Shelly, who wasn't menopausal, not yet anyway. God help Alden when she did enter that phase of her life; she could already be such an explosive terror with him. Always with a sharp reprimand, Alden this, Alden that... He just took it in stride as if his spine was made of wet noodles. Diana jumped off the boat into the warm, salty water and swam up to Curt, who was playing his usual cat and mouse game. She was able to catch up to him since he was drunk, and she eyed him with a stone-sober glare.

"What is going on with you and Shelly?" She looked into his eyes as if she would find the truth.

He faced Diana, treading water, and bugged out his eyes to mimic her without a word. She waited for him to say something, anything at all. Instead he swam away back towards the boat. As Diana's heart sank, she plunged down under the water to find a respite from the pain of his rejection. She imagined swimming after him and throwing all of her weight on top of him, holding him down until he lost all his breath. She hated him at that moment. And she knew deep down this would only be the beginning of what felt like a new form of emotional torture.

During the week, Curt acted a bit more like his old self again, bringing her coffee in the morning and taking a swim with her before he headed out for the day.

"Well, this is a nice way to start the day, isn't it luv?"

"It sure is," she said cheerily, afraid to say anything more, as it might break the moment's spell. It was so confusing to Diana; she did not understand the constant turnaround in behavior and mood from absolute disdain to near adoration. It was driving her insane. She sat on the edge of the step, closed her eyes, and lifted her chin to the sun. She was enjoying the sound of the birds happily chirping while Curt continued his laps. He was starting to get into good shape again with all the swimming.

"Well, I must be off." He pecked her on the cheek as he walked up the steps, covering her with fresh droplets of water, too few to quench her thirst for him.

* * *

The following weekend they had planned to go up to Alden and Shelly's mountain house with Elizabeth and Ted, and given Curt's unpredictable behavior towards her, she was hesitant to go. But nonetheless, Diana found herself shopping, which she rarely did, for a few items that she hoped would get Curt's attention. She had lost quite a bit of weight, since she hadn't been drinking in weeks, and she was starting to see and feel the benefits. Maybe even a new bathing suit or a nice dress would make her feel feminine and wanted again. She hoped a weekend away would help them reconnect, to recapture what seemed to have been lost between them, especially since they were headed very close to the place where they were engaged all those years ago.

Curt seemed to be in a rush to get up to the mountain house; he was driving faster than normal, and there was no talk of stopping on the way to enjoy the journey.

"Hey, Curt, how about we stop to hike Pineview Hill? It's such a beautiful day, and we can grab a bite at that organic market we like so much." She suggested the spot of his beautiful proposal. Maybe that might jog his memory of the intense love they had felt for each other. But that was met with a quick "No, Di," the two words that seemed to go so well together.

Nevertheless, Diana was content. Vermont had always been one of her favorite states; she delighted in the view of the Green Mountains, the smell of pine drifting through the open window. No stranger to where they were headed, she had been coming to this particular mountain to ski since she was a little girl; spending time here in the summer would bring a new set of activities she hoped to enjoy with Curt. It was rare to go anywhere as a couple since he proclaimed there would be no vacations without his kids. This was an exception, and she wasn't going to let his moodiness ruin it for her.

Elizabeth and Ted were headed up with their two boys and would be arriving at the same time. Diana talked herself out of her concern; she had a talent for glossing over the situation and diminishing her own feelings. Shelly's warm and friendly greeting helped to put her at ease; she was being so gracious leading Diana to the largest bedroom she had set aside for Curt and Diana, with a picture-window view of the green mountainside.

"Oh, Shelly, this is lovely, but I don't want to put you out of your bedroom."

"It's fine, Diana. You and Curt should enjoy yourselves. You deserve it."

"Oh, that is really sweet of you, Shelly. Thanks." Diana gave Shelly a quick hug.

"No problem at all, Diana. I want you to have a nice time. Plus, we rented the unit next to this one so we could have some privacy. It might be a little noisy with the boys."

"Oh no, I don't think so. They're really well behaved. They're good boys."

Shelly shrugged. "Honestly, I don't know how Elizabeth does it. Those boys would drive me crazy."

Diana turned to leave the room. She did not want to carry on this conversation with Shelly. As generous as Shelly was, Diana did not like the way she always seemed to be poking around in people's personal lives; she wanted nothing to do with that. Elizabeth was a kind and trusting friend, and Diana was loyal to her.

The adults were all in the kitchen, where the alcohol had already hit the counter for consumption. Diana plopped down on the comfy couch in the adjoining living room and sat back to watch them drink. As the afternoon wore on, they were clearly starting to get a bit out of control. Shelly was the first to get animated; Elizabeth and Ted kept one eye on the boys who were occupied by video games. Diana was the observer, and she started to realize that this was not fun. She remained sober and could see things for what they were, an absolute waste of time.

"Hey, Diana, don't you want a drink? Alden has your favorite."

Shelly was trying to bait Diana to drink, which she seemed to do every time they were all together. Diana thought Shelly could get nasty when she had a few, and seemed to direct that energy mostly onto her.

"No thanks, Shelly. I'm trying hard to be good." She forced a smile and raised her hands to form a halo around her head.

"Are you judging us, Diana?"

"Of course not," Diana said. "I just don't want to drink." Diana could feel herself getting angry at Shelly's goading. It was hard enough not to join in on the festivities; Alden was so sweet, and he always got her Artemis, the Cabernet that she could never seem to get enough of. Once again, instead of putting Shelly in her place, she chose a more diplomatic response. "But you go ahead, Shelly. I'm not stopping you."

Shelly smirked and turned to walk out onto the balcony over-looking the mountainside. Curt soon followed. Everyone sat in the living room while Shelly and Curt stood side-by-side with their backs to the group. Diana could see how Curt turned to smile at Shelly, his hand just inches away from hers on the deck railing. That smile that had always been for Diana, the hand that had been unusually absent of late. She knew that look of his; her skin began to crawl, a chill washed over her, and she could feel herself getting nauseous. She needed to break it up.

Diana cheerily bounced out onto the deck. "What are you guys talking about?"

Shelly whipped her head around with a sharp retort, "Nothing," as if Diana was rudely interrupting them. Diana stood in between them, and they stood there silently. She resisted the impulse to punch Shelly in her ugly, little rat-like face.

"Well, we'll be serving the birthday cake for Tom, if you guys care to join us." She turned on her heel with an air of defiance. Making her way back into the kitchen, she found Elizabeth alone, out of earshot, preparing a snack for the boys. Diana walked up to her, and without any filter, she nodded over to the balcony and said, "There is something going on between the two of them." Elizabeth looked aghast and stared at Diana with her doe-like brown eyes.

"Are you serious, Diana?"

"Yes, look how close they are standing." She nodded over to the balcony. "And did you see them on the golf course the other day? Curt had his arms around her showing her how to swing the club. It made me sick."

"Yes, I did see that. Maybe he was just trying to be helpful," Elizabeth said in her usual positive manner, and somewhat convincingly. "And you know how Shelly is, she's just a big flirt. Everyone knows it," she added with a giggle.

"I think there's more to it than that."

"No, Diana, that couldn't be. Curt loves you."

Diana stood next to her long-time friend, trying to soak up her optimism as rationalization. "You're probably right. I guess I'm just being silly."

Diana decided that it was not worth making a scene. She could only base what she was feeling on her intuition—there was no proof. And Shelly, really? Shelly was supposed to be Diana's friend. She wouldn't do that, right? And Curt was the love of her life. Perhaps she was being paranoid and ridiculous.

But she couldn't stop the heavy feeling of trepidation weighing down on her. Things were not right. Every time Diana would enter the bedroom to be alone with Curt, he would leave. When they went to bed that night, he just rolled over and immediately fell asleep. She expected that behavior at home but thought he would make some attempt to be closer while they were away. Always looking for a rational explanation, it occurred to her that maybe with her sobriety came awareness, and she was just noticing his true behavior for the first time.

Regardless, her body seemed to know what her mind would not allow her to confirm. After two days of witnessing his behavior, the tears came as she showered to get ready to leave; she knew in her gut something was terribly wrong. There were quick goodbyes as everyone got into their cars for the three-hour drive home. She felt so sick she wanted to crawl out of the window.

After nearly an hour of silence, Curt finally spoke, "Sorry this wasn't the romantic weekend you wanted, Diana."

She was flabbergasted. *What the hell. He's going to be nice and apologetic now?* He never apologized. "What were you and Shelly talking about on the balcony, Curt?"

"Nothing really, just silly stuff." He focused on driving.

"Silly stuff? Like what?"

"I said nothing, Diana," he cut her off more sternly.

"Well, I don't like what I'm seeing, Curt. You are being disrespectful to our relationship, openly flirting with Shelly." Diana turned and waited for a reaction. Nothing but silence. "And why did she come out in that negligee last night to play cards? It was disgusting with her tits hanging out, and in front of the boys." No response. "If you care anything about us or your friendship with Alden, you will cut it out."

"I'm not doing anything wrong, Diana."

They sat in silence. Diana wanted to scream to the top of her lungs, "I hate you, I hate you, I hate you… for all the years of pain, the disrespect, the times you were not there when I needed you, when you undermined me with your children, when you ignored Abby and me as if we were inconsequential, for all the important decisions you made without me, for your lack of attention, support, and kindness. I hate you!"

"Not to change the subject, Di, but what do you want to do when Sammy and Rose come over?" Curt glanced over, waiting for her answer.

She whipped her head around. "How about getting along for a change?" she blubbered, the tears pouring out.

He went to reach for her, and it was her turn to shrug him off. Her skin burned at his touch. She inched her body away from him and closer to the door, her face pressed against the window; she wanted to fly out of the car to get away. Instead, she returned to her silence the entire journey home, listening to the cruel thoughts running around inside her head.

<h1 style="text-align:center">11</h1>

Janis was really starting to uncover the painful stuff. Even after all these years, it was hard to talk about. Diana wondered why she was compelled, locked inside this jail cell, to tell a complete stranger the gory details. For Diana, it was a test of how far she had come in her healing. Could she tell the story without getting upset? And it wasn't like she had anything to hide at this point. Talking to Janis was better than silently sitting here in worry, fear, and doubt.

"Who are these people you were hanging out with, Kung Fu? They sound like real assholes to me."

"Some very twisted people, for sure."

"What's up with that, then? Why you hanging with people like that?"

"That is a good question." Diana thought for a moment. *Why did she? Bored, lonely, out of obligation?*

"Those were not friends, I can tell you that. Backstabbers, I know the type."

"You're right. I should have stayed away."

"You're not too good being on your own, are you? Don't you love yourself, Kung Fu?"

Diana had to think for a moment. She was so isolated in the woods and thirsty for connection, friends to hang out with. She had been happy with the small crumbs Curt would give her now and then, but it wasn't enough to fill the void.

"No, it's not that. I guess I was happy to go to parties and such. It gave me something to look forward to, and it got Curt out of the house. Besides drinking at home, working in the yard, he never really wanted to do anything except run, golf, and shop."

"Yeah, he was shopping, alright, but for what exactly?" Janis chuckled. "Sounds like maybe your gut was right. So, was he cheatin' on you or what?"

* * *

After fourteen years of marriage, this was the first time Curt refused to go to the beach house for summer vacation. Like Diana, he loved it there. It was a place that allowed you to be a kid again. The water was warm and the surf was high, allowing for hours of play, building castles in the soft white sand, taking long walks to collect shells while your toes happily received an inadvertent massage. The kids had always loved it, too, and Diana made sure they could spend part of their August vacation there together. Except for this August; they would not be coming over. Curt's children were growing up and planning vacations with their friends, and Candy's new husband was wealthy enough to take them to exotic and exciting locations. The beach house had lost its appeal for Sammy and Rose.

So, it wasn't completely surprising that Curt had chosen not to come. He had been acting a bit strange and distant lately; this was just another addition to his weird behavior. Diana had been on high alert since Vermont, and she was watching every move he made. Now there were new passwords on his phone that did not leave his pocket, smiles at texts being sent to his phone, and an amplified cold and distant attitude with no rhyme or reason.

Mornings spent together eating breakfast and taking laps in the pool were all of a sudden not happening. He did everything in his power to avoid her.

Diana's stomach had been tied in knots since the weekend in Vermont with Shelly and Alden, wondering what was going on with him as he refused to speak to her. It was just a few months ago that they had been looking for beach houses closer to where they lived, enjoying the exploration of the area for the next phase of their lives. They had finally agreed to get their own house near the water, which had been Diana's dream for a long time. The search came to an abrupt end when Diana had refused to consider a gutted home ridden with mold and smelling of dead carcasses. Diana met Curt and the realtor to tour it at his insistence, and although a good investment as a knock-down, there was no way Diana was signing up for more work. Fixing up two houses together was enough. It would take a lot of cash that Diana was not willing to shell out and a lot of work that she no longer had the patience to coordinate. Curt became frustrated and just gave up the hunt. "You figure it out," he bluntly told her.

And it went downhill from there. Curt had been harping on wanting to retire early and, out of nowhere, wanted to go visit a financial advisor "to find out what *they* had." Diana found this insulting, since Curt never wanted to commingle funds, and all housing expenses were split down the middle. Even when Diana had returned to school so that she could change careers, Curt was not alleviating the financial burden; Diana had to cut into savings to make her monthly bills. She retorted, "Perhaps you should go see someone, Curt," since she suspected he didn't save a dime and spent money quicker than he got it, more recently on new clothes, golf clubs, and of course, lavish gifts for his children to ease the guilt of his absence. She really didn't know what his financial situation was, but more importantly was the fact that he did not know her net worth since her mother's passing, and she was going to keep it that way.

On the morning Diana was due to leave for vacation, she tried one more time to talk to him while he sat eating his breakfast. "What's wrong, Curt?" No answer. He sat grimly at the kitchen table, the sun catching his sparkling blue eyes, a sight Diana still found hard to resist. "Why won't you talk to me?" Diana was standing over him now, demanding a response. She was getting desperate; she wanted answers. "Is there someone else, Curt? Just tell me."

"No," he replied quickly.

"Did someone say something to you about me?"

He looked up briefly and narrowed his eyes. That seemed to hit a mark. "No."

"Don't you love me anymore?" She was pleading for some answers.

He looked up again, and his voice softened. "I'll always love you, Diana."

Diana paused and waited for the "but," as this was something you might say when you were going to break up with someone. "What is it then?" No answer. Now Diana was getting angry. She couldn't leave on a ten-day vacation like this. When she asked if he wanted to make love the night before, he just said, "I'm good, thanks" and smirked. It was so cold, not like Curt at all. He never refused sex, and neither did Diana. Great sex had been a cornerstone of their relationship.

Diana took a deep breath and laid her cards out on the table. Her voice was clear and strong. "Let me see. You hate your job, you miss your kids, you're worried about your health, and you're feeling old. Does that pretty much sum it up?" She stood in the light of the naked truth she saw in him.

"I can't talk to you about this now. Go on vacation, Diana, and I will talk to you when you get back." He pushed himself away from the table and gathered his things for work. He silently moved past her with no kiss or embrace to say good-bye. He opened the door to the garage, and just left.

Now she was supposed to happily get into the car for vacation without him? This was the absolute bottom for them; she really didn't know what to do. *Should I stay?*

She had to go; they were supposed to be celebrating her nephew's engagement. And Abby was bringing Mike, her new boyfriend from college. Maybe it was best if they had some time apart? Perhaps this was normal for couples who had been together for so long. What did she know? She didn't make it past five years in her previous marriage. She was about to triple that, and she couldn't give up now.

Days went by, but no word from Curt. She kept wishing that he would call her and declare his undying love. A wave had swamped the beach on the first day and took out her phone, so Diana could pretend there would be numerous messages from him once she was able to retrieve her data. But there was nothing. He did text Abby to see how things were going, but no call. This was not how things usually went; it went from "I always want to be able to reach you" when he gave her the first cell phone she ever had, which was about the size of her shoe, to absolute silence. Diana decided to give him space, remembering what a girlfriend once told her about men, "Just let them be, and they will come back to you."

Diana walked the beach for solace and some time to reflect on what had been transpiring. These walks brought her closer to her mother. They'd both loved it here; it was a special place.

Diana really needed her mom now; she'd always had a soothing word, especially when Diana had been in turmoil. As a bonus on these clarifying walks, Diana was convinced that her mother would leave items in the sand for her to find; they were deeply meaningful to her, and much too coincidental and personal for it to be rationalized. She was thinking about Curt, looking for guidance, searching for answers, when she spotted something poking out of the sand. Diana bent down to pick it up and could not believe her eyes. It was a toy soldier holding a shield bearing the red cross of England, sword held high, ready for battle. She thought, *I am fighting for my life.* She rushed back to the blanket to show Abby.

"What is it, Mom?" Abby was clearly annoyed that her mother had interrupted her beach nap with Mike, but she sat up to grab her water and provide some halfhearted attention.

"Look what I found in the sand, Abby." Diana held out the plastic figurine for Abby to inspect. Abby reached up to take the item from her, then looked up to Diana to give her the warmest smile—the kind that lit up her beautiful, woody-green eyes.

"Awe, Mom, you deserve a knight in shining armor."

"I think I need to be my own knight in shining armor, sweetie."

* * *

Diana had tentatively decided to leave on a Tuesday to avoid traffic, but she was not confirming that with Curt. On the day they were supposed to come home, On the day there were supposed to come home, Curt finally broke his silence. He contacted her on her new phone via text after ten days of no communication:

Are you coming home?

She stared at the text. The hurt welled up, and she swallowed hard before texting back.

Probably not, it's pouring rain and too nasty to drive.

In actuality, she was sitting in the car waiting for Abby, who was picking up a tub of the caramel popcorn she loved, before heading back.

How's Nutmeg? Please take a pic, I miss her.

She snapped a quick photo of Nutmeg in the back seat, in a moment of disbelief since Curt never really cared about the dog, but sent it to him anyway to convey nonchalance.

So, you are in the car?

We're just shopping.

He was obviously trying to find out whether or not they were on the road. Something told Diana not to tell him; it didn't take a rocket scientist to know that this was definitely not right.

That was the end of that, no more messages.

She looked up from the phone and saw Abby and Mike approaching the car.

Abby opened the car door. "Hey, Mom. Curt is texting me about when we're coming home."

"Don't respond. Just turn off your phone, Abby, please. You can just say it died." Diana hated to put Abby in a position of lying, but she wanted to get back without him knowing.

They left directly from the parking lot to go straight home. Diana was driving as if she was on a mission, which she was. A mission to find the truth. There were no coffee stops, no bathroom breaks; she passed cars with the finesse of a race car driver at Le Mans. She shaved almost an hour off the usual five-hour trip.

Diana's heart was beating out of her chest when they pulled into the driveway, and she reached up to press the clicker that would open the garage door. She had been wishing all week that she would come home, and he would have missed her and freshly declare his love. Instead she was faced with the first oddity: his car was in her garage bay, and his bay was empty. What was on the floor on his side, however, were puddles of AC condensation, meaning a car had been parked there recently but was now gone.

They walked in the house together, and Diana's eyes darted around to take in the scene. Curt was in his usual position, asleep in the recliner in his underwear, mouth open, passed out. She noticed that he was freshly showered. *Perhaps he had gone running? It was Tuesday, a running day.* He did not wake up despite the hastened activity to settle into the house—the three of them pulling their luggage in on wobbly wheels across the hardwood floor, dumping stuff on the island that separated the kitchen from the living room, the dog jumping up and down around him looking for affection as he stayed in full sleep mode. *He must be absolutely trashed!*

Diana moved around the house as quickly as possible like a machine gathering data: she took note of the bed unmade and the quilt folded down, one of Curt's habits after sex. Diana's heart sank into her chest; she looked at her daughter, and a deep concern reflected back into her eyes.

"We're going to the diner, Mom." She grabbed Mike's hand and moved to leave.

"Okay," she said, swallowing the lump in her throat, knowing it was best that she and her boyfriend not be there when she woke up Curt.

Diana took a deep, racked breath and walked up to the recliner. She laid her hand on Curt's shoulder to wake him, bending down to closely meet his face. He stirred as he opened his eyes and asked in a sleepy, come-hither voice, "Where have you been?"

Diana pulled back with a furrowed brow and looked at him, perplexed. He shook his head, snapped to, and said in a panic, "Oh, oh, you've been at the beach." The recliner thumped into position with its back upright, so he could take a more offensive posture to interrogate Diana. "I thought you weren't coming home?"

"Well, we decided to come home because of the rain." Diana slowly moved away from him, as she could sense that he was about to get ugly.

"Oh, so the car was just magically packed while you were shopping?"

His voice got progressively louder as he shouted in her face, "You're a liar, a liar, a liar!" Lifting himself out of the recliner, the footrest came down with a thunk, like the sharp blade of a guillotine that had just made its final cut. He pushed past her and went to bed, slamming the door behind him.

Diana stood in the middle of the room, thunderstruck. She tried to shake herself from the disbelief and slowly walked by the closed door to their bedroom, listening for a moment for some hopeful recall, then carrying herself up the stairs to the guest room as if she were wading through quicksand. She tried to find comfort in the room that contained the inherited furniture that her mother, and subsequently Diana, had slept in as a child. The mahogany, pineapple-topped bed posts that were so familiar to her provided no solace and no pathway to sleep. At 5 AM, she heard her mother's voice in her head: "Everything is going to be alright, sweetheart." She told herself to go downstairs, get into bed, and give him a big hug, that she was just imagining it all.

Diana moved to her side of the bed and slipped in so she would not disturb Curt. She smelled the sheets. *Hmmm... that's a new scent. Maybe he used a new laundry detergent. Why did he wash the sheets? The cleaning lady was just here.* She moved next to him, and he pulled her close to him and hugged her like he hadn't in a long time. Still in some form of denial, looking for hope, Diana thought, *maybe it will be alright.* He stirred and then abruptly disengaged from the hug to move away from her. He threw the sheets off, silently got out of bed, and started moving down the hallway to get ready for work. He didn't even turn to look at her.

Just before he left, Curt stood over the bed and asked, "Do you want coffee or are you going to lie in?"

Diana briefly thought, *oh good, he's trying to be nice again, to be normal.*

"I think I will try to sleep some more. Thanks." She reached for his hand, but his fingers slipped through hers as he walked out the door.

* * *

Diana did her best to move through her morning as normally as possible. After her dip, she went to dance class, followed by coffee with friends. She didn't mention a word and just claimed "exhausting trip" when asked why she seemed so low. Heading to Trader Joe's she thought maybe if she made a nice dinner, she and Curt could talk. She gave Curt a call to check in. After all, he was still her husband, and she was allowed to call him; he was not off limits.

"Curt here."

"Hey, are you coming home for dinner?" Diana asked sweetly.

"Didn't you get my email? I'm going out after work." He spoke quickly and succinctly.

"Oh, okay, I'll see you later then." Diana quickly hung up before bursting into tears. She had been away for ten days, and he wasn't coming home for dinner? It was not going to be okay. She pulled into the driveway and started to unload the groceries. She scurried into her office to check her inbox to find Curt's email; in the subject line it read: *Out for drinks tonight Di won't be too late.*

She started moving as if in a whirlwind, swirling around to identify menial tasks that would take her mind off the panicked feeling she had. As was her way when she was emotionally uncomfortable, she started moving at superhuman speeds. After putting away the groceries as if they were on fire, she hustled to clean out the car from the trip. She gathered the popcorn bags and empty seltzer cans into her arms and quickly crossed the garage to put them in the garbage can. Since the pickup service had been the day before, the can was empty but for a small, tightly-sealed bag that lay in the bottom.

She looked down into the garbage can as if it was a long, dark tunnel containing the mysteries of life. She lifted the bag out of the can and decided she should open it to find out what was inside. Untying the first knot to look inside, she found another bag, and then like Russian dolls, inside that, another. Inside the third tightly-knotted bag sat the remnants of a sushi dinner. Diana started adding up what she had found. Four eaten trays of sushi (plus a half-eaten one in the refrigerator, that makes five). That's a lot of sushi for one person, even for her husband. Add to that clue the two little square saucers they used to mix wasabi with fresh ginger and soy sauce she found dirty in the dishwasher. A finished bottle of sparkling wine, which Curt didn't drink, in the recyclables plus the nearly-finished large bottle of sake she found next to Curt when she walked in the night before. The scrunched-up paper bag in the recyclables contained a receipt that told her both had been purchased that same evening from the local wine store Curt usually "called into" on his way home. And the kicker, two fortune cookie wrappers. One cookie had been eaten and one was left uneaten, soggy in the bottom of the bag (Curt hated them), and two sets of chopsticks... both used.

Oh my God, someone was here! She wasn't imagining this. *Maybe he had the neighbor over. No, there was someone parked in the garage. That's why there was condensation. I had just missed them? And they were in my bed! That wasn't the smell of new laundry detergent! Oh, God. Who was here?* The question screamed in her head.

He walked in that night at 8 PM. Diana was standing on the other side of the garage door in the mudroom, waiting in response to the sound of his car pulling in. She had noticed that he hadn't been running the night before because there were no dirty running clothes in the washing machine that he usually left soggy to be dealt with. If there was one thing she knew for sure, Curt was a creature of habit. *It's always the details that reveal the story.*

She opened the door from the garage and was practically on top of him when he walked in. He struggled to get by her.

"Did you go running last night?" she asked him as she followed him into the kitchen.

"No, my leg was bothering me. Why are you asking?" He walked past Diana with a sudden limp and went to greet the dog. He started gushing over Nutmeg, saying how much he missed her. *Is that just another sligh?* Diana followed him to the living room to continue her interrogation.

"Who did you have drinks with, Curt?" He wouldn't look up from his play with Nutmeg, intending to inflict further pain.

"Guys from work."

"Really, that's interesting." She recalled how he complained that his co-workers always left early to go home to their families and did not drink for religious reasons. Diana sat down in the recliner and watched as he lowered himself to the floor. He was within arm's reach—she could easily grab him by his hair, or ear, or throat, or something to gain his attention. She took a deep breath and calmly said what she'd had hours to practice.

"You know, Curt, we've been together for a long time, and I'd like to think that we've been happy along the way, but I feel like you're hiding something. Why won't you talk to me?"

He stopped playing with Nutmeg and looked up at her. The smile changed to a cold, hard stare. "You're right, Diana. I told you I would talk to you when you got back from the beach house." He didn't skip a beat as he got up from the floor to tower over her. "So, here's the thing. You know how you always ask, oh honey, are we going to grow old together?" His eyes narrowed and mouth twisted into a sneer. "Well, I don't want to grow old with you, and it's over."

Diana's jaw dropped as she watched him walk into the kitchen with his back to her. "Are you serious?" She nervously chuckled in disbelief.

He just turned to look at her with a blank stare.

Diana's face was on fire as she started rifling questions at him. "You don't want to talk about it? You don't want to see someone? Talk to somebody?" Her voice started to rise in pitch with each question as if to enunciate the panic that was welling up inside her.

"Not everything needs to be talked about, Diana." And with that, Curt started to walk out of the room.

"Is that it?" Diana cried out; her tortured heart was crumbling.

He turned to look at her with a frigid glance. "I only have one question."

"Yes, please tell me?" The hope rose in her that maybe this might be a way into some revealing dialog.

"Are you sleeping in the guest room or should I?"

* * *

Diana woke up dazed, confused, and upset; she hadn't really slept. Even though she changed the sheets, she could still only imagine what might have happened in her bed only hours ago. But she would be damned before he kicked her out of their bed. She felt nauseous; the pain in her stomach wouldn't subside. Curt opened the door to enter the bedroom and moved past her to get ready for work. She listened with half an ear as he went through his morning routine in the bathroom they had carefully renovated to their tastes: showering in the large walk-in shower with river stone to massage his feet, primping in front of the mirror over the golden granite counter, then dressing in the large walk-in closet they shared.

As he passed by, he stopped to stand over the bed and said sharply, "We need to put the house on the market this weekend." He waited for a reaction. "The only realtor I know is Ed, my running mate, and I wouldn't do that to him."

Diana looked up at him and thought, *you wouldn't do that to him? Are you kidding? But you will rip my heart out and stomp on it without cause or explanation, that's okay?*

"You just brought my world crashing down around my feet, and you want to talk about putting the house on the market. I'm sorry, Curt, I'm not on your timeline." She thought quickly and said, "Give me ten sessions of therapy, and then we can talk about putting the house on the market."

"I'm not negotiating with you," he sneered, then walked through the bedroom door, closing it on her as he left.

She didn't know what to do. Frozen in place, she sobbed uncontrollably. She wasn't equipped for this; she did not see this coming. Diana knew he had been flirting with Shelly, but could he really be involved with her?

She tried to stay focused on the work she had to do. She had agreed to teach a sales training class at the local university that would start in a few weeks. She sat in her office, staring at the phone, trying to think who she should call; who could help her? Bing! An email came in from Curt. She hoped that maybe he would tell her this was a joke, but her husband was not the joking type. For some reason, the entire message was contained in the subject line.

Subject: *I know you would prefer that I moved out, but I can't afford to fund two places, and in the end, it just hurts both of us financially. Besides, I want to help clear out and sell the house. If you really don't want to list the house, the process will just drag on. We should get it on the market this weekend.*

He can't be serious! What is going on? Diana was frantic. She had to find out who had been here. She started running around the house playing detective. She ran up the stairs, taking two at a time, and started her investigation in his office. Looking through his scant files, Diana started analyzing his Amex credit card bills for any clues of expenses that didn't add up. Nothing. She turned on his computer and, by some miracle, it was left up and running. She clicked on his Skype account to look at his contacts. Not much there. Wait! What was this *sexforme* account? Was he looking at porn? And why was Shelly Reid listed as a Skype contact? There were only a few: his mum, his brothers, Diana, the porn site, and now Shelly? Another piece of evidence to suggest there was something much more going on, something that he was not admitting. If he would just tell her, it would somehow take the sting out of this abrupt ending. *Is he trying to make me crazy?*

* * *

Diana was barely awake; she had finally fallen asleep sometime around four in the morning. Curt jolted her awake when he opened the door, and then quickly followed with a new declaration to deliver his daily blow.

"I have signed a lease in SoBo, and I will be moving out by the end of the month." He didn't wait for any reaction, just moved on to begin his tedious routine.

She lay in bed in her relentless state of shock, disbelief, and debilitation, listening to the rainfall from the showerhead. *SoBo? South Benton on the water. Near where he works, near where Shelly and Alden keep their boat. How convenient.* Once she knew he was out of the shower, she lifted herself out of bed to confront him once more. She needed answers, and he was going to give them to her.

"Why are you doing this?" she sobbed as he was primping in front of the bathroom mirror. He finished spraying the heavy cologne between his legs and slammed it on the counter. As he spat out, "I, WANT, OUT," he thrust three fingers in her face in unison to each word to assert his crippling message.

"Just tell me who was here," she further pleaded as she tried to breathe through the fog of the cologne's perfume. She used to love his natural smell; this new habit disgusted her.

He rolled his eyes at her. "If it makes it any easier for you to accept, I'll get someone." He pushed past her, hurried out of the bedroom, and went off to work.

She threw herself onto the bed as the garage door slammed down in finality.

12

Diana could still sense the ghost of the pain, that initial shock she experienced. It was traumatic for her and sent her into survival mode. Pain is so personal, and healing is not a straight line nor does it have a timeline. Even after all these years, and all the attempts at healing, it was hard for her to resurface the details, albeit cathartic to do so.

"Okay, you got me now." Janis shook her head. "Now mind you, I've seen and heard much worse, but I get how that would have thrown you, Kung Fu." She nodded her head and looked straight at Diana and asked, "Why did you stay with him all those years?"

"I loved him… and I thought he loved me." A lone tear escaped and slowly rolled down her face. "I desperately wanted us to be happy, and yes, to grow old together. That's what everyone in my family had done. I didn't want to be a failure."

"Wow, Kung Fu, I actually feel sorry for you. That growin' old bit he said must've really cut deep."

"I don't want your pity. As shocking and painful as it was, it forced me to wake up and take control."

"I guess you didn't have much choice, did you?" Janis swung her legs from side to side as she cushioned her legs against the sharp metal edge of the bed.

"No, he left me with no choice, you're right. I guess I could have cozied up with the hurt, but I was determined I wasn't going to let it destroy me." Diana raised her chin. "It took all my strength to pull it together and move on with my life."

"Well, if you don't mind me sayin', seeing as you're in here, I'm not sure how that's worked out for you."

Diana smiled and pointed at Janis. "Good point."

"What I want to know, Kung Fu—did you go after that bitch? I would have killed her." Janis slid a finger across her neck.

"Well, at the time I wasn't completely sure what was going on. He wasn't telling me anything, and I had to find out."

"I hope you finally got off your ass and did somethin' about it then."

* * *

Shelly bounced down the ramp of the fitness center and out into the parking lot, her ponytail trying to bob as it held back her thin red hair. She was gleaming as she looked down at her newest iPhone. Shelly looked up as Diana pulled up next to her in the car.

Her face lit up. "Oh, Diana. What are you doing here?"

Diana had circled the parking lot going in and out again, wondering if she should do this. Was she crazy? Could the person that was in her bed be Shelly? It seemed impossible, but Diana had been soberly watching her and Curt all summer long, flirting, casting glances (she knew that look of his), caught in what seemed to be intimate conversations. And there was the weekend in Vermont with Alden, Elizabeth, and Ted. Her gut knew then that something was going on between them, but could it really be? The man who recently told her, "There's no other woman for me," and the woman who said, "You're so good to me, Diana. You know I've always got your back." She had to find out; she was going insane.

Diana didn't know what she was doing or even what she was going to say, but as the summer breeze hit her face, a calm strength came over her. "Get in the car, we need to talk."

Shelly's smile faded as she got into the passenger seat. Diana locked the doors and started to drive to the back of the parking lot, behind the storefronts that lined the main street.

Shelly turned to her, and looked directly into her eyes. "What's up, Diana?"

She never noticed before, but Shelly's eyes were intense, almost inhuman, more like a wild animal, when illuminated. Diana tried to remain calm, but her heart was pounding in her ears and the heat of anxiety rose to the surface. She parked the car behind the red dumpster where no shoppers would ever venture, making sure they were out of sight from any employee who might be taking a cigarette break out back. Diana decided to tread lightly because she didn't have any proof, just her gut.

"So, did you go on the boat this weekend?" Diana knew Curt had gone because she spotted him in the kitchen walking by, clutching the usual towel and bathing suit he brought with him on the countless boat rides they went on with Alden and Shelly that summer.

"Yes." She enunciated the "s" to answer definitively.

"Who did you go with?" Diana wondered if she would mention Curt.

"Oh, it was just me and the dogs."

Diana knew that was a lie because, unlike Diana, Shelly was not a confident enough helmsman to go out on her own. "Oh really," Diana said sarcastically.

"Oh, and Alden," Shelly hastily added. She seemed to squirm in her seat, but she was a smooth cookie and a practiced liar. "Why do you ask?"

Diana took the plunge. "You better tell me what's going on with you and Curt... or I'm going to Alden."

Shelly recoiled. "I don't know what you're talking about. You're crazy," she spat. "You have been accusing me all summer, and it has thrown a wedge into our friendship." Shelly looked out over the dashboard, her eyes darting around like a trapped animal.

That comment stopped Diana in her tracks. She said nothing to Shelly about what she was seeing. She had told Curt that their flirting was making her uncomfortable, and it was disrespectful to the relationship. Curt had just denied his behavior and laughed it off, not taking Diana seriously at all. Perhaps he had delivered the message to Shelly himself.

Her anger welled up. "Then who was in my bed, Shelly? Why is Curt all of a sudden telling me he's moving out?" Diana could feel her anger surfacing, and she started to worry about what she might do to Shelly.

"Oh, so it's all my fault?" Shelly took an insulted posture.

"Well, maybe you shouldn't flirt with other people's husbands, Shelly." She started poking her in the ribs, mimicking what she observed Shelly doing to Curt on the last boat ride Diana had to endure before her trip. Shelly quickly got out of the car and slammed the door behind her. Diana sped away, suppressing the desire to mow her down. She kept saying to herself as she tried to breathe, *grace and dignity. Grace and dignity.* The air entered her system in sharp, ragged breaths.

Diana sped out of town down to the beach to see if Curt was running. This would be a good time for them to meet. That's probably why Shelly was smiling looking down at her phone. Making plans, plotting their next fuck. She looped around the parking lot down at the beach where his running buddies met; no sign of Curt's car. She drove around the route they usually ran.

He was nowhere to be found. He was probably somewhere comforting Shelly from their altercation in the parking lot. *Unless I'm wrong? Maybe there's no one else?* Maybe it was just Diana; she was getting old, and he was done with her. It still didn't feel right. Some things just didn't add up. She had to find out.

* * *

Curt marched into the kitchen while Diana was downing an espresso to counter the effects of another sleepless night.

"Have you lost the plot?"

Diana looked up at Curt with narrowed and questioning eyes, observing his aggressive flurry while suspecting what was coming.

"Shelly called me last night and said you accused her." He nearly spat in her face with the venom he was seething.

"Well, of course she did," Diana retaliated, as she leaned on the granite kitchen counter to steady herself. *That certainly sounds like another admission of guilt. Calling the husband of the accuser, that's just what a concerned, innocent girlfriend would do.* If it were the reverse situation, Diana would swear to her innocence and pledge her allegiance to help her friend find the culprit. This is not how a friend "who has your back" behaves.

"Diana, have some pride."

"Pride? Really, Curt? How about the truth?"

"I'll tell you why this is happening," Curt snapped. "You haven't made a family dinner for five years."

Diana couldn't help but laugh. *That's the best he can do?*

"And you're jealous, and, and miserable, and..." He seemed to be rattling off whatever came into his mind like a five-year-old on the playground.

Diana shot back, "Miserable? That's the word you used for Candy, and yet she seems to be happy, and with a nice guy... according to you."

He started to scamper off, his usual solution when Diana had a valid point to make.

"You're just like your father," Diana shouted after him, "but I'm nothing like your mother."

That remark should hit its mark and, hopefully, sting. Curt would know exactly what she was referring to—his father had taken off to Australia with his landlord lover, leaving five teenage boys for his mother to raise, and, despite this betrayal, she never stopped loving him. Diana would never forget the first time she met Curt's mother; she went into detail about how his father left the house to work in London for the week, told her to order mulch for the weekend, and then, without a word, just never came back. Thirty years later, he showed up on her doorstep, sick and penniless with nowhere to go, and she took him in.

That comment temporarily stopped his exit, and he turned with a hateful look in his eyes. "We can do this the hard way or the easy way, Diana."

"I don't have to listen to you anymore, Curt. You can stop threatening me. I'm not afraid of you. All you are is a liar, a drunk, and a cheat."

Still within earshot, he shouted over his shoulder, "You're bipolar." Diana laughed at that comment: *that makes me sad, no, that makes me happy...* "And you're a sociopath!"

She was left standing alone in the kitchen faced with another day of absolute crazy. She could not understand how she and Curt went from looking at beach houses to begin their next phase of life together to him moving out at the end of the month. *What happened?*

She waited for Curt to leave for work and now had only minutes before garbage pickup. What had he been throwing out? She started looking through the large trash bags Curt had been filling from his office and were now lined up like zipped-up body bags waiting to be collected. They contained cards and letters, photos and other personal effects that he would just toss away along with the rest of his life. As she frantically dumped the papers out on the pavement, she thought how embarrassed she would be if the garbage men pulled up to find her rummaging through papers that were now strewn across the driveway. This was crazy, and she was getting nowhere fast. She picked up one of the bags and started swinging it around her head, beating it on the ground, her anger rising with the bag and then moving through her body to come crashing to the ground into complete devastation. Years of anger, resentment, and frustration began moving through her body. She lifted her head and heard the truck coming up the road. Only moments to put everything back! She scooped the garbage up and then calmed herself to appear as if she had just put it out. She waved to the driver and walked through the garage to move into the house, realizing at that moment she needed to protect herself, emotionally, physically, and financially. No one was going to save her, least of all him. He went from being her knight in shining armor to her biggest nightmare.

Diana launched into action and picked up the phone. First, a call to the lawyer a friend had recommended. Her heart was pounding as she tried to remain calm. *How do you even explain what was happening? What should the first sentence be? 'I just got home from vacation and my husband informed me that our relationship is over, and I think he is having an affair.' How do you say that calmly?* You don't, and she didn't. After unleashing the details of her insane situation, she arranged a time to meet with him for a consultation. He assured her she would feel much better after she had met with him. She composed herself, hesitated, and then asked, "Also, I was wondering if you knew of any good private investigators in the area."

13

Launching into action had saved Diana in that moment, although it took some time before she would give herself credit for taking over the reins of her life. Curt had made his last unilateral decision—the final blow—the relationship was over. He had refused to talk to her, to provide some explanation, but she had been determined to find out why. "Not making family dinner" had not been good enough.

"So wait, Kung Fu, you hired a Sherlock?"

"A Sherlock? What's that?"

"A PI."

"Yes, I did. I needed to know what was going on."

"Wow, I didn't see that one coming. Good for you." Janis soaked that in with a big grin on her face. "Wait, is he the guy who's helping you now?"

Diana nodded. "Yes, that's him. He saved my life back then, and I hope he can do it again."

"He cares about you, that's easy to see. You lucky you got him on your side. Janis raised her eyes to focus on Diana as she said, "I would be seriously worried otherwise."

Diana rolled her eyes. "Thanks, that makes me feel so much better."

"It's okay, Kung Fu, at least you have good company."

"Oh, who's that?"

Janis pointed her thumb at her chest and exclaimed, "Me!" She smiled her broad grin that had been buried to show the prize she had become to Diana.

It was a brief moment when Janis' tough exterior was dropped, and Diana saw a glimpse of the little girl she must have been—happy, playful, loving.

"Yes, of course, I'm just teasing." Diana smiled warmly.

Janis sat up and leaned in and whispered, "So, are you gonna tell me? What did he find out? Were you right?"

* * *

The lawyer had given Diana the name of a PI, Robert Abbott, a local retired cop who he had used before in "these types of cases." She wondered what qualified as "these types:" husband abandons wife without explanation, husband cheats on wife with girlfriend, husband lies about the whole thing and tries to make wife seem crazy. *What type of case am I?* It didn't matter, she called the PI right away; she was geared up with a momentum of conviction and an unbridled need for the truth.

"Hello." His voice was deep and measured. "Abbott here."

Diana took a deep breath and cut right to the chase. She began with a confident, professional voice. "Yes, hello, my name is Diana Wall. Scott Sage suggested I give you a call."

"Oh, yeah, sure, I know Scott. Great lawyer. How can I help you?"

"Okay, well." She hesitated then blurted, "I think my husband's having an affair, but he won't admit it, and I need to know." Her voice quivered as she tried to hold it together from the edge of absolute breakdown. She walked around the gunite pool as if it was a labyrinth; she lost count of laps she had taken during the morning's hysterical phone calls to family and close friends in a series of pleas for help.

"Okay, sure. I can help you with that. Would you like to meet tomorrow?"

Diana was taken aback at the speed in which this would occur. She wondered if she really needed to do this. Maybe this was all just a mistake. But then she remembered the hateful look in Curt's eyes when he told her he wanted out. "Yes, let's meet." They arranged to meet the next afternoon at a coffee shop in town.

Diana was shaking when she pulled into the parking lot along the river. She had spent the entire morning getting ready for this meeting and trying to figure out what else she needed to do to protect herself. Her mind had been ricocheting like an excited bee trapped in its hive, wanting to get out for its next source of pollen. *Passwords on accounts—he had access to my financial files while I was away—need to change those. What about mail? Open a PO box in town. Valuables? And a safety deposit box. What about my personal check books and statements? Did he have access to my email?*

Diana was still shaking as she moved from the car to the coffee shop. She looked around to make sure she didn't see anyone she knew. She never thought in a million years she would be hiring a PI, but she had to find out what was going on for her own sanity. Curt was hiding something from her, and she knew in her heart there was someone else, and most likely it was Shelly. Why couldn't he just tell her when she asked? He was being so cruel.

It was a beautiful summer day, which didn't seem fair, given how Diana was feeling. It should be raining and windy, the trees swirling around her like her emotions spinning out of control. She had to hold it together; she needed to be professional. *After all, I don't want to come across like some crazy housewife. Ha!* She spotted him in line at the counter. It had to be him; he just looked like a detective: big and tall, probably in his fifties, with sharp watchful eyes, totally aware of his surroundings, quickly sizing up the shop patrons like a sophisticated surveillance device.

Of course, he spotted her as soon as she walked in. He extended his hand to her as she entered the line. "Diana, Robert Abbott. What can I get you?" He had a sympathetic manner about him despite the harder edges written on his face. Known about town for many things, including a bit of a sucker for a damsel in distress, he was reputed for being good at his job.

She straightened her white blouse and quickly checked that nothing was hanging out or showing through, then shook his hand. "Hi, I'm Diana."

"Yes, I know. What would you like?"

"I'll just have coffee, thanks. I can get it." She wondered how he knew it was her. *Is there a caged-animal look about me?* She joined the line next to him and ordered a nonfat latte, extra hot with cinnamon on top. He took his coffee large and black, nothing fancy.

"Where would you like to sit?" he asked. Abbott looked directly into her eyes and, as a trained investigator, would have to notice their unusual color. Blue, green, gray... there was a little bit of everything going on in Diana's eyes, and they seemed to change in the light.

"Can we go outside? It's so nice." Diana started moving nervously towards the door. She didn't want to be spotted by her dance friends, who would come in for coffee about this time. *Better to be outside by the river where it's quiet.*

They picked a park bench along the river and sat side by side.

"So, tell me what's going on, and how can I help?" Abbott asked sympathetically.

"A week ago I got home from vacation with my daughter, and I found..." her face contorted, and the tears started slipping down her cheeks, spilling onto her blouse and collecting in the fabric to account for her misery. "I'm sorry." She tried to pull herself together. She hated how emotional she was being; this was far from professional.

"Don't apologize." He handed her a napkin to dry her tears, which calmed her down, as it reminded her of how her father would tenderly hand her his clean handkerchief out of his pocket when she was upset.

She took in a short breath and started in again. "I think he is having an affair, and he won't tell me. I think it might be with my friend." Abbott just shook his head. She took out a photograph of Shelly taken with her and Elizabeth at one of the many parties they had been together. When she handed it to him, she noticed what she thought was tobacco-stained fingers from years of smoking. What she didn't know was that he was a painter, and had been working with yellow ochre that morning.

"He's having an affair with this? What, is he crazy? She looks like something you might find under a bridge." She knew he was trying to get her to laugh to lighten the mood but was only rewarded with a small smile. "Listen, I know how hard this is. I've been there." He pulled the top of his shirt down to show her a puncture wound in his chest. "My wife of twenty years stabbed me with an icepick. That's after I found her outside an AA meeting screwing her sponsor in a car."

Although he spoke of what Diana considered a horrifying scene in a matter-of-fact tone, she could sense the undercurrents of pain and anger that had been suppressed over the years. She wondered why he was spilling his guts, but she just listened intently and without judgment, her eyes never leaving his. *Is he someone I can trust?*

"Okay, so here's the deal, I'm going to take it easy on you... $100 an hour plus expenses. I've handled this type of case thousands of times, so it shouldn't take too long. Men are ignoramuses when they are carrying on like this, and they are easily caught."

"Thank you," Diana said. "I appreciate that." She briefly wondered what this would cost, but she didn't care. She needed to know what was going on. She put a number behind his words and figured it was worth it. You can't put a price on sanity.

"The more you can tell me, the quicker this will be. I need both their full names, and if you can tell me anything about his habits or hobbies. What kind of car does he drive? Also, if you have the license plate numbers of their vehicles. And addresses, home, work. Okay?"

Diana started giving him the information she had. With each piece she felt better as she was taking action, and this man Abbott seemed to know what he was doing. She didn't know why, maybe because he showed his vulnerability with his story, but she trusted this guy and thought he could help her. She would play it cool at home and back away from Curt. She was done trying to talk to him; he was not telling her anything anyway.

* * *

After weeks of following Curt, the PI was getting nowhere fast. It seemed the PI spent hours sitting outside Alden and Shelly's house, hiding behind the long row of whatever the landscaper planted to give them privacy from the road. Abbott would follow Curt there to watch his car sitting idly in their long driveway while hanging out with Shelly. The PI also observed that he would often go out with Alden when he got home from work. This made Diana even more suspicious and wondered if the three of them were involved in some strange tryst. In a community like this one, it wouldn't be that hard to believe. She remembered someone telling her there were "swingers" in town. Diana was so naive, she had no idea what that actually meant.

"Robert, this is getting frustrating. I think maybe we should try something else besides following him. Why not follow her?"

"You mean that toad? Why would he want anything to do with her? She is really hideous."

"That aside, let me look up when she gets out of her Y classes. It seems to me she would want to be with him during the day while Alden is at work."

"He seems pretty friendly with both of them. Are you sure..."

"I know what you're thinking, you don't even need to say it. Just follow her, please."

* * *

When she got the call from the PI reporting in a week later, Diana was thankfully with her good friend, CeCe, who she met at the dance studio years ago. Dance had become a joyful savior for Diana, helping her get through some tough times—the difficulties with her stepchildren, the three miscarriages, the loss of her mother, and now this absolute nightmare.

CeCe was about ten years older than Diana, but she was young at heart and full of energy. Her bobbed snow-white hair did not give her age away, and her beautiful skin was free of wrinkles. Of course, they were both in great shape from going to dance nearly every day, which was good for the body, mind, and spirit. They had also become playmates outside of class—golf, kayaking, tennis in the summer, skiing and hiking in the winter months. On weekends, they would go out to dinner or a movie with friends and their respective partners. They had even taken a few trips together, so CeCe knew Curt quite well. She always told Diana how she thought Curt absolutely adored her.

CeCe had been through her own marital drama through the years, and she was trying to help Diana get through this one with sound advice and loving guidance. "So, how ya doin', baby?" CeCe had a way of talking to Diana as if she were her little sister. CeCe was used to taking care of others since she had four sisters of her own that were scattered about the country, and even though she was in the middle of the lineup, she seemed to carry a strength that her sisters relied on. She had become a trusted and treasured friend to Diana.

"Well, I hired a PI." Diana sat down at the kitchen counter to look out the picture windows that framed the view of the rocky river that ran past CeCe's backyard.

"Good for you, Diana."

"Yeah, I just couldn't take it anymore. Curt won't tell me a thing."

"What a creep." CeCe handed Diana her coffee and sat down next to her. "So, has he found anything?"

"No, not yet. It's been pretty frustrating." Diana shifted in her seat to continue the report. "He's been following Curt. The other day, he spent hours outside Shelly's house because Curt was parked out front. I found out through the grapevine that he was with Shelly and Alden at the U.S. Open. He's been hanging around them a lot lately."

"What a jerk." CeCe was great at taking your side, no matter what.

"Yeah, so I've been doing my own reconnaissance." Diana thought about how she had carefully steamed open his bank statement earlier that morning.

"Uh-uh. So... what did you find?"

"Well, it was very interesting. There were some charges from the Walgreens near his work for hundreds of dollars. I thought it was either for Viagra or painkillers. I don't think he ever got off of those from when he hurt his back this past Spring."

"Really? Oh, that's not good, Diana. He could easily get addicted to those."

"I wouldn't be surprised, CeCe. He gobbled down Abby's painkillers for her broken nose when the doctor refused to give him anymore. They had been sitting in the cabinet for years."

"Okay, so listen. You don't want to get obsessed with this. You may not be able to figure it out. You have to move on, sweetie."

"I know. Maybe he just wants out like he said." She was looking for clues but only finding shades of possibilities; it was filling her head with theories, not answers. She felt like she was teetering on the edge of a cliff.

"But I told the PI that maybe he should follow Shelly instead of Curt. Shelly teaches a lunchtime class at the fitness studio. So, who knows, maybe she goes to him afterwards."

"Well, that would make sense if it is that little bitch. But I can't believe he would be into her. She is so heinous." CeCe looked like she swallowed a bitter pill.

The ringtone of Diana's cell phone caused her to jump. She looked at the screen—*Robert Abbott*. "It's him, CeCe!" She picked up the phone and moved away from the counter.

"Hello?"

"You would not believe the way this bitch is driving." Abbott had called Diana to tell her that he was 'on her tail.

"I can barely keep up with her. She's headed down 133 to the coast." That made sense to Diana, as Shelly was headed in the direction of Curt's office.

"Stay with her, Robert." Her voice broke as she tried to breathe.

"Oh, I will, don't you worry. I'll call you back."

Diana's adrenaline started pumping; she could feel the blood coursing through her veins. This was it. He called back minutes later. He started to give her a blow-by-blow description of what was happening. Detail, pause, reload, fire one. Detail, pause, reload, fire two. Each detail felt like a bullet to her gut or, more appropriately, a stab in her back. "They're at the marina. She's parking right next to his car... they are getting out of their cars and moving to a picnic table." Pause. "They are sitting down across from each other. She is pulling out a stack of papers. Boy, this is some serious meeting." Pause. "Let me call you back."

Diana bent over and held her stomach; rocking back and forth, she wailed like someone who had just lost their loved one in a car accident. It was that quick and unexpected. She couldn't breathe. In fact, she hadn't breathed properly for months. *This is absolutely crazy! Curt is in love with me! He left his children for me! He said I was the only woman for him.*

CeCe came over and gripped her shoulder. "Calm down, breathe."

Diana pursed her lips and started pushing out air in short bursts. Now she knew why she had taken that Lamaze class all those years ago. Her friend acted as a doula, reciting calming phrases she remembered, having survived a similar situation. All the blood drained from Diana, and she was white as fresh-laden snow.

Abbott called again. "He's moved from around the table. It's starting to get touchy-feely." His voice rose in pitch to mock the moment. "He's stroking her cheek." That bullet hit close to its mark. "They're kissing. Let me get photos."

After what seemed like a lifetime, he called again. "Oh, you're not going to believe this. They are fucking in his car. What a piece of shit this guy is."

"You have to get photos," Diana cried.

"I can't. I'll blow my cover. The back windows are tinted; I'd have to take them from the front of the car. They'll see me."

"Do whatever you have to do, please!" She hung up.

She turned to CeCe and started crying uncontrollably, shouting in between sobs. "They're fucking in his car."

"What? Are you kidding me? That's disgusting." CeCe's face contorted and grew red with anger.

Diana managed to eke out in staccato between sobs, "He destroyed my family, CeCe… and now he's going to do it again."

"Get in the car, I'm taking you to get your things. You can stay with me tonight." CeCe took her hand to pull her up, and Diana shot out of the chair. She couldn't breathe, but she knew she had to move. She gathered up her stuff from dance class and raced for the car, tears pouring down her face.

"That mother fucker." She got into CeCe's red convertible. The day was clear and sunny, so the top was down. She thought, I will never be able to enjoy this ride again. Life was over as she knew it; it would never be the same. She couldn't fathom, absorb, or understand what had happened. Surely, this was not meant to be. This was not the promise that was made. She didn't know this man, and she didn't know whose life this was. Reality hit her; the image of his body on top of Shelly's. The image of that bitch being touched by her husband in the way she wanted to be touched by him. *Did he ever tenderly stroke my cheek? Did he ever love me like he said? Is it to get Alden's money?* She couldn't understand. Everything she thought she knew was undone. Everything she tried to build with him had just tumbled to the ground. The arrow of destruction hit its target, but she would not let him break her. She would not allow this to define or destroy her.

When they got to the house, she ran around grabbing the things that really mattered to her. It was like she had five minutes before her house would burn down; she had to quickly decide what was really important and could not be replaced. In the end, she took financial records, photos of Abby when she was a baby, her journals, the small ivory Buddhas that sat on her shelf, her laptop, toiletries, and a few items of clothing she would need for the weekend. She was in a panic and could barely think. She just knew she could not stay in that house with him while he destroyed everything they had built together. *For what? Shelly? She's despicable.*

* * *

Diana had a week to pack up and take Abby back to college, while she also prepared for her own classes, which would start in days. She ducked in and out of the house while Curt was working and Abby was staying with her father. Diana didn't know how she was going to get through the semester. Instead of being excited about starting this new teaching assignment, she wasn't sleeping, she was barely eating, and she could not stop crying, falling to pieces every time she figuratively slapped herself awake with the reality of what was happening. She did not want to be in that house while Abby was gone. She didn't know what to do. She couldn't stay with CeCe forever.

Her heart was beating out of her chest as she drove up the long drive to the house; she needed to pick up the remainder of Abby's things, including the poorly-sewn duvet cover. She prayed that Curt was not there. Her prayers were answered. She was able to get in and out without confronting him. She wasn't sure what she would do to him if she saw him now. Armed with the information from the PI, she knew she would not be able to control herself, emotionally or physically. She glanced in the rearview mirror as if to take a last look at the house before pulling into the street. She waved to the neighbor in a weak attempt to indicate that everything was normal.

Abby was anxious to get back to school. She had been away from Mike the last week and needed his soothing presence. He had left for home right after Abby's birthday, which was not the celebration they had planned. Diana had tried to make the most out of it by taking them to Abby's favorite restaurant, but she could barely hold it together. None of this was fair to poor Abby. She couldn't tell her father what was going on, even though he had been asking questions. Diana told Abby that she'd be the one to tell him the truth.

She stepped onto the back deck that overlooked Dave's manicured yard. Abby had chosen to stay with her father for a few days so that she could collect some things and spend time with him. Abby had told Diana, "He's always outside pruning and fussing, which is fine with me—it gets him off my back." It always sent shivers down Diana's spine when Abby recounted these stories of his behavior. He had not changed over the years, and now his special form of abuse was directed at their daughter. Another source of guilt for Diana, even though Abby seemed to weather it from a place of strength.

Diana looked through the plate-glass door to see Dave approaching; this was her chance to come clean.

"Hey, Diana."

"Hey, Dave."

"Thanks so much for taking Abby back to school. I've been so busy with work and the house." He posed this as if she was doing him a personal favor, which usually got under Diana's skin, but today it didn't matter. "Are you okay? You don't look so good."

She ignored the insult. "Dave, I need to tell you something."

"What?"

"Curt is leaving me. He's having an affair with my friend."

He didn't say anything. He just looked at her as if to calculate the consequence.

"I guess you can say, what comes around goes around." She started to tear up.

"I would never say that." He moved to embrace her, and she couldn't hold it together.

"I'm sorry, Diana."

"Me too," she said through tears. "I thought I was making the right decision."

He pulled away from their embrace to look into her eyes. "It's okay, Diana. You weren't feeling loved. It's not your fault."

She never expected to hear that.

* * *

On the way up to college, Abby provided some welcome relief playing music and singing, which were two of her favorite pastimes. Diana was thankful that she was in a good mood and figured she had Mike to thank for that. He would be meeting them at the other end, ready to unload the car. Regardless of what happened in their relationship, Diana would be forever grateful to Mike. He had stood by Abby with his calm and caring demeanor and shown a maturity beyond his years—most 20-year-olds would have run in the other direction. Abby had chosen wisely, and she was glad that her daughter seemed to have better judgment when it came to men.

When they turned off the Mass Pike, Diana turned down the music. "Abby, listen, I have to tell you something."

"What is it, Mom?"

"I hired a PI."

"You did what?"

"I hired a private investigator to find out what was going on with Curt."

"Okay..."

"He found evidence that Curt is having an affair with Shelly."

"No way, Mom. That is messed up."

"Yes, I know. The PI got photos of them kissing and whatnot."

"What a scum. Mom, you are so much better off without him. Let him have her, they deserve each other."

"Thanks, honey. It's just really hard." She fought back the tears wanting to show some strength for her daughter.

"I know, Mom, it will be okay." She reached over to tenderly stroke Diana's arm.

They rode the rest of the way in near silence; it would be extremely hard to say good-bye. Diana held her daughter tight and looked at Mike, who stood behind Abby, willing him to take good care of her. He nodded as if he understood, picked up a suitcase, and took Abby by the hand to bring her to the safety of her new home for the semester.

As Diana headed out of Boston, she received a call from her friend, Mary, from dance class. Mary was a generation older than Diana and an inspiration to her. Not only was it admirable that she was still shaking it on the dance floor, but she was a published author and a fine artist. She and Diana had become good friends while spending hours painting in her studio in town. Through a haze of tears, Diana proceeded to tell her everything that had been going on in shocking detail.

"I don't know what I'm going to do, Mary. I can't go back to that house while he's still in it, watching him destroy the life we had together."

"You don't have to, sweetie."

"What do you mean?"

"You can come here. We have a spare apartment over the garage. No one is using it. It's yours if you want it."

"Really?"

"Yes, I'm sure of it. I could use the company, too. You know Richard is not doing well, and he's really depressed. He's making me crazy."

"Oh, well I'm not sure if I'd be good company. I'm a bit of a mess."

"Don't you worry. I'll take care of you. You do not need to go anywhere near that heinous man."

"Okay." she sniffled and regained her composure. "Thank you so much, Mary. I'll come. You don't know what this means to me." She choked back the tears, this time from a sense of relief and gratitude. "I should be there in three hours or so."

"Take your time, sweetie. We'll have dinner ready when you get here."

They said she could stay for as long as she needed. Diana felt safe, loved, and cared for. Mary and Richard listened to every detail of her story. They let her work through her shock, her pain, her disbelief. They tried to feed her and make sure she got to where she needed to go. Every day was a new revelation about how unreal this truly was. But she was given a safe haven, a quiet room, and a warm bed. She was able to sleep for about four hours, and she marched through each day with lists of what she needed to do to survive.

While Curt was at work, she would go up to the house so she could get into her office, collect some more clothes, and check on what was happening. She pulled into the driveway and cringed when she noticed his car was there. Pulling up to the garage doors, she spotted him inside, rummaging around and packing up boxes to add to the long row in the third bay. She backed the car down the long drive and entered through the front door to avoid him. It seemed he was mostly packed in less than a month—hard to believe given all the crap he had collected over the years. The boxes she saw staged at the front door were carefully numbered and labeled with hints of the inventory in each one. Mostly, it was tools from his cherished workshop that he outfitted in the way he had "always wanted."

Diana moved through the kitchen and opened the garage door to find him looking overheated from running around; he was busy stuffing a green garden tarp into a box.

"What's the panic, Curt?" Diana held the handle to the door so that she could slam it shut in his face with a moment's notice. She didn't know if he would come after her; he had been so unpredictable. She was afraid of him, although she refused to show it. It occurred to her that he might also be afraid of her. It wasn't that long ago that she had woken up from a dream in which he was cheating on her, and she playfully told him how mad she was about it. "If you ever do cheat on me, I will kill you." He had nervously giggled in response, and she said, "No, I really mean it. Don't forget, I prepare your dinner."

"I'm trying to get out of here!" he shouted at her as he hurriedly taped up the box.

"Are you going to be done after this?" She stood firmly, challenging him with a strength she never knew she had.

"Yes." He didn't even look up at her, just continued to spread tape around the box containing his beloved garden tarp.

"Good." She slammed the door to the house. That would be the last word she would say to him in their home. He finished and drove off; still no admission of what he had done, no apology for his behavior, no goodbye. That's what you get after a life together—a big, fat zero—and worse, no explanation.

Moments after, her cell phone began to play its cheery song. It was Robert Abbott. He had been calling her almost every day to check in on her; he seemed to know exactly when to call, like he could sense when she needed him.

"How ya doin', kid?"

She couldn't even answer. She sobbed into the phone and managed to blurt out an apology for her weakness. She told him everything, as she had been doing since the very beginning. He listened and reminded her of what a 'piece of shit' he was, and that she was going to be so much better without him. She knew that he was right, but her emotions were so twisted, it was hard to believe that she would ever be the same. *I guess I won't be. I've never experienced such pain.* Even with the loss of her mother, Diana could at least see that coming given the nature of her mother's condition and the slow and steady demise. But this came out of nowhere, and she could not digest the magnitude of what was occurring, especially given the speed.

"He just left for good," she was shouting into the phone through the tears. "With no word at all. Nothing. I get nothing."

"You don't deserve this, Diana. Do not beat yourself up. The guy's a narcissist. I'm telling you. I know the type."

She wasn't sure whether to believe that or not, but she did see a cruel and black-hearted side to him that she was never exposed to before. Where did that come from? She knew he could get nasty, but this was extreme. It would be one thing if she had cheated on him, or abused him, or didn't bend over backwards to make him happy. It just didn't make sense, or did it? She would spend many hours looking at this from every angle like studying a masterpiece for its secrets of technique. There was no manual for this experience.

"Look, kid, I want you to call me anytime, okay?"

"Okay," she managed to say through her tears. She wiped her nose with the back of her hand and sucked up the snot that liberally flowed. She was a mess.

After hanging up, she allowed herself to cry, letting the tears fall wherever they wanted with no cause for concern. She was not going to falsely stifle these emotions; she was going to let them escape from their hiding places to rid them once and for all. How long that would take, she had no idea. She figured it would be a long haul.

14

It had taken Curt less than a month to pack up and move out. Diana remembered how devastating it was to watch him destroy their lives together. It was gone with a snap of his fingers, so Diana focused on making it official and recommended mediation to get the divorce process going. This had surprised Curt, as she never revealed that she had proof of his infidelity, which fueled her decision-making.

"So, that was it. He just packed up and left." Janis softened her gaze on Diana in empathy. "What an asshole. At least I got to fight it out with my ex."

"There was nothing to fight for. He was gone. I had to focus on my welfare, and that meant getting out from under financially and legally. I had no idea what he was capable of."

"Yeah, I get that. Seems like men get all business-like while women are so emotional, they end up getting a raw deal."

"Not this time." Diana shook her head. "No, ma'am. He wasn't going to get the best of me. But it was tough, and it was hard to keep it together."

"How so?"

"He made me face my biggest fear in life."

"What's that?"

"Fear of abandonment. It stems from a childhood trauma I experienced when I was very little."

162

"Well, I guess we have that in common." Janis' eyes began to tear up, and she flinched to shrug off the deep-seated pain.

"I'm really sorry." Diana thought for a moment of what she could say to Janis. She knew she could be explosive, so she didn't want to pry. She also knew that Janis did not appreciate a show of weakness. "We all have a story, I suppose."

"Yes we do, Kung Fu. So tell me more of yours."

* * *

She couldn't look at him as they sat in the reception area. He disgusted her. Diana could not believe they would be meeting with a mediator just one month after Curt's proclamation. She woke up that morning thinking: *Curt is dead to me.* It occurred to her that she did not stay to fight it out with him; she did not demonstrate any rage. She was done with his lies, manipulation, and lack of care. She would turn to herself for self-preservation and protection. She did not want anything from him; she knew that getting as far away from him as possible was the right decision. To her, he was not in his right mind, and Shelly was even worse. *Who pretends to be your friend, and then fucks your husband behind your back? What sick human being finds pleasure in that?*

They were ushered into the office of Adam Rothstein, a mediator who had been recommended to her by the same lawyer who recommended Abbott. She hoped she would be in good hands. She sat down at a small round table and tried to quell the shaking in her hands so that it did not come through in her voice.

Curt was very charming with his British accent; she wanted to puke. "Well, this is a lovely corner office. Beautiful views overlooking the pines."

"Well, thank you," said Rothstein. "So what can I do for you folks today?" He was trying to be casual. For some reason, the term folks made Diana cringe; this was not the local jamboree. Far from it, there was nothing fun about what was happening here.

Diana blurted, "Several weeks ago I came home from a family event, and my husband informed me that our marriage was over." She said it quickly; she didn't want to lose her composure.

"Okay," said Rothstein, "and how can I help you?"

Curt took his turn. "We want to avoid expensive lawyers, and you were recommended."

"Well, that's very nice. By whom, may I ask?"

"I spoke with Scott Sage, and he recommended you," Diana quickly interjected. She didn't want Curt to get the credit. She was hoping the professional connection might garner a level of sympathy towards her. Even though mediators were supposed to be objective, they always tended to side with one party over another. She was not thrilled that he was a male; she suspected that most were wired to think, *She must be a nag or a hag if the husband had to stray.* She didn't like thinking that way, but she could be pragmatic when necessary.

Diana's head was swimming, and she sensed sharks around every corner. She never thought in a million years she would be in this position again. She thought she and Curt would be together forever, that he would never leave her, as they had been through so much and were once so passionate about each other. She could not shake the feeling of being kicked in the gut... not lightly, but with enough force to crack all the ribs in her cage.

"Okay, so let me tell you folks how this works, then." Another cringe.

"Oh, Diana knows. She's been through this before," Curt snickered.

What a complete asshole! She wanted to fly across the table and take his neck into her hands and squeeze hard until his blue eyes popped out of his head. If it wasn't for him, she wouldn't be going through this again. And she may not have gone through it the first time.

"Well, we have to take a look at your financials. This may be an alimony case," said Rothstein.

"That's not going to work for me." Curt sat stiffly in his chair to indicate that he would not budge.

Diana laughed. *What a joke. Of course it isn't going to work for him. He's in this for the money; he isn't going to shell it out.*

"I don't want anything from him," Diana snapped. "When this is over, I never want to see him again." Against the promise to herself, the tears began to well up. She turned her head away from the table to look at 'the pines' as she fought them back.

Curt continued with no concern for her pain. "What about her assets? I know she got money when her mum died, and part of the beach house."

"Yes, those would be considered joint assets if acquired while you were married."

Diana already knew what the upshot was, having met with the lawyer.

"And what about the diamond ring she has? That's worth quite a bit of money, probably fifty grand or so."

Diana's jaw dropped. This was so disgusting. He wanted her to put up the family ring her mother had given her just before she passed away. He knew how awful it was for Diana to watch her mother fade away with Lewy Body Dementia—a gruesome way to go, and such a gruesome posture he was taking. *What a pig!*

The pit in Diana's stomach grew. She had to take control.

"You take nothing, none of my assets, or I go for alimony."

"Well, this is going to be the quickest divorce in history, folks." Rothstein smiled as if this was something to celebrate.

* * *

"So, which one of your folks wants to be the one who files?" Rothstein was ready with papers in hand on the second visit; there would be no delay.

"I do," said Diana. *How ironic*, she thought. The last time she said that, she was exchanging wedding vows with Curt. She sat forward with pen in hand, reaching for the papers to sign. Since she found out about Shelly, she knew she had to get away from these people as quickly as possible. She had focus and clarity around that if nothing else.

Curt looked surprised. Perhaps he thought Diana was going to make a scene, maybe even fight for him.

"I didn't see that coming," said Rothstein, showing his surprise as well.

"I think we should take a hiatus," Curt said, "and let the emotions calm down." He addressed Rothstein directly, still unable to look her in the eye.

"What are you talking about, Curt?" She was taking nothing from him, and he was still playing games.

He directed his answer to Rothstein. Such a coward; he couldn't speak directly to her. "Yesterday, my friend Alden received a letter that accused his wife of cheating on him with me!" He paused for drama then exclaimed, "And she has two children!"

"I have no idea what you're talking about," said Diana. "I don't know anything about a letter. Furthermore, I want nothing to do with you or your sordid affair."

Curt stood up from his chair. "I'm done here," he said, and left the room.

Diana signed the papers and left without a word. I suppose she could get some pleasure out of the fact that he would be served. *The fucking bastard.*

She rushed out into the newly-paved parking lot and hurriedly got into her car. Her heart was pounding like the steady beat of a galley's drum propelling the oars forward through the sea. She pulled out and looked in the rearview mirror; Curt was behind her. She quickly thought about all the times he followed her, a little too closely, and she figured this would be the last time she would feel that discomfort. She called Robert.

"Hey kid, what's going on?" He always picked up quickly when Diana called.

"I just signed divorce papers." She said it in a matter-of-fact tone, which was somewhat off-putting, given all the high emotions and tears that usually accompanied these conversations.

"Oh, wow... you okay?"

"Yes, I'm fine. I'm pissed though. The asshole almost blew the whole thing with some letter he said I sent Alden accusing him and his wife of having an affair. How ironic is that?"

"What? That's just crazy."

"I didn't send any letter, Robert. If I wanted to tell Alden, I just would. Something doesn't seem right."

"What do you mean?" Robert cleared his throat and settled in to listen.

"Who would send a letter like that? What would be the purpose?"

"Maybe one of Alden's friends or a neighbor. Someone who has it out for Shelly."

"Huh, maybe..."

"What? What do you think, kid?"

"Well, there was a rumor floating around that Shelly had been fooling around with another one of Alden's friends. Maybe it was the guy's wife, Ophelia."

"Oh, jeez. So she's done this before? What a piece of shit that woman is. Those two deserve each other."

"You are right," Diana enunciated. "Why would I send that, anyway?"

"So, what did you say?"

"I told both Curt and the mediator I wanted nothing to do with their sordid affair. Then I signed the papers."

"Good for you, kid. You're gonna be alright."

"I know. Thanks, Robert. Gotta go…" She hung up quickly before Robert's calming tones sent her into tears. She needed to get off the road. She headed for her sanctuary, the place where she could breathe and find some peace, the beach.

She sat on a rock overlooking the water and felt the salt air on her skin. She closed her eyes and took in a deep breath. *I think I have cried my last tear… but the hurt is still unbearable. The absolute betrayal.* She gathered her tears and regained her composure. *Remember, Diana, it's not how you fall, but how you get up that matters most.*

* * *

Diana was in the middle of teaching a class when she glanced down to check the time on her phone. She stared at the screen and read it over and over to be sure, a voice message from Shelly. She looked up to see her students' perplexed expressions as she had abruptly halted the flow of conversation. She quickly snapped out of her trance to call for a ten-minute break. Moving to the exit, she stepped outside to listen to the message. Each venomous word that Shelly spat out shot through her like crippling poison.

"Diana, writing that letter to my husband was absolutely despicable. How could you try to break up my own marriage, my family, my kids? Oh my gosh, you've really taken it to another level here, and it's unforgivable. You need to take some responsibility for the breakup of your own marriage, Diana. I understand now that it was a long time coming, and I know that you saw it. You wrote this letter based solely on speculation. Zero proof. There isn't any, because there is nothing going on. Shame on you. Do not write another letter to my husband. He does not believe you, Diana. We can all see everything now. It's very crystal clear."

That bitch. How dare she! Diana's heart was pumping so much adrenaline through her system, she could not control herself. After months of taking the high road, knowing what she knew, with the evidence she had, it was too much for her to handle. She pressed *Call Back*, and Shelly picked up.

"Hello, Diana."

"I am going to tell you the same thing I told Curt," she said with her own venom. "I want nothing to do with your sordid affair. I did not write that letter…"

"Yes, you did. You threatened me. You said you would go to Alden."

Diana cut through her rant of lies and accusations and said in a loud, firm, and measured voice, "Maybe it was Ophelia, Shelly."

A moment of silence cut through the hatred. "You wrote it," Shelly tried to interject.

Diana yelled to the top of her lungs, "FUCK YOU, FUCK YOU!" and pushed the button to hang up. She looked up and saw one of her colleagues passing by; she prayed that she did not hear the conversation but feared that the last line was delivered with such velocity and volume that she probably did. This was her place of employment. She couldn't risk losing her job, too. She was mad at herself for letting that wretched, home-wrecking, slime-ball bitch get the best of her. She vowed to herself that she would never react to either of those two scumbags ever again. Diana scrolled down her contacts and blocked Shelly's number.

Diana had decided she was not going to stoop to their level right from the beginning, but they continued to needle her, testing her strength of conviction. She knew in her heart it would not help to lash out for revenge. It might feel good for a moment, but really, what was the point? It wouldn't change anything; it would only make things worse. Giving them the ammunition to prove that they had good reason to do what they had done.

But she had her fantasies of revenge. Marking Shelly's front door with red spray paint something akin to a scarlet letter for all to see. At Christmas time, she could send her a card that said, "HO, HO, HO" inside. Gather up the gifts Shelly had given her and return them with the note Shelly had given her saying, "You're such a good friend, I'll always have your back." Diana would add her own note to the package. "Have my back? More like my husband's back, front, and middle. You bitch." She came across a site where you could anonymously post photos of homewreckers and expose their identity; what a great idea! So many ways to take out her vengeance, none of which she would carry out. Instead, she held onto grace and dignity, her new mantra.

Diana could have called Alden at any point in time during the months that she knew what was going on, and she did not. This almost provoked her, but she was not going to be the woman who broke up that family. Let someone else tell him. Plus, he didn't seem to believe whomever sent this letter. And she received no call from him, so maybe he was aware, maybe he was just happy that someone was entertaining that shrew. Shelly was so emasculating to Alden, maybe he really didn't care, or maybe all three of them were involved. *Who knew?* It was best to stay away from it all and focus on the divorce.

* * *

It wasn't as easy as Rothstein had hoped, but it was fast. Diana was determined to make the first date that was available to them, five months to the day from when she pulled into the garage to find her life had been turned upside down. Curt had tried to get them to put it off until the spring; perhaps he wasn't sure, or maybe he needed more time to make sure Shelly would actually leave Alden, especially given the letter. She didn't know, but every time he indicated he would drag his feet, the bitter bile of betrayal would rise up for her to spit out before it settled in her throat.

If there was one thing she did know, she was not going to be bullied anymore. She had faced her biggest fears with him, and they had come to fruition. He was abandoning her, not to go back to his children, which would be understandable, but leaving just the same. She decided he would only respond to an ultimatum, a hit where it mattered most, his wallet.

He had been trying to bully her into putting the house on the market from the very first day. She knew he wanted his money. So, when he said they should put the divorce off, the simple statement, "As soon as you sign the agreement, I will list the house," worked like a charm. She was satisfied with her approach, having him on the ropes for a change. He wanted his money, she wanted out.

Despite his past offenses, Diana did not recognize the monster he had become. Even Curt's mother was shocked by his behavior. She had contacted Diana via Facebook (not even a telephone call), and wanted to know what was happening. When Diana did not want to give her the details of what he had done but said, "Suffice it to say, it was shocking," her first reply was, "Did he rape someone?" *Why in God's name would that be the go-to reaction from his mother?* Perhaps Curt's heinous behaviors went deeper than Diana ever imagined.

* * *

It was the day before they were due to appear in court. Diana was sick to her stomach, exhausted from lack of sleep, but still resolute on going through the legal finalization of the destruction of their marriage. Checking her emails to make sure there were no last-minute hiccups, her already upset stomach dropped to her feet, seeing an email come across from Curt:

Hey Diana, I blocked out the whole day for court and was wondering if you would want to get coffee or lunch afterwards. I would really like that.

Is he insane? He acted as if his behavior was perfectly normal and that she should be thrilled to spend some time with him! Oh, how she wanted to respond. She typed out a series of responses, "Are you mad?" Delete. "Of course, let's have lunch. That would be so nice. What a charming idea." Delete. "You are a sadist. I will barely be able to look at you in court. I would vomit if I sat across the table from you." Delete. "What's the matter, Curt? Having second thoughts? Is Shelly not all she pretended to be?" Delete. Delete. Delete.

* * *

Chills ran through her to reflect the cold and gray winter day. She stayed focused on the task at hand—getting to the courthouse, finding a parking spot without hitting anyone or anything on the way. Remnants of the last snow storm were scattered as reminders of how harsh it had been to winter in that house by herself. It had been months since she had laid eyes on Curt. This would be the last time. She meant it when she said she never wanted to see him ever again.

They sat stiffly, waiting for their turn with the judge. Diana thought how ironic it was that the last time she sat here, not too long ago, she was watching Curt take the vow of citizenship. That was a day of celebration for Diana, a sign that Curt was committed to her and to staying in this country. He always said emphatically that he did not want to be a U.S. citizen, and then out of the blue, he went for it. As Diana thought about the timing of it now, she realized that it may have been in preparation for this day. *Was he calculating this even back then?*

Diana gripped the PI report in the dark blue binder as if it could give her strength to get through this. She wanted to shove it in Curt's face and say, "See, I knew two weeks after I came home." She would thrust two fingers up, the English way, "You fuckin' liar!" Her rational side prevailed; for some reason, she felt that report was better kept under wraps. She didn't need it for the negotiation, as she was able to get what she wanted without it. The important thing was she would have no reason to connect with him once the house was sold; he wasn't giving her alimony, she negotiated to keep her savings and assets from her mother's estate, they would split the proceeds of the house supporting its maintenance equally until sold. Fair enough. The judge just needed to confirm the agreement and then it would be done.

Her hands shook as she sat at the heavy mahogany table. Opposite the aisle sat Curt. She tried not to notice his crisp white shirt and freshly-shaven face and refused to register the intensity of his blue eyes that fell on hers when the judge asked her a series of questions. She remembered, instead, his cruel nature and the intention she had set for herself. Carving him out of her life like a cancer that had been slowly spreading through her body over the years and would accelerate if she let it. This bleeding from the stab wound in her back had to stop.

The judge brought the gavel down to announce the next case, "Someone vs. Someone," and continued cycling through the many unhappy couples who were going through hell to move on with their lives. *The stories the judge must hear every day.*

As they left the courtroom to take the elevator down, Curt hung back and stood in the hallway, watching Diana. She frantically reached over and pushed the button to close the doors quickly, and then realized that would be the last time she would ever look into his eyes. For once, she didn't cry, but nothing that had happened over the past months had truly sunk in. Including the walk out of the courthouse, where she divorced the love of her life.

** * **

The house was her last connection to Curt. Once it was sold, there would be no reason for them to communicate. Diana wanted to sever all ties, physical and emotional. He was sick and toxic, and she needed to get him out of her life for good. Breaking his hold on her would make her stronger and more attuned to her needs of self-preservation, love, and nurturing.

She sat on her meditation cushion, pen and journal in hand, closed her eyes, and breathed as deeply as she could. She opened her eyes again to look out over the snow-covered yard and thought how beautiful this jail had been. The beauty now forgotten, it was a place where her emotions and feelings were trapped in a cell, built on a foundation of manipulation and lies. She began to write.

Today, I am divorced again. Today, I am single for the first time in nearly 20 years. I am hopeful about my future. I do not need to ever feel so unloved, so uncared for, so hurt. Now, I am free. I don't own his story, I own mine. What will it be? There are so many questions, but I am not afraid. I have faith that I will figure out the lessons in this and move forward stronger, happier, and clearer about my path. And it will be mine.

I am starting to spread my wings. Just six months after that glorious homecoming, I know I am getting better. I feel less resentful, almost grateful. I will create a brighter future for myself, and I will not be a victim. I will fly.

All these years, I was afraid that the shame of Curt leaving his children would ruin our marriage; perhaps it did. I was afraid to lose him because he would 'go back to England'—a threat he used so often to get what he wanted. Finally, I had the strength to say, "Then go." But he isn't going back, is he? The real threat was infidelity, alcohol abuse, cowardice; the real threat was a home-wrecking pathological bitch.

Diana would find some way to get closure. It wasn't going to be through Curt or through Shelly; above all, she would maintain her dignity. She wouldn't confront Shelly, even though she was a liar, a homewrecker, and a horrible human being; she had everything coming to her. Diana supposed whatever the universe had in store for Shelly would be much more eloquent than whatever she could devise. She would not call her nor would she write her a letter. There was only one letter she knew she needed to write, and that was to Sammy and Rose, the stepchildren that she helped to raise to adulthood and tried so desperately to love. But she knew in her heart, she would most likely never see them again.

Dear Sammy and Rose,

You probably know by now that your father and I are divorced. I'm not sure how much you've been told, but I would guess not a lot. It has been quite a shock.

If I had known that your visit in July would be the last I would see you both, I would have said so much more to you; I would have hugged you tighter.

I know that you didn't ask for me to be in your lives. I tried to be loving and kind to you, but I know you blamed me for your father's absence. I understand—you were children, and you were hurt. I am sorry for that.

The truth is, your father has inflicted pain on us all with the choices he has made for his own selfish gain. He is not the victim.

Despite that, I choose to be happy, with forgiveness in my heart, and hopes of a brighter future. I wish you both the very same. I realize we may never see each other again, but I want you to know that you have been loved, and I will remember the good times and loving moments we had, nothing else.

If you ever need me for any reason, I am here for you both.

With love,

Diana

P.S. Please tell your mother she was right.

Diana hoped that this would bring Sammy and Rose some peace of mind. She also hoped that Candy would read the letter and know exactly what Diana was referencing in the postscript. When Curt first came to America, Candy had phoned Diana with some nasty things to say and a long list of all the gruesome characteristics that Curt had displayed in their relationship. At the time, Diana didn't believe her and had pleaded with Candy to stop spreading her hatred to the children, to leave them out of it.

Candy's parting shot to Diana was, "Just you wait, he'll do it to you, too." Candy was right. Curt had treated Diana the same way he had treated Candy; the parallels were frightening, including the timing and longevity of each relationship. In the end, he was cruel and black-hearted to them both.

PART THREE

15

The sound of keys jingling and clanking against the cell door lock woke Diana from her distressed sleep. She had fallen asleep in a huddled position, with her head resting on her arms and knees. She was so exhausted, her body had just given in. She picked her head up, but the female cop said nothing as she shuffled the keys to find the one that would unlock the door. She sleepily watched as the cop dropped the ring into a jumble, picked it up with a huff, and began sorting through the keys again.

"Diana Wall?" She heard the sound of her name, muffled as if against a strong wind; it pulled her out of her stupor. She did not know how long she had been out; Janis, of course, was taking a rest from the storytelling, sleeping off the last of her hangover.

"Yes, I'm here." *Well of course you are, dear, where else would you be?* She actually chuckled, as it reminded her of the time she got stuck in an elevator, and the guys who responded to the call said, "Just stay put, don't go anywhere, we'll get you out." *Control what you can, give to the universe what you cannot.* She had to have faith that she would get out of this cell. There had to be some justice in the world.

Diana stood up and moved to the cell door. "Yes, I'm Diana Wall."

"Your lawyer is here to see you."

"My lawyer?" She wondered who it was. The only lawyers she ever had or needed was for a real estate transaction, to write-up a will, or for one of her divorce mediations. This would have to be a criminal lawyer; she shuddered at the thought. Robert must have called this guy for her. *What would I do without him?* With Robert, she had confidence that the lawyer would be good and could help her out of this jam.

The cop cuffed her and walked her through the cell door, back down the hallway that she had come through just a few hours ago. Despite her nap, the nausea had not subsided, the feeling of having her hands locked behind her back did not help. She thought she might throw up. *Where are they taking me?* She walked with her head held high as they led her to a bleak room with a gunmetal desk, two worn wooden chairs, and a naked fluorescent lamp overhead that made everything look green and depressing. A handsome young man dressed in a blue suit, crisp white shirt, and light blue tie stood up as she entered and greeted her enthusiastically.

"Ms. Wall, I'm Steven Obermeyer." He guided her to sit in the chair opposite his. "It seems we have a mutual friend." He smiled. "Robert Abbott gave me a call and told me about your situation."

Diana nodded in affirmation. His manner was professional but not cold; he had a calming way about him, and Diana liked him right away. However, she also learned the hard way not to trust anyone too easily.

"I'm here to help you, if that's okay with you." He paused. "I'd like to represent you. Abbott has spoken very highly of you and is quite confident of your innocence. I have a great deal of faith in his intuition for reasons I won't bore you with."

Diana listened as he spoke and finally responded. "I have come to learn that as it relates to Robert, there are no boring stories."

"Well, yes, that is quite true." He laughed. "But let's use our time to focus on you. I want to give you an understanding of what's happening and what to expect going forward." He nodded. "Shall I proceed?"

"Yes, please." Diana took a deep breath and exhaled slowly through pierced lips.

"I know you must be very frightened."

"No, just confused," said Diana. "This is a mistake, but I have faith that you and Robert will figure it out."

"Well, thank you, Diana. May I call you Diana?"

"Yes, of course."

"Thank you, Diana, for that vote of confidence."

"Can you just tell me how much longer I need to be here?" She was ready to get down to business.

"Okay, so here's the story. The detective on the case has information that puts you near the scene of the crime at the time the crime was committed. Ordinarily, that alone would not be enough, but they have an eyewitness who apparently claims he saw you do it."

He waited for her reaction.

"Well, I didn't," said Diana. She was firm and calm about it, although she wasn't sure why. She should be freaking out, but at this point, she knew in her heart that it was going to be okay. This was just another challenge that she would have to face, as it related to the whole ordeal. She wasn't angry, she wasn't afraid, she was at peace in the knowledge that she would get through this..

"Okay, I believe you." He nodded and opened a folder. "Now, here's what will happen. The judge is most likely going to see you on Monday, so I don't think you will have to stay much longer." *Okay, I can get through this.* She had started to enjoy her alone time, but usually it was sitting in sand by the water, not on a cold, concrete floor. Plus, there was Janis to pass the time.

"My guess is he is going to set bail at $1 million."

"What? A million? I don't have that kind of money!"

"Well, let's hope that he will call for a bond, in which case you only have to come up with a minimum of 10 percent, or $100,000. I will argue that you are a citizen of this town with no previous arrest record and no offenses, except for a speeding ticket, and that you are not a flight risk." He wrote a few notes on the pad.

"Furthermore, there has been no lineup, so the eyewitness is sketchy at best. He is old and has a history of drinking. I will argue that he is not a credible witness. And don't forget you have an ace in the hole."

"What's that?" She looked hopeful for the first time.

"Robert. He will not rest until he figures this out." He started to organize his papers. "Do you have any questions?"

Diana shook her head and simply said, "Thank you, and please, thank Robert for me."

"Okay, we'll be in touch. Stay strong."

16

Back in the cell, Janis was sleeping soundly. How could she do that? She didn't seem to be worried about anything. Diana needed to practice a bit of that and called on her optimistic nature to assure herself that everything would work out. No sooner had she begun to feel at peace for a brief moment, Janis woke up and jumped right back in.

"This doesn't look good for you, Kung Fu. I hope you gotta good alibi, because man, you for sure got motive."

Diana sat up, glared at Janis, and pointed a finger for emphasis. "I'm only going to say this to you one time. I did not kill my ex. And furthermore, I did not do anything to Shelly. I was sure the universe would take care of them both in its own way."

"Well, it seems the universe has taken care of your ex!" Janis hopped up from the bed and started pacing the cell. "So then, if you didn't do it, who did?"

"That's a good question."

"C'mon, who do you think? You must have some idea."

"I really don't know. It could have been quite a few." Diana began to make a list in her head of all the people that Curt had hurt in the past. She thought about all the families that he broke apart—his, hers, theirs, and now Alden's.

"What about your ex-husband, what's his name?"

"You mean Dave? Abby's father?"

"Yeah, him. He would definitely have reason to do it, right? "That creep broke up his family and then ended up leaving you? Man, that is double whacked." Janis was clearly thinking through Dave's motives.

"How did he take it when you decided to stay with Curt?"

"Not well." Diana shook her head. "He was very angry and quite threatening. I thought at one point he might try to take Abby away from me."

"Oh man, I would have killed my husband if he even thought he could get close to that. What did you do?"

"I talked to a lawyer. They said not to leave the house, that would be considered abandonment. So, I had to stay there during the entire divorce process."

"Well, I guess that's one good thing about my man taking off." Janis paused for a moment. "It wouldn't be easy to be in the same house through that."

"No, it wasn't. And there was this one time," Diana shifted in her seat, "when he really did scare me."

"Please, do tell. This is getting juicy."

* * *

Diana didn't wake up when the door to the guest room slowly opened, nor did she wake up when Dave quietly stepped up to the bed and hovered, watching Diana sleep. He stood over the bed with his hands behind his back, his fingers gripped tightly together as if they might have a mind of their own and he had to fight hard to control them. The look on his face suggested he was calculating the consequences of his next steps.

Diana woke up with a start as Dave menacingly leaned over her. It took a second for her to realize the situation. This was not a nightmare; it was happening in real time. She jumped out of bed and yelled, "What are you doing?" Dave seemed to shake himself out of his nefarious trance, turned, and silently left the room.

Diana's heart was pounding. There was no lock on the door, she had no protection, and she would be no match for Dave if he tried to get physical. She thought quickly and grabbed the little wooden chair in her room and lodged it under the door handle. At least it was something. She couldn't go on living like this. She had told Dave they needed to divorce, but he refused to move out, and her lawyer told her in no uncertain terms that she should not abandon the home.

She picked up the new cell phone that Curt had bought her. He said he wanted her to be able to reach him whenever she needed. And this would be one of those times. It would be early in the morning for him, but this was an emergency. He picked up on the third ring.

"Curt, Curt…"

"Diana, what's wrong? Are you okay? What's happening?"

She attempted to explain through an outpouring of tears. "Dave, was standing over me while I was sleeping. He looked like he was going to strangle me."

"Where are you now?"

"I'm in the guest room. I barred the door. I don't know what to do."

"What can I do for you, Diana? Just say it."

"I don't know," she cried.

"It's going to be okay, sweetheart. Shhh. I am here for you."

Curt tried his best to calm her down, and his soothing voice in her ear made her feel protected. After she quieted, he simply said, "Do you want me to move to America, Diana?"

She hesitated briefly. "Yes, I do."

That's all he needed to hear. With those words, everything changed. She wanted him, and he was coming to America for good. There would be no stopping him.

17

Diana watched Janis as she seemed to be processing this new information. Janis was no dope, she had a lot of common sense, and Diana was beginning to appreciate her wisdom and perspective. Although she was stuck in a jail cell, going through the possibilities with Janis of who might have killed Curt seemed to help. There were so many people who could hate him, and although not an admirable thought, it was a validating one for Diana.

"That last bit was spooky, standing over your bed like that while you sleepin'." Janis shimmied as a shiver went down her spine.

"It was definitely scary, but I don't think Dave has it in him to actually hurt anyone physically. He's actually a good person with morals. He's just a tortured soul, and that rubs off on everyone around him."

"But didn't you say he said he would kill that creep?"

"That's true, but I'm pretty sure that was just in the heat of the moment. I think he's actually been happy lately, or as happy as he can be. He has a girlfriend now—stick thin, platinum blond. Just what he always wanted."

"But men get real angry when another man takes his woman. What about that bitch's husband? Wasn't he that creep's friend?"

Diana was enjoying how Janis referred to Shelly as "that bitch" and Curt as "that creep." She wasn't too sure about the nickname, Kung Fu, but she didn't really mind. She thought of herself as a fighter, a survivor even. And she would survive this.

"You mean Alden?"

"Yeah, what's his story?"

"I only know what he told me," explained Diana. "So, I really can't say for sure. Plus, I would hear things from the grapevine about what was going on."

"Well, let's hear it."

* * *

Alden and Shelly were standing in the gourmet kitchen on opposite sides of the long island that sat eight. The counter was a natural golden limestone and cold to the touch, like their marriage had been for some time.

Alden pulled out a small envelope from his pocket. "Where did this letter come from, Shelly?" Alden unfolded a typed eight and a half by eleven-inch sheet of paper. He was watching her intently as she took a healthy gulp of her Cakebread Chardonnay.

"What letter are you talking about, baby?" Shelly cooed as she came around the counter to embrace him.

Alden gently broke their embrace and thrust the letter into her hands and waited. He would get her to talk. He was smarter than most and was good at stirring the pot then just waiting to watch where the chips would fall.

As Shelly read each sentence, her eyes widened, and Alden could see them darting back and forth across the page.

She tossed the letter on the counter. "How ridiculous. Diana must have sent it, baby. She is really crazy, isn't she?" Shelly gave him a peck on the cheek, as she continued to chatter in his ear. "We all knew she had a problem with drinking, but this is nuts. Poor Curt. No wonder he left her."

"So, it's not true?"

"Of course not, silly." She threw her arms around his neck, "You're the only one for me, baby."

Alden looked at her and shrugged. Diana may be a bit whacky, but she always seemed so happy and smart as a whip. And as far as he knew, she was still on the wagon, which was more than he could say for his wine-guzzling, pill-popping wife. "You're right, sweetie. I just don't understand. Why would she do this?"

"Who knows, but I think you should take Curt out with you and the boys tonight. He must be so lonely. Plus, I'm going out with Debra, so I won't be around."

"Yeah, you're right. I'll give him a call now." He figured if there was any truth to it, it's better to keep your enemies close.

Alden pulled out his cell phone, which was always handy in his pocket. He had it out more than not, which was one of Shelly's biggest public complaints. "Even when he's around, he's not really there for me." Shelly's back was to him as she busied herself at the sink.

"Yeah, come by the house around seven. I'll drive, we can take the Porsche. We're going to meet up with the other guys at The Pub." Alden paused. "Great, glad you can make it. See you then."

"He's coming." Alden laid his phone down next to hers and moved to give her a hug.

"You know I love you, right, my love?" He moved to kiss her, and she turned ever so slightly so his lips connected to her cheek.

"Yes, of course, sweetie." She made a big fuss over him, and then flashed her expensive white teeth at him. "I'm headed upstairs to get ready for tonight." She moved around him to position herself on the other side of the island, out of reach.

"Okay, my love." Alden picked up his phone and started scrolling through his messages.

Shelly moved quickly up the steps to the master suite, slamming the door tight behind her. She threw off her workout clothes, and made her way to the shower to remove the day's sweat from a morning of tennis followed by leading a weight class at the local YMCA. Drying herself off, she glanced in the mirror and cupped her breasts to check their buoyancy.

She chose a black, low-cut wrap dress with tall stiletto boots that could not fully compensate for her lack of height. While she was slipping on her dress, Alden came bouncing into the bedroom, glancing down at his phone.

"What are you thinking about, my love? You look really happy."

"Oh, I'm just excited about going out tonight."

"You look really nice. And smell good, too." He came over to hug her from behind as she was picking up the Chardonnay for another swig. She cringed and held her glass away from her body so none would spill.

"Don't mess up my hair, Alden." She gently shrugged him off. "I'm going down for another glass of wine. Do you want anything?"

He followed her down to the kitchen. "Sorry, sweetie, this must be really hard for you. Diana was such a good friend." He plopped on a barstool and started spinning side by side against the counter as he watched Shelly move around the kitchen. He decided to change the subject. "It's been a while since you've seen Debra. Is she alright?" Alden feigned concern. Out of all of Shelly's friends, Debra was his least favorite—recently divorced and always flirting with everyone.

"Oh yes, we're still friends. She's just been a little depressed since the divorce. I'll probably have to keep her out of someone's bed tonight. You know what a slut she is." Shelly had a look of disgust on her face.

He chuckled, but had nothing to say. The moment of silence was interrupted when the doorbell rang. "That's Curt. I'm out of here." He got up from his perch.

"I'll get it," she quickly said. "Why don't you get the car out of the garage and pull it around? I'll have Curt meet you outside. You don't want to be late, my love."

She waited until she heard the door to the garage close and opened the front door to Curt, who was standing there with a big grin on his face.

He looked around her to check the hall. "Hello, my love."

She grabbed him and pulled him into the foyer. She pulled his head down to hers and kissed him while she worked her other hand down to his crotch. It didn't take a lot of time to get a reaction. He grabbed her wrist hard and said, "No."

"But I want you, baby."

"Well, you can't have me. Just stand there and be still. Don't move."

She pretended to obey. He quickly turned her around and took her breasts into his hands while he squatted to work his hard penis under her skirt and into the crevice of her buttocks. "How does that feel? That feels good, doesn't it?" he prompted.

"Take it out," she commanded.

Just then the horn of the Porsche blared from the driveway. Alden was revving the engine, showing off the power of his cherished toy.

"Later," Curt said and headed for the front door.

Shelly turned around and slapped him in his face. "How dare you?"

His hand came up to his face to feel the heat from the slap. He broke into a smile and walked out the door, laughing. He got into the car, and Alden peeled out of the driveway before he was fully in his seat.

"What an ass." Shelly headed back into the house to straighten her hair and grab the keys to the Land Rover. A wicked smile crossed her lips as she headed back to the kitchen. She picked up the letter from the counter and headed for the lavish home office. She made a quick copy, and then placed the original letter back in its spot.

* * *

Diana had waited patiently for months after Shelly had accused her of sending that letter, and then it finally happened; she received a cryptic message on LinkedIn from Alden.

Subject line: *You were right. I'm sorry. If you feel up to it, can we talk?*

Her heart began to pound, and she broke out in a cold sweat. She noticed her armpits smelled something like spring onions, which she thought was really odd since she didn't even need to use deodorant ordinarily. What strange hormones must be running through her system from the foreign emotions triggered by this contact?

She agreed that she would talk to him, but only if it was in person. Diana wanted to stare into his eyes and see into his heart. All these months, she suspected that he had been involved, spending time with her soon-to-be ex, boys' night out, and such. She thought maybe they were all having sex. But no, he was just completely oblivious. He had no idea. She found out through the grapevine that he had actually invited Curt to Thanksgiving with his family because Shelly thought he shouldn't be alone. *What a guy!*

They agreed to meet at the library. Diana wanted to meet in a public place because she really didn't know what she was in for. She reserved a conference room so they could have privacy. They sat across from each other at a roundtable reserved for business meetings. As he told her his story, she could feel herself getting sucked back into the dark pit of betrayal, double betrayal. She felt sorry for him, and part of her wanted to know the details. After staring at him in silence for what seemed a very long time, she just got up and gave him a hug. She had listened and wanted to help him, but it sounded as if he was just going to roll over. Not fight. He said he was concerned about his safety. She wasn't sure if he was afraid of Shelly, or Curt, or both. He mentioned he had a lot of life insurance and that he had changed beneficiaries "just in case." In the end, he knew he would have to give her half of his millions. It was over. Shelly was in love with Curt, and she told him he had abandoned her and she deserved to be happy. She played the guilt card with him and took no responsibility for her behavior. *Typical sociopath.*

Diana broke her silence and asked the first question that was burning in her mind. "Alden, why didn't you contact me?"

He shrugged and tried to explain. "Shelly told me she tried to call you and you wouldn't answer her calls. She said she felt sorry for Curt because you were crazy."

"And you believed her."

"Yes, I did." He looked down at his feet and then up again. "She is my wife, why wouldn't I? And then when I got that letter..." He shook his head and rolled his eyes. He looked as if he might be on the verge of tears. "She said that was proof that you were crazy, that you were the one who sent it."

"Oh, so you did get a letter? I swear to you, Alden, I did not send it. I didn't even think it really existed. I thought Curt was trying to start trouble in mediation, and then I got the call from Shelly."

"What call?" he picked up his head in surprise.

"She accused me of sending the letter and denied everything. It was ridiculous."

"I'm sorry," he repeated again.

"Do you have a copy of the letter with you?" Diana was very curious and wanted a chance to try and figure out who sent it.

"Yes, actually, I happen to have it right here." He pulled a piece of paper out of his front-shirt pocket, and it looked as if it had been folded and unfolded many times to be reviewed again and again.

"Here you go, Diana." He nodded. "You should find it very interesting."

Diana's eyebrows raised as she read through the letter.

Alden,

I write to you with a heavy heart. You may be already aware that Curt and Diana are now breaking up and that the cause of this is Shelly.

This is not the first time Shelly has cheated on you. In fact, across many of your friends, she has a nickname to reflect her behavior with married men, showing no respect for you or the other partners.

Shelly and Curt have been having a long-term affair behind your back. Everyone has noticed the chemistry between the two of them at many of your parties, and Diana was clearly aware something was happening.

How did they get caught? Diana returns with her daughter to find Curt with empty bottles of champagne in the unmade bedroom (still warm from Shelly). Curt eventually admits that he has been sleeping with your wife.

Curt and Diana are now splitting up, and it is all down to your sleazy wife, who yet again satisfies herself with married men.

It is important that you are aware. Suggest you call Diana and ask her outright.

Diana had been trying to figure out for months if there really was a letter, and if so, who sent it. She had her suspicions that Shelly or Curt had done this to move things along. But she had heard from the grapevine that Shelly had messed around with Tim, Alden's friend and the husband of Shelly's friend, Ophelia. That means she had done this before, and there were other women who would want to see her go down.

"Oh my God, Alden, I cannot believe this. I swear to you again, I did not write this. And you received this at work?" Alden nodded slowly. "So, it has to be someone who knows your work address. And someone who doesn't know the story well—Curt never confessed to me." She thought a bit more. "I'm looking at this language, Alden, and I'd bet you it's a woman."

"Why do you say that?" He sat up in his seat expectantly.

"Well first, 'with a heavy heart,' no guy is going to say that. Also, there's a turn of phrase that is British, '...it is all down to.' So, maybe it's someone with an English accent."

"I always said you were smart, Diana. You're good at this." He tried to smile at her, but it was strained.

"Could it be Ophelia, Alden?"

Alden glared at Diana with a quizzical look. "Why would it be Ophelia?"

The poor guy, he had no idea how his wife had carried on. He really was a cuckold. Again, Diana felt sorry for him. She tried to explain as gently as possible, but he just couldn't grasp the concept that his wife would fool around with one of his best friends. Diana gently relayed what she had been told by people in their circle of friends.

"Alden, Shelly was caught kissing Tim at a party."

"Oh, I didn't know that." His head turned away to a distant point beyond the walls.

"Yes, and on another occasion, she was caught playing footsies with him under the table." She paused to let that set in. "And didn't she arrange a family vacation to follow Tim and Ophelia over to China right after they relocated?"

"Oh, yeah. I forgot about that. That was weird. She was so insistent, almost panicked, about going there."

"And wasn't there some letter that Tim received from Shelly that he wouldn't show Ophelia? That's what I heard."

"I don't know about that one," said Alden. He stared into space.

Diana was on a roll; she was going to try and confirm as much about Shelly as she could. It was her attempt to understand what had happened. Still trying to find some rationalization when there was none.

"And didn't Shelly steal you away from one of her friends when you met her in college?" Diana remembered how Shelly had gleefully told Elizabeth and her all about it, as part of her story of how she and Alden first met.

"That's right. I forgot about that, too. I feel like such an idiot." He shifted uncomfortably in his seat and ran his hand across his forehead and through his hair.

Diana could tell that Alden was a broken man not up for the fight. "Look Alden, I'm so sorry this has happened to you. I want to help you as much as I can. I think you should talk to my PI."

"You have a PI? Wow, Diana."

"Oh, yes. I hired him right after I discovered someone had been in my bed. Curt was pretending there was no one else, and I had to find out. So, I did."

His mouth twisted in disgust as if he might be sick. Then his eyes brightened. "So you have evidence? With photos?"

"Yes, I do, but Curt doesn't know it."

Alden sat up straighter with a look of vengeance crossing his face. "Well, that could be very useful to me."

"Would you like to meet my PI now?" Diana paused for the dramatic effect. "He's close by; he came just in case I needed him. We weren't sure what your state of mind would be."

"Yes, I would like that very much." Alden's mood had shifted, and there was a glimmer of the cut-to-the-chase persona that had made him such a success in his career.

Diana picked up her cell phone. "Hi, Robert." Pause. "Yup, I'm fine. So, can you come to the library?" Pause. "We'll be in the first conference room on the right. Thanks. See you soon."

"So, he's coming?" Alden said excitedly.

"Yeah, he should be here in a few minutes." Diana would make the connection and then walk away.

* * *

It was just a few weeks later when Diana was making her way through Grand Central Station, scurrying to the platform in her usual fashion, head down on a mission to get home. Alden nearly bumped into her doing the same. They were both headed out of the city on the same train, and after a few pleasantries, decided to ride together. Alden seemed to be doing a bit better, and he had plenty to tell Diana once they settled in.

"So, Diana, you are not going to believe this." Alden shifted in his seat like a two-year-old being bribed with candy to behave. "I had to go to Manila for business, and guess who I bumped into?" There was no opportunity to either guess or respond, he launched directly into his story.

* * * * *

Alden walked in through the front door of the Manila Hotel and down the length of the red carpet to find the bar. He was exhausted. Between the long flight, which he would normally enjoy as a respite to what had been happening at home, he anxiously approached the bar in sore need of a drink. He sat at the bar, contemplating what he left at home. *How could she do this? After 24 years of marriage, two kids, giving her everything she asked for... Why would she do this? What does she see in him? How could she love him more? It just doesn't make sense.* He lifted his head from his drink and could not believe his eyes. Waltzing into the bar was Tim Truell, his best friend, the husband of Ophelia, and the man that Diana suggested Shelly had been involved with before Curt. Alden stood up and waved Tim over.

Tim's face lit up when he noticed and hurried over with his larger-than-life greeting, always the salesman. "Hey there, mate. What are you doing here? In for the Money Summit?" They exchanged pleasantries, then Tim nonchalantly asked, "So, how's Shelly?"

Alden could not hold it together and blurted much louder than planned, "She's leaving me for Anderson, Tim." Alden looked into his friend's eyes in search of the truth.

Tim pulled back as if he just dodged a bullet, but Alden was too deep in misery to notice. "Oh man, I'm so sorry, mate." He patted him on the back. "What happened?"

Alden picked up his drink and turned to Tim with tears in his eyes. "She says she deserves to be happy. That she's in love with him. We tried for a month to work it out in therapy, but she was talking to him the whole time."

"Really? How do you know that?" asked Tim.

Alden took a sip of his martini to keep the tears at bay. "I found another phone."

"Oh man, I'm so sorry," repeated Tim.

Alden could not stop thinking about what Diana had said. He looked deep into Tim's eyes, searching for a clue. He took a deep breath and said, "Did you sleep with my wife?" This almost sounded like a Dr. Seuss line (Do you like my hat?), the way Alden pushed the question out.

Tim sputtered his Maker's Mark all over the bar. He slowly turned to Alden, and his eyes began to dart around. "Alden, I can't believe you would think that. I'm your friend. I wouldn't do that to you."

"Anderson was supposedly my friend, Tim. I had him over for Thanksgiving dinner with my family, for Christ's sake!" Alden was getting progressively agitated. "He sat there and ate the meal my wife had prepared for us..." he gulped, "...to give thanks for everything we had." He swallowed hard and wiped his wet eyes. "Just wait, he'll get his someday."

Tim bowed his head to the floor while he formulated his response. "Listen, Alden, I'm not even attracted to Shelly. I don't know what Shelly is doing with Anderson, but it was never me."

They finished their drinks in near silence. The conversation turned to the more mundane business discussions, a more comfortable place for both of them to land. Tim finished his drink as quickly as he could, feigned the effects of jet lag, and gave Alden a shake of the hand and a slap on the back with his good-bye. "If you need anything at all, mate, you let me know." Anyone reading his face as he turned away would see the slow release of the breath he had been holding.

* * *

Alden asked Diana to come over to help him figure out what questions should be asked during the deposition. He said he was having a party with a few close friends and was calling it, "Deposition Jeopardy." In the end, it was just Diana and his new girlfriend, Tracy, whom he met online. It was only a few months since he had separated from Shelly, and he was hot and heavy with this woman. She had practically moved into his new apartment. For Diana, it was strange to watch, to see someone able to transfer love so quickly. Or maybe she was the one who was wacky. *How come I'm not in a new relationship?*

It didn't matter. She was here to help in any way possible, so those two horrible people wouldn't get what they wanted. She was happy to know that Curt would be deposed along with Shelly, and that the lawyer was asking for all his financial records—that should keep him busy. The idea of him sweating it out was sweet. Before she headed over to the party, she made up a list of questions that should be asked and a calendar of events that should help the lawyer with the timing. She wasn't sure if the PI report was going to be used, but she had to have faith in Alden's lawyer to have it handy and take it out at the right time.

"Do you know who she is going to question first?" Diana had joined them at the glass dining room table that Tracy had picked out for Alden's new apartment. This felt like a business meeting, and Diana was the facilitator.

"Probably her, I would imagine." Alden was tapping away on his Mac, barely looking up, as he seemed to be in the role of scribe.

"Oh, I would question him first," Diana said emphatically.

"Really? Why?" Alden had a way of asking questions in a sharp staccato that bee-lined straight to the heart of things. That was probably why he was successful in his investments.

"Shelly is probably a much better liar than he is." Diana was sure of this; she could usually tell when Curt was lying, but Shelly was much more gifted. Even though she came across as not being very bright, she was extremely cunning, like a rat hunting its way through the restaurant pipes in search of the finest leftovers.

"When faced with authority, he is quite a coward and will cave," Diana added. "I would ask each of them who started the affair and when. This way they might finger each other and blame the other party." Anything that would create discord between the two of them seemed to be a good strategy to Diana. Although she wouldn't admit it to herself, she didn't want them to be happy.

Alden was more focused on the financials of the matter, specifically the amount of money Shelly had spent during the affair to entertain Curt. That seemed to really get under his skin. He started listing all she had been doing with him under the guise of time spent with girlfriends: concerts, sporting events, weekends away. He even paid for a certification course that the two of them had taken together at the local community college to become CNAs, Certified Nurses Aids. When Diana heard this, all she could think of was Shelly as Nurse Ratched in *One Flew over the Cuckoo's Nest*. She had the same nasty, under-handed, holier-than-thou manner. Diana shivered with the thought of her taking care of the vulnerable elderly. But for Curt to join in; that was even more bizarre to Diana.

"Why would they do that?"

"Who knows. All I know is I paid for it, books and all. It's probably so Shelly can get more access to those pills she takes. Stealing from little old ladies, that would be her style."

"She takes pills?" Diana knew Shelly took a sleeping pill every night because she had told her once, "Alden snores too much." *Ha, ha, ha, she's in for a real treat with Curt.*

"Oh, yeah. Look at this." He thrust his phone into her hands to show her a photograph of about five or six bottles of prescription medication.

"What's all this for?"

"Sleep. Depression. Pain. You name it."

Tracy lifted her head up from her iPhone. "Oh yeah, she's a junkie… and an alcoholic," she said, and then returned back to her phone. "I know the type," she added.

"Hey, Diana, you want to see something funny?" Alden turned his computer towards her to show her footage from the cameras he had set up in their matrimonial home. "You should see this, Diana. They fucked like five times in one night—in our master bedroom, of course." He snorted the last words out through his nose like it was a disgusting piece of dirt that had been lodged up there and was making its way into his brain.

"Alden, I really don't want to see that, thank you." Diana averted her eyes so she would not catch a glimpse. Too late, she saw a frame of Shelly sitting on Curt's lap.

"Aw, come on, it's fun." He forced a laugh out. Diana couldn't think of anything less fun then to see the man she thought she would love all her life fucking one of her so-called close friends. That was not an image she wanted imprinted on her brain; her imagination was bad enough.

"This one time, they were hanging out in the living room, and he was playing with the dogs. As soon as she left, he pushed the dogs away. What a phony."

That did not surprise Diana at all. Curt didn't really like dogs in general, and hated dogs that shed their hair everywhere. Shelly's dogs shed like crazy. For some reason, this was entertaining for Diana. Caught on tape, he couldn't escape his true self.

"How about when she found the cameras? That's a really funny scene," Tracy said.

"Oh yeah, Diana, you have to see this." Alden turned the computer towards her, and it was already playing. Diana's curiosity got the better of her as she watched Shelly frantically looking around the master bedroom for a camera similar to the one they had found in the kitchen and family room. Alden must have planted them before he left.

Diana watched as Shelly moved around the large room quickly, phone to ear, bending over to look under the king-sized bed, scraping the hardwood floor in her high-heeled boots. She looked up and her eyes widened wild in anger.

"Oh my gosh, Curt. I think I found it."

"You're kidding." His surprised tone transmitted from the phone speaker to be picked up by the camera audio.

"No, I'm not kidding," she snapped. "It's behind the speaker." Her scary face loomed large as she tried to reach the camera from its hiding place.

According to Alden, the one in the master bedroom had footage of them "fucking countless times." According to Alden, Curt had popped quite a few Viagra that weekend.

"What are you going to do, Shelly?" Curt's voice had an edge to it; he was a bit worried about what Alden might do to him once he actually saw Curt giving it to his wife.

"I'm going to call my lawyer, that's what I'm going to do. He can't get away with this!"

"But won't that just run up the bill?" Curt was thinking about the money; the more they spent on lawyers, the less Shelly would get in the end, which meant the less she had to spend on him.

"What do I care, Curt? Alden is paying for it, the jerk." She crossed the master bedroom with a speed that would seem unusual for such short legs in high heels.

"You're right, sweetheart, just calm down."

"Don't tell me to calm down!" she shouted into the phone. That was one of her many hot buttons that she had developed over the years; anything that even hinted at someone telling her what to do was the one that really sent her into a rage. She grabbed a wooden hanger from the closet to further her reach.

"I'm sorry, sweetheart. Are you alright? What can I do for you?"

"Later," she said, and hung up the phone.

The screen went black, followed by a dark silence as if to memorialize the death of the camera. "What time is it?" Diana looked over at the clock on the kitchen wall. "Oh, I've got to get going."

"What for?" said Alden. "You haven't even had any wine."

That again? Why does everyone want me to drink? "I have to teach in the morning. And there's Nutmeg—she'll be crossing her legs." Diana used her old joke to lighten up the mood as she picked up her bag and stood up from the table for a quick exit.

She gave Alden a gentle embrace. "I hope this was helpful to you, Alden."

"Yeah, thanks for showing up, Diana. I hope you're okay."

"I'm fine. Take care, Alden. See you later, Tracy." Tracy lifted her head once more.

"Yeah, bye." She didn't miss a beat and continued typing with her thumbs.

Well, she is much younger, Diana thought, *of a different generation.* Diana still used her right index finger.

Diana was feeling very unsatisfied on the drive home. Looking up at the stars through the moonroof, she took a moment to reflect at the stop sign. She had been looking forward to this evening, thinking somehow it would help her get closure, but all it managed to do was upset her more. The image of them to add to those from the PI report tore at her heart, a heart trying so desperately to heal. She vowed to be done with Alden; she had helped him as much as she could, but this wasn't doing her any good. Alden was out for revenge, it was clear to her, and it was toxic. Seeking justice in this way was not a good use of her time or energy.

* * *

Diana was proud of herself for letting go; she did not care what happened to Curt and Shelly. She was really starting to believe that what happened to them had nothing to do with her or her happiness. But Alden was not giving up that easily. He and Shelly were divorced now, and she had gotten half of everything. It really bothered him that Shelly hadn't worked a day in her life, and he had to send her money every month in addition to the millions she received per their agreement. On top of that, she wouldn't even be taking care of the kids because they preferred to be with him.

Alden had heard that Curt had proposed to Shelly, and despite his moving on with his own engagement to a younger, more attractive woman, he was not happy about it. Alden called Diana to see if she might be able to provide some relief from his sorrow, as a parallel victim in the ordeal.

"Hi, Diana. It's Alden."

Diana had almost ignored the call but thought he might have some information that could somehow help on her long healing journey. "Hi Alden, what's up?"

"Well, I was wondering how you've been doing and all."

Wow, now he's concerned with my welfare. "I'm doing well, thanks. I finally sold the house, which is good. It's been rough being stuck here."

"Oh, that's good. Will you stay in the area, then?"

"No, actually. I just received an offer for a full-time teaching position. She didn't want to tell him where; she did not want to be found by any of them. "I'll be moving at the end of the summer."

"That's great, Di. Congratulations!"

"Thanks. I'm pretty excited about it."

"Will you be closer to Abby then, too?"

"Yup, it's all good." She abruptly stopped, not wanting to provide any more information.

"Well, listen, the reason I called, it's about Curt and Shelly."

"Okay." The last thing she needed was more details about those two. *Can't these people just let me move on with my life?*

There was no stopping Alden, as he was fixated on his end goal and wanted to share in his pain. "Apparently, they're engaged and I heard they might be living together."

"Okay." That didn't surprise Diana at all. She predicted Curt would want to seal the deal as quickly as possible with all that money on the table.

"I talked to the lawyer, and she said if I can get the evidence that they are cohabitating, then I might have a case to renegotiate the agreement. Maybe I wouldn't have to pay alimony anymore."

"Okay." *Would that be justice?* "So, what do you need from me, Alden?"

"Well, I was wondering if your PI friend could help me."

She took a deep breath to think. "I really don't know about that."

"Well, could you ask him if he can do something to help me?"

His whiny voice was like nails to the chalkboard. "Honestly, Alden, I really don't want to get involved. Don't you have his contact information?"

"I lost it." He shuffled the papers on his desk searching for the missing clue.

"Okay, I'll ask him if he can help you. But then I will have him call you directly if he's able. Will that work?"

"Thanks, Diana. I appreciate it, I really do."

"No problem." She thought, *please let this be over.*

"Take care of yourself, Di." His voice wavered.

"Bye, Alden."

"Bye."

Diana hung up, hoping that would be the last time she would have to speak to Alden. She had worked so hard to rid herself of this drama, to dissect this cancer from her body. She did not want to go into remission and get caught up in this tangled, hateful web again.

"Hey, Robert."

"How ya' doing, kiddo?"

"I'm good. Just getting ready for the move and all." She exhaled as she breathed the words out in relief.

"Yes, I know that's coming. Let me know what I can do. My back isn't great, but I wanted to help you."

"Robert, you have helped me so much already. I don't know what I would have done without you." She giggled. "You are officially off the hook."

"Nope. I'll always be on the hook for you, kid."

"Awe, Robert, thank you so much. That means a lot to me." She paused to let the feeling of care settle in. "But no worries, I think I hired a couple of hunky movers to help." She delivered the line in a weak attempt at a joke to hide the stress she was feeling. "So, listen, I got a call from Alden. He needs to prove that Curt is living with Shelly."

"Hmm. Interesting. They didn't wait too long, did they?" He coughed as if to rid himself of a bitter bug trapped in his throat. "Where are they, do you know?"

"Alden told me that they are living on some posh golf course in Arizona."

"Yeah, I have a guy. Ex-FBI. He can take care of it."

"Can you call him? I really don't want to get involved."

"I don't blame you, kid. Don't worry, I'll take care of it."

"Thanks, Robert. You truly are the best."

Diana was sincere, and he knew it. "Yeah, yeah, take it easy, kid."

18

There were moments that Diana would suffer the thought that everyone had moved on but her—Curt was living with Shelly, Alden was engaged to his latest arm candy, but she remained alone. When she thought about this more positively, she realized she was taking the time to heal, to reflect on her life, and to take better care of herself in hopes of a better future. She was going to translate her mistake into lessons and move forward on her own.

As if Janis was reading her mind, she broke the reverie. "What about you? Did you ever get with anyone after your ex cheated on you?"

Diana hesitated. Janis was getting a little too personal, and she wasn't sure she wanted to share all her secrets. *Oh, what the hell? Considering the position I'm in right now, it really doesn't matter.*

"Not exactly." Diana's heart started racing as she thought about Dillon.

"You're getting all red in the face, Kung Fu. What's that about?"

"Well, there was someone else who did a good job of helping me recover from Curt."

Janis sat bolt upright with a look of discovery. "Maybe he did it!"

"No, uh-uh. That was a long time ago."

"What happened to him?"

"I had to break it off with him. He was way too young."

"Ooh. Robbing the cradle. I want to hear about this."

* * *

Diana strolled around the house to make sure things were in order before the realtor showed up. She hadn't been spending much time there; it just seemed unfair that she was left with the burden of selling the house when she never wanted it in the first place. It was a lot to take care of, but she was doing it, and without any help from Curt. After all the years and all the projects to build a beautiful home together, there was something empowering about that. She even changed out a faulty light switch by herself. Yes, it turned off when you flipped it up instead of down, but she chose not to fix the error that stumped her every time. It made her laugh and demonstrated to her the previously misunderstood notion of being perfectly imperfect.

It was a crisp fall day, and she looked up at the clear blue sky with a smile, always appreciating the gifts from nature. And then she saw it, a big gaping hole at the corner of the roof line at the highest point of the house. She wasn't going to be able to fix that herself. Just what she needed, another project to deal with in this godforsaken money pit. She wondered whether or not animals were getting into the attic. *Calm down*, she thought, *just call the handyman*. He was a nice old guy, and he would know what to do. CeCe had introduced her to him, and he had been helpful with the things that had started failing once Curt had left.

He told her there was no way he was getting up on a ladder to fix that, but he knew a very nice young man named Dillon who had just started his own carpentry business and was looking for work. She called Dillon right away. In a warm, friendly voice, he agreed to come the next day.

When Dillon stepped out of his bright red truck, he greeted her politely with an easy-going smile and bright green eyes. "Diana? I'm Dillon. So, I hear you have a repair for me?"

Diana laughed to herself at her reaction. *Yeah, my heart, can you help me with that? What a babe! Calm down, Diana. There is no way this guy is available, and uh, by the way, he's a bit young, isn't he?*

They arranged a time for him to come back with his brother to complete the job. Diana made sure she would be there (to check on the work, of course). In the end, he did a nice job, patiently answering Diana's questions about the materials and any possible animal encroachment into the attic. He didn't charge her much, and she had the added benefit of the eye candy. His parting words stuck with her as he handed her his card, "Call me anytime, and I'll be here to help you with whatever you need."

* * *

Looking for an excuse to see him again, Diana had called Dillon to claim some of Curt's tools he had left behind that she thought he might like; he was a carpenter, after all, and he had been so nice when he repaired her roofline. One trip had turned into several, as he volunteered to help her get the house ready for selling. In the process, she found out that he had separated from his wife because he had found her cheating on him. They had something in common to commiserate over, and the more they talked, the closer they became. When Diana told him her story, she couldn't help but delight in his reaction.

"Well, that guy is clearly an idiot. Why would he ever want to leave someone like you? He probably never deserved you in the first place."

Diana giggled and blushed. "Keep it coming."

Dillon's last visit ended on a high note when he pulled her to him for an incredible kiss that sent tingles straight down to her toes. Now, the relationship would develop into something exhilarating and healing for Diana.

* * *

Dillon held out his hand to pull her up into his truck. Even that small gesture was sexy; she really liked this guy. She was exhausted from the move but wanted to see him, and she definitely wanted to kiss him again.

"So, how did it go?" Dillon was asking about the move. He couldn't help her because he was too busy at work, but he had been receiving updates via texts and was keeping her in good spirits with his easy-going banter.

Moving out of a four-bedroom house loaded with a half a lifetime of stuff was quite the task, emotionally and physically. It had been a major lesson in letting go, probably the toughest one she had to face. Letting go of what she had hoped her life would be, living in her dream house in a timeless love that she could count on forever. With all her moves in life, this was the one she did not expect but probably needed the most. She marveled at how much stuff she had accumulated, carried around with her, and how little she would take into the next phase of her life.

"Oh, it went pretty good." She shrugged. "It was supposed to take the movers a few hours, but it took seven… in the pouring rain, of course." She giggled at that. "The movers were a day late—yesterday it was beautiful, and today it poured like crazy." She didn't really care; she was happy to finally be out of that beautiful jail. The house that was supposed to make Curt so happy. The house that those two creeps had fucked in. How many times, she would never know. Nor did it matter.

"But I had to get a bigger storage unit because the stuff that was left from the sale just wouldn't fit. I'm just so glad it's all done." She hesitated and smiled as she stared into his amazing eyes. "Time to celebrate."

"What would you like to do?" He smiled back. "I'm easy, I just want to loaf around with you." He picked up her hand and kissed it to express his tender desire to be with her.

"It's such a nice day, let's go to the beach." She was being a bit selfish because she knew he wasn't a big fan of sand, but it was all she could think of at the moment. And for her, it was always a place of respite.

They took a ride down to the local beach and sat talking. She laid her head in his lap and looked up at him as they chatted. He caressed her face, carefully removing a piece of hair blowing in her eyes from the cool breeze playing off the water so he could look into them without interruption. She thought of the countless times that she had hoped these scenes would occur with her husband, but they were fleeting. Here was a man who had been dropped into her lap, and she was now in his. Even if this could not last, and she knew deep down it could not, it was a memory that would be everlasting. After a few minutes, he pulled her to him and kissed her.

Releasing himself from their embrace, he gave her a sideways glance. "You know, I am kinda mad at you." He stared into her eyes and tried to look tough, but it just didn't work with that baby face of his.

"Oh, really, why is that?" Her heart dropped. *What could she have possibly done?* She sat up to take a more serious posture and peered in the back seat. There was a blonde wig that had been tossed. As he started explaining, she was distracted by the thought, *maybe I don't know enough about this guy.*

"I think all your love of the water is rubbing off on me. I was driving by the coast on the way home the other day, and I was thinking, wow, that's really nice." He smiled as he teased her. "I blame you for that."

"Oh, sorry about that. Well, not sorry." She paused, then jokingly asked, "By the way, why do you have a blonde wig in your back seat? Is there something you need to tell me?"

He laughed heartily. "Oh, that's my daughter's. She was recently in a play."

"Well, that's a relief." She smiled and giggled shyly.

This is how it went between them. It was easy-going, it was light-hearted, it was relaxed. Nothing was forced. There was something more than just the physical compatibility; they were somehow spiritually aligned. She didn't want to get too carried away, but it was his nature that she was responding positively to. It felt natural to be with him; it was refreshing.

Diana hesitated for only a moment. "I need to stop by my friend's house around the corner. They are away, and I said I would bring their garbage cans in for them. They also said I was welcome to stay if I needed a place." She waited for his reaction.

"Sure, I can drive you over there. Let's go."

* * *

He traced his finger along her collarbone and asked if she liked to be kissed on her neck. "Well, yes, I do," she said invitingly. She was nervous. He kissed her tenderly and moved down her neck to nuzzle in the crevice. Dillon was taking his time, and Diana moaned as he worked his hands under her shirt to touch the arch of her back. It had been so long since she had been touched, and never in this way. It was a beautiful mix of tenderness, sweet and sexy at the same time. After being with the same man for so long, this was foreign to her, but she began to relax into it. She had been unsure that she could even be with another man, let alone feel these sensations that had been buried in the last years of marriage.

He kissed her passionately and said, "I'm sorry, my hands might wander."

Diana smiled and thought, *I'm okay with that.* She didn't care if he was 17 years her junior. He was delectable. Kind, smart, talented, spiritual, she was attracted to him on many levels. But he was not free. He had been separated for several years but not yet divorced. Diana had to think seriously about whether or not she should get involved. She did not want to even be remotely involved in a breakup. For now, it was a gift to know that desire had not left her body; she would enjoy the present moment. *Does this officially make me a cougar?*

"I'm sorry, I'm a bit nervous," Diana confessed.

"I know," he said. "I can feel that. It's okay. I'm nervous, too."

He was tender and sensual, not rushed the way Curt had always been. This was exactly what she needed. Dillon held her close, kissing her neck, nuzzling her. In broad daylight, Diana was self-conscious of how old her body must seem next to his. He didn't seem to mind—he only told her how soft she was all over as he touched her. He lifted her from the couch without effort and picked her up to bring her closer to the well-endowed proof that he was turned on. He made Diana feel young and alive, but she couldn't have sex with this man. She was simply not ready, and he was not going to do anything to push her into it.

After three hours of kissing, touching, and pressing against each other, it was time for Dillon to go. It would have been so easy for her to go all the way and prove that she could indeed be with another man. But she was worried about how she would feel afterwards. She reminded herself, *there's no rush, no panic... it will either be or not. Every decision has its time.*

* * *

She finally moved into what she referred to as her "new single's pad," which was less notably her friend's one-room efficiency over their garage that Diana furnished with various items that she donated from the house. She and Nutmeg would stay there for the summer before making the big move out of the area. When Dillon came over to check it out, Diana began chatting nervously about whatever came into her mind. Dillon sat on the barstool and intently listened. He winced as he pulled her stool closer to him.

"Are you okay? You seem like you might be in pain?"

"No, I'm fine. I've just been having a bit of back pain but don't you worry." He moved to kiss her.

"How about a massage. Would that help?"

"We could certainly give it a try."

Diana shyly laid the fluffy, white bath sheet down and grabbed the coconut oil she had handy. *This should work like massage oil*, she thought. *There is nothing like the smell of coconut.* It reminded Diana of the beach. Dillon removed his shirt and laid down. She began to move her hands up and down his strong back. Her fingers drew a line down his spine to trace its curvature.

"Oh, I think you may be out of alignment."

"Could be, but whatever you are doing feels great." Nutmeg started jumping around Dillon's head, thinking it was playtime. He took it with good humor. Diana thought this was a clue that he was kind. She suggested a hot shower as an alternative to the haphazard massage; he suggested she join him. He began removing the rest of his clothes and moved to the bathroom to get the hot water going.

Practical as always, Diana thought about how she had just showered and did her hair and make-up. Something she never liked to go through twice in a day. *Oh, what the hell? I won't get my hair wet.* He was too tempting and delicious to deny. She pulled her hair up in a tie, then slowly pulled the curtain back to step in. He gently caressed her under the spray of water, and as it cascaded down their faces, they kissed, deeply, passionately. No words were spoken between them. Diana briefly thought about the oversized showers for two she had designed in the houses she had owned with Curt. Her intention had been to do just this. The hot and steamy showers with Curt never really panned out and were a novelty rather than a habit and always short-lived.

Diana slowly sucked in her breath as he turned her to the wall to soap her back. His hands trailed up and down her sides, and as they slid between her legs, she released a small moan. She pressed both hands against the cold tiled wall and arched her back in response. He was taking his sweet, sweet time. He pulled her head back against his shoulder as he kissed her neck and cupped her breasts with his soapy hands. Diana could see the suds on his muscles moving under his wet skin as he lathered her up and down. She breathed in deeply as he dropped to his knees. He gently placed her leg over his shoulder and began darting his tongue in and out. Diana's eyes rolled back into her head; incredible and so much better than it had ever been with Curt. They stayed in the shower until they were satiated and waterlogged.

Diana was compelled to validate her sexuality and honor her womanhood. It was part of her awakening. She needed to know that she could love again and prove to herself that there was more than one man for her until the end of time. She wasn't drunk; she was sober and thoughtful about what she was doing. Somehow this gave her closure; she could make love to another man with intention. This was another turn in the wheel of healing, sending her forward to a destination of freedom where she would honor herself and her needs. For once, she was not putting anyone else first. This was about what she wanted. At first, she didn't know how she would feel. And then, as she thought it through, she realized that this would feed her ego, which had taken a severe blow. *But will it feed my soul?*

* * *

After the unforgettable shower scene, Dillon had been extra attentive and wanted to carve out a whole day to be together, "Maybe hiking in the woods." For some reason, the idea of that made Diana a little nervous. *What did I really know about this guy?* Diana was spending way too much emotional energy thinking about him, and she knew in her heart she had to break it off. It didn't feel right, so it wasn't right. He wasn't really available, and he was way too young and she knew it.

Dillon responded to her text right away with the usual pleasantries and adding, "…busy, as usual." She asked him if he would be available to meet her because selfishly she wanted to kiss him one more time before she brought the hammer down. But more importantly, she also wanted to see him face-to-face when she told him it was over. He couldn't see her, but he wanted to talk to her "desperately."

Diana had just gotten in the car to meet a friend for lunch, but she picked up the phone when he called and asked him to wait a second while she parked the car and moved to the garage for privacy.

"How are you?" Diana decided to start the conversation on a light note.

"Oh, busy as usual, but never too busy for you."

"How's your back? How did it go with the chiropractor?"

"It's still bad, but it gets better every time I go."

"What did he say the problem was?" Yada, yada… more talk about his back.

"Listen, Di, I have been missing you something terrible. I can't stop thinking about you, and I want to talk about next steps."

"Dillon, stop. I have to say something before you say any more." Diana absentmindedly grabbed the tennis ball that hung from the garage rafters to mark where to stop the car and started tossing it from side to side. Like a pendulum counting beats, her heart was pounding in rhythm. She took a deep breath and started to talk about the real reason for the call. "I can't see you anymore, Dillon."

"What? No, Diana. Don't say that. I think I'm falling in love with you."

"You can't be, Dillon. You barely know me. You really don't know anything about me."

"I know enough. You're smart, funny, kind… and sexy as hell."

That made her pause, catch and swing, catch and swing. "But, the age difference."

"I don't care. It doesn't matter to me."

"Well, it matters to me, Dillon."

"Why? Don't you know, I will always be there for you. When you get old, I'll be there. If someone hurts you, I'll be there. No one will mess with you, Diana. You're mine."

That last line and how it was delivered caused her to deliver her last line, "I am no one's." The phone went dead. Diana, shaking as she drove to her luncheon, could not help the tears from falling. Thank goodness the lunch was with a dear friend who always knew what to say. She left the lunch feeling better but still upset. Diana realized that she had gained something very important from the relationship, albeit short-lived, and she wanted to remember it fondly. She needed to send one more message to let him go with grace and dignity.

> *Dillon,*
> *I want you to know that I do not regret the time we spent together. Thank you for making me feel so wanted again. I wish you much happiness.*
> *Diana*

She did not expect to get a response back; that was not why she sent the message. It was for her. As soon as she hit send, she felt better. Now, she could move on in a more positive way. To her surprise, she received a message from him early the next morning:

> *I'm glad to hear that. I will never regret the time we spent together. I just regret that it couldn't be forever. It was like an arrow through my heart, Diana. I will keep a watchful eye out for you, and if you ever want me, I am yours.*

19

Diana closed her eyes and luxuriated in the aftermath of telling that part of her story. She had been carrying it around for a long time, and now it was out in the open as she inexplicably revealed her secrets to her cellmate.

"Man, Kung Fu, you broke up with that? Although that last bit sounded a little too possessive."

"I know, I'm crazy. But it was the right thing to do."

"You know what, you got too many shoulds in your life. Why you should so hard on yourself?" Janis laughed at her clever turn of phrase.

"It wasn't that so much, but it just didn't feel right. It's like what I tell my daughter, if it doesn't feel right, it's not."

"Yeah, that's what you call instinct. It's gotten me out of some jams before." Janis hung her head for a moment. "But lately, I think it's been a bit dull... not making the right decisions for myself."

"I hear you. My choices and me," Diana shook her head, "they're not always in sync." Diana chuckled to cover the truism in the statement. "But, you know, sometimes, when I don't know what to do, I think about what advice I would give my daughter, and then I try to follow it."

"That's good, 'cause we at our best and worst when it comes to our daughters."

"You got that right. So yeah, I had to go with my gut. And my gut was telling me that this was not going to be good for me in the long run."

"Why?"

"I don't know. There was no future in it. And as much as I'd like to say I can, I just can't have casual relations."

"No, but you can marry the wrong guy. Is that a better future?"

"Touche."

"So, you never saw him again?'

"No, I didn't. But you know, this is probably going to sound whacky. I always felt his presence somehow."

"Hmmm. Interesting. I'm not gonna ask exactly when."

"Haha, very funny. No, really, it was like he was never that far away. Like he was watching me."

"Ooh. Another creepy thing. So, you don't think this guy was getting back at you? He said he was in love with you. Maybe he was, like, defending your honor or somethin' with your ex?"

"No, no. I don't think so." Diana thought a moment longer. "You know, there was one strange thing." She hesitated to continue. "There was that wig in his car one time. He said it was his daughter's, that she was in a play."

"Wait, what?"

"He had a blonde wig in the back seat of his car."

"Well, isn't that interestin'? Is he a big man?"

"No, not especially."

"So, he could pass for a woman?"

Diana thought for a minute. *There was nothing womanly about him.* But one fact came to mind. If she was in here because someone pointed her out, wouldn't the killer be a woman? That would be logical. Of course, this assumed that the said witness was in their right mind and actually saw someone in that much detail. She was not ruling anyone out as of yet.

"Hey, Kung Fu, I'm thinking about that wig. Don't you think maybe it's a woman, since they think it's you?"

"I was thinking the same thing, and yeah, that is a strong possibility."

"How about Curt's ex-wife, the first one?"

"No, it wouldn't be her. She's probably feeling validated that Curt did to me what he apparently did to her. Plus, she's in the UK remarried to a 'bloke' who provided her a 'posh lifestyle.' Diana used her English accent for comic relief.

"What about Curt's kids? He has a daughter, right?"

"You mean Rose. I don't know about her. Last I knew, she was studying art nearby."

"So, she's in the area. That's interestin'. Would she have any reason to do it?"

"All I know is she must have been very upset when Curt decided not to go back to England. I think she was always hoping all those years that if she got rid of me then he would come home to be with her. Although she hid it well, and pretended to be so sweet, the disdain oozed out of her pores for Abby and I."

"Maybe she was mad enough to push him?" Janis thrust her two arms out to mimic the movement.

"I guess it's a possibility, and come to think of it..." Diana hesitated, as she did not want to accuse her stepdaughter even though they hadn't been in touch since the breakup.

"Tell me, Kung Fu," Janis prompted.

"Well, it's just that I could see how you might confuse the two of us. We're both blonde, both about the same height and same size. We used to trade each other's clothes and shoes."

"Very interestin'." Janis rubbed her chin. "But you don't talk to her, right?"

"No, not a word. All those years helping to raise them, and not a single word."

"That's tough, Kung Fu. So whatcha think then?"

"I don't know, like I said, she's obsessed with him."

"Well, if she's obsessed with him, then maybe she was angry with him. Angry that he left them to be with you, and then angry again that he didn't come home to her and chose that bitch instead."

Diana hesitated. Rose had always been so sneaky. *Could she possibly be that angry?*

"I really don't think so. Rose never held Curt responsible for leaving England. His children always blamed me."

"As if you held a gun to his head. So, you were the evil stepmother."

"Right, exactly. It didn't matter what I did. I tried so hard, but they were always focused on punishing me. That was really tough for me, especially since Curt never defended me. It upset Abby, too. They weren't very nice to her either."

"Speaking of which, is there any way your daughter…"

"Not a chance. She's an angel. She wouldn't hurt a fly. Honestly."

"Well, of course you're going to say that. I get it. My daughter can do no wrong." Janis bowed her head and smiled. "So, what other women would possibly have a reason?" They sat in silence for only a moment.

Janis popped her head up in revelation. "Oh, I know. How about that Ophelia chick? Could she have done it?"

"Not sure about her. She's a wild card. I heard she was in Hong Kong with her husband. It's so twisted. Alden and Shelly would spend a lot of time with them, just like they did with Curt and me. I guess that's how Shelly does her thing."

"So, you mean it's like a pattern?"

"Yup. I think the term is serial homewrecker. These women get off on taking other people's husbands, and then when they get bored or rejected, they go on to the next."

"Oh man, I know some women like that. I didn't know there was a name for it. Like a condition."

"Well, apparently that's not the only condition Shelly has." She thought about Shelly's self-destructive behaviors and how they had apparently caught up with her. From what she understood, Shelly was in a bad way.

"Kung Fu, it's gotta be Shelly."

"Nope, not possible. Not based on what I was told."

* * *

"Mr. Anderson?" Curt looked up as the young, female doctor headed down the fluorescent-lit hallway, and he raised his hand to identify himself while he stood up. "I'm sorry, Mr. Anderson, your wife has had a stroke."

"She's not my wife." He raised his eyebrows in defiance and used a tone of voice that suggested that the doctor was not that bright.

"Okay, but you are the one who called 911 to bring her in, right?" The doctor raised her eyebrows in response.

"We live together," Curt said quickly, "but don't tell anyone that." He winked as if this was a charming little secret between the two of them.

The young doctor took a step back and looked down at the clipboard. "That's okay, sir, we don't need to know the details. Is there someone else, family perhaps, that we should call for her?"

"No, her family doesn't talk to her." He smirked. "I'm all she's got."

"Okay, well, sir, we need to explain what has happened. It appears that Shelly has had a stroke that has caused a condition which is quite rare. It is commonly referred to as pseudo-coma or locked-in syndrome."

Curt took a moment. "What does that mean, exactly? Will she be okay?"

"It is a neurological disorder that causes complete paralysis except for the muscles that control the movement of the eyes. This means that Shelly is conscious and awake, and is cognitively aware, but she will not be able to speak or take care of herself." The doctor looked down at her clipboard to make a few notes.

"Will she be able to hear me and understand what I'm saying?" He seemed to brighten up with the question.

"Absolutely. And we can teach her to communicate through eye movements."

"How does that work?"

"Well, for example, she can look up to indicate yes and down to indicate no."

Curt's eyes widened as the severity of the situation seemed to sink in.

"…and we can get her to indicate the letters in the alphabet so she can spell out words. I'm sorry, Mr. Anderson, are you okay? Do you understand what I'm telling you?" The doctor observed a self-satisfied look about him.

He pulled his eyes back from looking into the distance and returned the doctor's serious tone. "Oh yes, indeed, I understand."

* * *

Curt got up to answer the door. Shelly was watching him as he waded through the mess of the condo. She was disgusted by his standards of cleanliness, which had dropped precipitously now that he was responsible for it. All he did was drink all day while he pretended to care for her. He was taking her painkillers, too. That should be good for his fatty liver disease, something he ignored because "he liked to drink." If it wasn't for the nurse that came in every other day, there would be little food, and she definitely would not be bathed.

He opened the door and was surprised to see Rose on the other side. When he moved in with Shelly, Rose had started studying art at the local guild, the one that Diana had introduced her to. She was doing well as a visiting artist but depended on his handouts to live there. Handouts that actually came from Shelly, since he had control of her checkbook.

"Hello, sweetheart, how are you?" He opened the door wider, welcoming her into the foyer. "Come in, come in."

"I'm fine, Dada." She brushed past him and took off her coat to reveal the contours of her body she worked so hard to obtain.

"What are you doing here? Aren't you supposed to be in class?" As they embraced, she kissed him on the lips and lingered a little longer than one would think appropriate.

"Are you ever coming home, Daddy?"

He hesitated, then broke into a million-dollar smile. "I told you, princess, never say never."

"That's what you said when you left Diana. You're not coming back, are you?" The question hung in the air with no response. "I hate you. And I hate Shelly." She started crying.

"Oh, darling." He hugged her again. "You don't mean that. You love Shelly. She's so good to you. Here, let me get the checkbook. What do you need?"

Curt had gotten Alden to change the rights on the account so Curt could pay the bills and take care of Shelly. Alden wanted nothing to do with it and was happy someone else was taking care of her. He had so much money, what he sent Shelly each month was a drop in the bucket, and it was well worth it. Her children wanted nothing to do with her either. Curt was the only one who would take care of her.

"Oh, just give me a thousand this time." Rose's tears quickly dried up as she bounced over to Shelly's chair.

Shelly was watching the sordid exchange, and her face progressively grew beet red with each moment. Because she couldn't talk, people assumed she was hard of hearing—quite the opposite—Shelly could hear better than ever.

"Hello, Shelly." Rose leaned over, her breasts spilling over, and pecked Shelly on the cheek. "How are you feeling, darling?"

Shelly's eyes narrowed as she looked at Rose, whose turn of mood once she had the check in hand was nauseating. *She is good,* Shelly thought. *Just play the guilt card so the other person thinks it's their idea to give you something. Never ask outright.*

"What did you do to her hair, Da?"

"I didn't do it, the nurse did," he snickered. "Maybe she thought blonds have more fun?"

Rose turned to look at Shelly and scrunched up her nose. "What's the matter, cat got your tongue?" She giggled.

"Rose, that is not nice. You apologize to Shelly." Curt rushed over and tucked Shelly's blanket around her legs. *Have to take care of the gravy train, toot, toot.*

"I'm sorry, Shelly." Rose leaned over and kissed her on the forehead, making sure she pushed her new tits into her face. She supposed she had Shelly to thank for those.

Shelly started blinking frantically.

"Wait, start again sweetheart." Curt reached for the pencil and pad. He didn't want to be blatantly cruel, not when there were other people around.

"Write this down, Rose. Let's see, A, B, C, D, E, F, G (Blink)... G, right?" Shelly blinked once for Yes.

"A, B, C, D, E... E."

"A, B, C, D, E, F, G, H, I, J... Oh, for fuck sake! K, L, M, N, O, P, Q, R, S, T...T"

"GET? Yes?" Blink.

"A, B, C, D, E, F, G, H... okay."

"A, B, C, D, E... E, yes?"

"A, B, C, D, E, F, G, is this another short one?" Blink. "Z, Y, X, W, V, U, T, S, R... R."

"HER?" Blink.

"Another short one?" Blink.

"Z, Y, X, W, V, U, T, S, R, P, O... O."

"Oh my God, Dad, how long does this have to go on? How can you stand this?" Rose stood up. She really couldn't take these two anymore.

"Rose, Shelly can hear you."

"Oh, I don't care. I told you, I hate her, and I hate you!" Rose stuffed the check into her bag and left, slamming the door behind her.

"Rose, darling, wait!" Curt went to follow Rose but thought better of it. He turned around and faced Shelly.

"Now look what you've done." He slapped her on the face with the back of his hand. "You miserable bitch."

Shelly began to cry. She wanted to die. She couldn't move, she couldn't fight back. She couldn't talk, fuck or play tennis. None of the things she liked to do. The only good thing about this was the seemingly unlimited supply of drugs. And she didn't have to go to that awful job wiping butts at the local nursing home to get them.

She didn't know how long she was going to be like this or how long she could even take it. But she was determined to get better; she would fight and beat it. As if her body was listening, Shelly felt her right foot come up in a small kick. *They will pay*, she thought. *They will pay.*

* * *

Shelly sat in the padded chair, stiffly braced as she watched Curt move around the room. She could see him in her line of sight preparing her dinner at the kitchen island. She rolled her eyes. She tried to shout to show her displeasure, but it came out as a slur, "Tomatho thoop an jello agin. Errrrrr," she grunted with anger.

Curt turned away to ignore her and went back to heating the soup. He shouted from the kitchen, "I liked it better when you couldn't talk at all, so shut up, you bitch."

Shelly grunted again. "Nowwww," she gasped. She was sick of sucking on this Ensure; it tasted like shit. She barely ate, but she needed to keep up her strength.

Curt slammed the ladle down and caught the edge of the pot, causing the hot soup to splash over the sides and onto the floor. "Shit!" he said as he stormed across the room to where Shelly was confined. He squatted down to lean on the arms of her chair so he was inches from her face. Piercing blue eyes penetrated hers with intensity as he squinted and sneered, "I'm done. I'm not taking care of you anymore. All the money in the world isn't enough to deal with this for the rest of my life."

"Waaiit," she squealed.

"It's over, and I'm going back to Diana." He cocked his head, glanced up as he stood, and said quietly, "She'll take me back."

Shelly spluttered and choked. She started to panic as she watched him grab his coat and walk out the door without a word. "Wait, don't leave me!" she said as the tears welled up. She realized this was it; he wasn't coming back. She thought about everything she had given up for him—her pampered life, her children who didn't speak to her now, a husband who had once cherished her, and now he had access to her money! He was not going to get away with it.

20

Diana had heard that Shelly had a stroke or something debilitating, and she was now confined to a wheelchair with partial paralysis. Not wanting to be inhumane, she tried to suppress any delight in this, but at times she could not help herself. Perhaps she was not as far along as she had hoped. Her therapist had said that forgiveness would be her last step in the process of healing. That was hard to come to grips with. Perhaps she could forgive herself, maybe him, but never her. She could not let go of all those moments when Shelly had pretended to be such a good friend, all the while collecting information that she would somehow use against her. As trusting as Diana had been, she had never revealed too much, but she was sure Shelly filled in the blanks in her underhanded, manipulative, and calculating manner.

"Well, isn't that somethin' else? I guess you were right."

"About what?" Diana asked.

"About the universe taking care of those two."

"I didn't want this. Curt is dead. There's no coming back from that." Diana held her head in her hands and the tears silently fell. She remembered how she declared that she would never allow him back in her life. Once again, he gave her no choice.

"Are you still in love with him, Kung Fu?"

"No! Certainly not!" She thought a bit longer and remembered what he had meant to her so long ago. "I guess on some level, there is a part of me that will always love him. A part that is long gone."

"Are you sure you didn't do it, Kung Fu? I mean, everything seems to point to you."

Diana lowered her head to cradle it in her hands.

"Diana Wall?" Diana jumped as she heard her name bellowed by the female cop, who clearly was not a happy person.

"Looks like you're up, Kung Fu." Janis threw her body back down to the bed since story time was temporarily over.

"You have a visitor." The cop was coming down the hall, she had hoped, to unlock the cell door, but this time someone was following.

"Abby." Diana sprang from her seat and rushed to the cell door.

"Stand back, ma'am. This is going to be a quick visit."

"Through the bars? Please, this is my daughter."

"Look, this is a courtesy, so you can take it or leave it."

"Mom, it's okay." Tears were streaming down Abby's face. "Are you okay?"

"Yes, yes, I'm fine. It's all a mistake, Abby."

"I know, Mom. I know." She wiped her tears away with the flannel sleeve she had pulled over her hand.

"Why are you here? How did you..."

"They had me in for questioning."

"What, no, that's ridiculous." Diana moved to the bars to get closer to her daughter.

"Ma'am, don't make me tell you again." The cop's formidable figure loomed over her daughter's tiny frame.

"Okay, okay." Diana took a step back physically, but emotionally her arms were wrapped around her daughter in a tight embrace.

"They didn't accuse you, did they?" She had a murderous look in her eye.

"Mom, don't worry. I was away for the weekend with Mike when it happened… and there were lots of witnesses."

"Okay, okay." Diana choked back the tears; she didn't want Abby to see her upset.

"They asked me a lot of questions, but it's fine. Mr. Abbott helped me so I could see you. And don't worry about Nutmeg, either, she's fine."

"Okay, sweetie, I just want to make sure you're okay. I love you, my angel."

"Time to go, miss."

Abby turned to the officer. "Fine." As she exited, she shouted, "We love you, Mom. You're gonna be okay."

Diana turned away from the bars and let the tears fall with no attempt to stop the flow.

* * *

Abbott entered the station house with a clear purpose. He greeted the Desk Sergeant, signed in, and made his way to Tom Kennedy's office. Abbott, and Kennedy had history, and it wasn't always good. Unlike most of the police force in South Benton, Kennedy did not always see eye-to-eye with Abbott and it had come to fisticuffs more than once in the past. To say they had a mutual respect for each other may have been an overstatement, but there was a recognition of the honor by which they served.

"Okay, Kennedy. What do you have?" Abbott handed Detective Kennedy a cup of hot coffee as a subtle bribe.

"Listen, Abbott, I know you're good friends with the captain, but I really can't discuss the case with you. This is an active investigation. You know that." Kennedy took the coffee and shoved his papers inside the folder labeled "Anderson Murder."

"So, I understand you guys found Anderson's body." Abbott continued ignoring the protests of Kennedy.

"Yup." Kennedy moved around his desk as Abbott continued his query.

"Did you find his cell phone?

"Yup."

"Did you get the records?"

"Yup."

"So, you know I can get a copy of those? You might as well save me some trouble and tell me the last calls he made." Abbott shifted in his seat and put his hand to his chin. He eyeballed Kennedy to watch his reaction to the last challenge.

"Okay, look, I will tell you that he called Ms. Wall, that went to voicemail, then sent a text message to her, and then he made another call, but that call never went through before the line went dead." Kennedy slammed the filing cabinet shut as if to end the conversation.

"We also went through his contacts. His daughter, Rose, and another woman named Shelly Reid were listed in Favorites."

"Oh yeah, I know her. She's Anderson's little tart." Abbott did not hold back his disdain for the woman.

"Well, we are trying to get in touch with her as we speak, so if you know anything about her, that could be helpful." Kennedy softened his stance when he thought Abbott might help shed some light to tie this case up.

"Well, what I know is that she is a known home-wrecker, she made a cuckold of her husband, and she's been shacked up with Anderson. Did you check his condo?"

"Yeah, we did go there, but there was no answer. The shades were drawn, so there was nothing to see. We are waiting for a warrant, which we should be getting in a few hours."

"Okay, Kennedy, thanks." He turned to leave. "One more thing, the captain knows that I'm on this case, and I'm looking for evidence that will clear Ms. Wall. I'll let you know if I find anything."

"Thanks, but…"

Abbott cut him off. "My advice. Don't jump to any conclusions based on the word of Walt. I think you'll be sorry if you do that."

"Fair enough." Kennedy sat back and took a sip of his coffee. Not bad, just the way he liked it, dark and sweet.

Abbott knew exactly where he was going to find out what he needed to know. He had a theory, and he was confident it would clear Diana. This was actually going to be easier than he thought, a piece of cake. All the more sweet, if he could get there before Kennedy.

* * *

Robert's first stop was to pay a visit to the nurse who took care of Shelly. South Benton was a small town, and Robert was well-connected and well-liked. He had done quite a few favors over the years for a lot of people in town, and Shelly's nurse happened to be one of them.

Robert stepped onto the porch of the Cape that Trisha had purchased after her divorce. It wasn't much, but she was happy and kept the place neat as a pin tending to her storybook garden. He rang the bell, and her little dog barked in response, with Trisha close behind.

"Hello, Robert, to what do I owe this pleasure?" Trisha's infectious laugh filled the air. She was a middle-aged woman with a big heart, which made her a fantastic nurse, but one that had gotten her in trouble with a man she had met online.

"Hi Trish, how've ya been?"

She opened the screen door with a warm smile. "Come in, sweetie. Can I make you a cup of coffee?"

"That sounds great. Just black, please." Robert sat at the familiar table in the middle of the kitchen surrounded by wallpaper of golden flowers and remnants of the past. Photos of her son hung on the refrigerator, highlighting the glory of his hockey days. Trisha placed the filter in the coffee maker and began measuring the grinds out for two.

"I remember how you like it." She smiled at him as she thought about the hours spent in her kitchen, pouring over financial records to track down the slimeball who tried to rip her off. He would have gotten away with it, too, if it hadn't been for Robert.

"So, Robert, I assume this is not just a courtesy call." She smiled and giggled flirtatiously as she turned to the counter to click on the pot. "Unless, of course, you've changed your mind about me?"

Robert became uncomfortable and wiggled in his seat at the playful advance.

"I'm just teasing, sweetie. Don't get nervous." She laughed. "I'm actually seeing someone, and I'm very happy."

"Oh, that's great. A good guy, I hope."

"So far, so good." She shrugged as her voice lifted in optimism.

"Well, if you ever need me to check him out, you just let me know. I'm always here for you."

"Thanks, but I'm pretty sure this one's a keeper. I checked him out myself, actually. I learned a lot from you." She giggled again. "Okay enough of this chit-chat, let's cut to the chase." The smell of fresh-brewed coffee filled the room.

"Shelly Reid. You take care of her, right?"

"Yes." Her smile quickly turned to a frown. "She's awful, but the money is good."

"What can you tell me about her?"

"Let's see. She has been confined to a wheelchair, so I mostly make sure she gets bathed, fed, and takes all her medications properly. That one likes her pills."

"So, she's on pain medication?"

"Yes, but I'm not so sure she needs it anymore."

"Why do you say that?"

Trisha poured the coffee and brought two cups to the kitchen table. "Well, oddly enough, she seems to be getting better, and some of her movement has been restored. She's been working really hard and doing her exercises. It seems to be paying off."

"So, the guy she lives with, Curt, is he helping her?"

Trisha scoffed, "That guy. Please. What a phony." She shook her head in disgust. "No, he is not helping. If anything, he just makes matters worse."

"What do you mean?"

"Well, he is not very nice to her, and he flirts with me right in front of her. He's a pig."

"That must make her mad as a hatter."

"Oh, yeah. I think that's what spurred her to work so hard. She said she wanted to keep her progress a secret... to surprise him. But I just don't buy it. I think she is fueled by hatred, that one."

Abbott lifted his head from his notes. "Interesting. So, let me get this straight. She'd been getting better but didn't want him to know. Have you seen her get out of the chair?"

"Well, not exactly, but she is regaining movement." Trisha thought for a moment. "Also, not sure if this is important or not, but I have been bathing her for awhile, and I can tell you that she has lost weight and has built up the muscle mass to get out of that chair." She hesitated. "What's going on, Robert?"

"Well, I can't tell you for sure… you don't happen to have the key to her place, do you?"

"I do, but I can't give it to you, sweetie. I could lose my job." She blew the heat off the fresh coffee as she peered over the mug.

"No, but we can go over there together, right?"

"Yeah, sure. I can say I've left something."

"Do you have time now? It's really important, or I wouldn't ask.

"Sure, sweetie, anything for you."

They pulled up to the condo complex that ran along the canal. When it first went up in this part of town, people were a bit worried about its location being a little close to nefarious street activity. But SoBo was one of those beaten-down towns that had benefited from the gentrification of the area, pushing the current residents further away from the center and on to the other side of the tracks. One of the benefits of the location, and the main reason why it received the investment of local developers, was its access to the Sound for boating, but it also benefited from the proximity to the train station and Amtrak that could quickly take you anywhere in the country you wanted to go.

"Hey, Trish, thanks for doing this. It's probably a bit weird for you."

"Look, Robert, it's been weird here for quite a while. These two are the nastiest people I have ever dealt with, so I'm happy to help." Trisha turned the key and nudged the door open with her hip.

The putrid smell permeated their nostrils as soon as they walked in. The place was a mess and had clearly been left in a hurry. They stepped through to the kitchen to be greeted with pots and pans left on the stove and dirty dishes piled in the sink.

The floor was caked over with some red substance that looked like tomato soup.

"Well, I guess the cleaning lady must have called in sick," he chuckled.

Trisha shared in the joke. You could always count on Robert to lighten the mood with his silly comments.

"Robert. Look." Trisha pointed across the room at Shelly's empty chair. "I knew it. That diabolical bitch. Oops, sorry." Trisha was a professional first and would never speak ill of her charges.

"Well, well, well. Seems like the chicken, or should I say, vulture, has flown the coop."

"I cannot believe it. Where did she go?" A look of concern crossed over Trisha's face. "Maybe she fell." They moved into the bedroom, and there was no sign of her. The bed was unmade, the closet door was wide open, and clothes were strewn everywhere.

"Don't touch anything, Trish. Let's get out of here."

Robert pulled out his phone and dialed the police station. He scanned the area for further signs of evidence as he waited for Kennedy to pick up.

"Kennedy here."

"Listen, Kennedy, I want to get something straight here. I don't like you, but I'm about to hand you a huge gift."

"Oh, really." Kennedy signaled to Suarez to get on the line.

"I think I may have solved this case for you. You can thank me later."

"Well, I don't know, Abbott. My advice. Don't jump to any conclusions..."

"Yeah, yeah. Here's the deal." He paused for effect. "So, I just happened to be with one of my clients who nurses Shelly Reid."

"You mean Curt's girlfriend, the one in the chair?"

"Yes. The nurse had left something behind and was nervous about coming over, so she asked me to escort her."

"Very convenient, Abbott."

"Here's the thing... you'll want to sit down for this."

"Yup."

"She's gone."

"Who? The nurse?"

"No, Shelly Reid."

"That's impossible, man. She's an invalid. Are you on something, Abbott?"

"Come over and check it out for yourself. The scene is clean, and the picture is clear."

21

The tears continued to pour out of Diana like Aquarius bestowing water upon the land for all eternity. It was ripping her heart out that Abby had to go through this, creating more drama and worry to fuel her anxiety.

Janis walked over to her and put her hands on her shoulders and gently shook her to bring Diana back into the room.

"Listen, Kung Fu, it's gonna be alright. Like your daughter said."

"But, but…"

"Come here, Kung Fu." Janis took Diana in her arms and held her like a child. "Shh, shh, it's gonna be alright. There, there." She began to pat her back with a tenderness reserved for mothers witnessing the pain of their children.

"Hey, look at me." She gripped Diana by the shoulders. "First of all, your daughter is gorgeous. I guess she takes after her father?"

A small giggle escaped Diana's lips as she quickly wiped the tears away.

"Now, let me ask you? How did you raise your daughter? To be weak and needy?"

"No, definitely not."

"No, she's strong like you. Much stronger than you think."

"I know, she's an incredible girl. The best thing I ever did in my entire life."

"That's right. And we live for them, and our love is stronger than anythin' else."

"Yes, I would die for her."

"You'll be fine, Kung Fu, and so will she."

"Thank you. That means a lot." She looked into Janis' eyes with returned care. "Are you going to be fine?"

"Nothin' can keep me down, Kung Fu. I've been through the worst of it. This is just a little vacation from life, that's all." Janis smiled at her secret pleasure. "So, let's just take a moment and do some of that breathin' you like to do. I think I'm getting the hang of it. I might even start meditatin' with you." Janis' laughter filled the cell and reverberated against the concrete walls to relieve the tension of the moment.

They sat in silence, just appreciating the stillness. A bond had formed between them, and Diana was grateful for the support that Janis had provided. She wasn't sure if she could've kept her sanity without it. Telling her story to Janis removed its power and gave her the perspective she needed to let go and carry on. Whatever the future would hold, she would survive it.

Once again, the sound of her name cut through the silence.

"Diana Wall?"

"Yes."

"You are free to go."

The cop opened up the jail cell, and just like that, she was free. It took a moment for it to sink in. She hesitated, as if this was some trick they were playing on her.

"Get going, Kung Fu." Janis gave her a little nudge towards the door.

As she walked through slowly and turned to go, there was Robert waiting for her. She took one last look at Janis and, with a little wave, said "Bye."

"See ya, Kung Fu." Janis hopped back up on the bed and started humming.

Diana looked into Robert's eyes disbelievingly. "Robert." The sound of his name cut through her hurt and pain.

"Hey, kid."

Now the tears flowed again but this time from the knowledge that someone truly cared about her and would be there for her when she was in trouble. No demands, no expectations of returned favors, no selfish motives. It was a relationship founded on trust, mutual respect, and a sincere desire to be supportive and loving. It was so simple.

"Thank you, Robert. I will never be able to thank you enough."

"I told you, Diana, I wasn't going to leave you in that jail cell." He turned to her and embraced her. He wanted to be there for her, to help her when she admitted she needed it, which wasn't often.

Robert reached into his pocket. "Hey kid, stop crying already." He handed her his clean, crisp white handkerchief. "I'm running out of clean handkerchiefs." Diana giggled at that, wiped her eyes, and blew her nose. "You're gonna be okay, alright?" He took back the used handkerchief and didn't think twice about putting it back in his pocket. He looked deep into her eyes. "You're free, kiddo."

Diana breathed a sigh. "He's really dead, isn't he Robert?"

"Oh yeah, that piece of shit." His body language changed from sympathetic to angry.

Diana winced at the image of Curt's body floating in the water. "Who do you think did this, Robert? Do you have any idea?"

"Yup. And you're not going to believe it." He paused and shook his head for drama, which he often unknowingly did. "It was Shelly."

Diana's eyes grew wide as she screeched, "What! I don't believe it. This can't be right, Robert," she said imploringly, as if he could make it all go away. "I thought she was in a wheelchair?"

"Yeah, that's what everyone thought, so she wasn't a suspect. Once they had the warrant, they caught that bitch on tape they got from the security camera outside Curt's condo complex. Shelly had some stroke, which left her in a chair, but the nurse found it empty and called the police. I guess Shelly's been faking how bad her condition was, probably trying to catch that asshole out on his bullshit."

"I didn't know any of this, Robert. You know I wanted nothing to do with those two. I had some idea what had happened to Shelly, but this is insane."

"Yeah, I know. Anyway, she's the one who pushed him in. They found her footprints along the canal with remnants of tomato soup that came off her shoes. How bizarre is that? It was the same set of prints that were all over the kitchen floor in the condo."

"I cannot believe this, Robert."

"Then Walt ID'd her and said he made a big mistake. He's really sorry, by the way. He feels awful about accusing you. I think he was just caught up in the excitement."

"So, did they get her? Are they bringing her in? Is she here in jail?" With each question, Diana's voice grew louder and more intense.

"Nope, that bitch is gone. They have an APB out on her, but I don't know, Diana, she seems to know what she's doing."

"What do you mean?"

"She was just biding her time, waiting for the right moment. Most of the money was moved out of her bank account, and she has gotten a solid head start on us."

Diana shook her head in sincere disbelief. She knew Shelly was despicable, but she never expected that she could do something like this. It took a second for it to process. Diana had thought those two might turn on each other sooner or later, but now Curt was dead. This was final; she would never see him again. She thought that's what she wanted, but this was forever. *Shelly needed to pay.*

"Honestly, Robert, I never wished him dead. I really felt sorry for him in the end, especially being stuck with that evil woman." She closed her eyes and took a sip of the tea that he had bought for her to soothe her pain.

"Right, I believe you, kid." He smirked to show his doubt, as he himself had been there before and knew exactly how dark your feelings could go at times.

"Robert, I think we need to find her before she does this again." He knew she was referring to the home-wrecking part, not just the murder. How difficult that must be for Diana to process, that this woman could continue to destroy lives for her sick entertainment without repercussion.

He turned to her and cupped her face with his strong hands. "We will, kid, I promise. But for now, let's get you home."

EPILOGUE

After everything Diana had been through, she decided she needed some time to just relax, and, of course, that meant going to her new beach house. Even after all the angst associated with Curt and the resistance to getting a house by the water, it did not destroy her dream, just as he would not destroy her ability or desire to love. She had done the work; she had walked through the fire of pain, and she was happy, from the inside out.

She woke up, opening her eyes to a beautiful morning. She decided to journal her thoughts before heading to the beach.

Lately, I have been getting up very early. This morning I beat the sun. The stars were still sparkling above and started to fade one by one with the morning light. Funny, I always thought that I wanted to live someplace where I could watch the sunset alongside my man. How many attempts to do that with Curt met with resistance! I realize now that the sunrise can be much more spectacular than the sunset. Waking up to that alone is pretty spectacular, too. I can choose how my day will begin. I can take a pulse of my mood and feelings and try to understand them. I can listen, empathize, motivate, inspire, or just be free.

It feels pretty good to be my own best friend. I am not saying that I wouldn't want to wake up with someone else again, not at all. Perhaps someday I will meet that person. But for now, I am content with starting the day on one's own, knowing it does not have to be lonely. It does not have to be sad. As I sit here overlooking the quiet and still marsh, listening to the sounds of the morning, greeted by puffy clouds pink from the sunrise and an elegant crane sauntering by, it is easy to say. Life is beautiful, and I find peace in the knowledge that happiness starts from within. I am proud of myself for not stooping to their level. I have found my faith in the universe to set things straight. I under-stand the strength of the human spirit, and it far surpasses any hurt, damage or destruction that can be done by another. Not to sound too crunchy-granola, and I'm not sure who said it, but it goes something like this: "We are not humans having spiritual experiences, but spir-its having human ones." I like that. So, I guess my advice is, find your spirit. Rise above the pain and let your time here be guided by your true nature. Listen and be guided.

She was anxious to get to the beach, as it was peaceful in the morning and not too hot. She quickly downed some breakfast with a cup of coffee on the deck. Hopping on her bike, she headed down to the refuge for a morning walk and swim, her absolute fa-vorite way to start the day. She loved it here on her little island. It truly was everything she ever dreamed of, so scenic and serene, around every corner was a moment of beauty. This was a place of peace for her and respite from the trials of life. And the people in the community that had befriended her in such a short time rep-resented what she would come to consider her little island family.

As she walked toward the surf to test the temperature of the water, she could see red pieces of something strewn on the beach. Pieces of busted-up balloon? No, they were flower petals creating a trail all along the water's edge. *How mysterious.*

Diana bent down and picked one petal up to study it. It seemed to be from an orchid or some other tropical flower. She wondered, *maybe from a wedding, perhaps it took place out on a boat.* She wasn't sure, but she decided that with their red color, it was a sign of love. A bit sappy perhaps, but she embraced her romantic side, never giving up on the idea of being happy again in a solid, supportive, healthy relationship.

With her white floppy hat secured against the wind, she followed the trail for fun, and a destination of sorts. It seemed to go on for miles, and when she looked up from spotting what she thought was the last petal, she nearly collided into a fisherman, who greeted her with a warm smiling face. Clearly, she had not been paying attention to where she was going and headed straight for his fishing line.

"Oopsie-doo," Diana reacted with an interjection she used with Abby, an annoying habit, according to her daughter.

"Good morning," said the stranger as he cast his line out. He had a distinct twinkle in his eye; he seemed to be tickled by Diana's reaction.

"Good morning," said Diana. "Catch anything?"

"No, not yet," he said with a chuckle, "I think they must be smarter than me."

Diana laughed and glanced down again, somewhat embarrassed by her near collision.

"Are you okay?" he asked with a somewhat concerned look on his face.

"Oh, yes, I'm fine. I was just..."

"Following the red flower petals, I noticed," he said and smiled again.

"I was wondering where they came from."

"Perhaps a wedding, off a boat," the fisherman said. "Where are you from?"

"Oh, the sea." Rolling her eyes, she had no idea why she said that.

"Oh, really? Well maybe my fishing skills are better than I thought."

Diana smiled and started to take him in. He was quite good looking, she thought. Maybe a little scruffy, but he was probably on vacation. His auburn-colored hair was wind-blown, but there was plenty of it, and he had a five o'clock shadow peppered with white stubble. *Kind of sexy. Let's see, no wedding ring, the right age...* He was smiling at Diana, and he had sparkling gray, no green eyes with hints of gold. Tall, too. Was that a tattoo? *Okay, maybe a bit more conversation.*

"Do you fish a lot?" She internally rolled her eyes at herself again. *You need to do better than that, Diana.* She was pretty bad at this, or at least unpracticed.

"No, not at all. I'm just down here by myself to relax for a few days. I'm thinking about buying a place here."

Hmmm, by himself. "You're kidding. I just bought a place here. I really love it."

"Oh, that's a coincidence, or maybe it's just the universe helping me make the decision." He smiled, revealing the slightest dimples under his beard, and started reeling in the line.

Diana couldn't help but notice his strong hands and the muscles of his arms working as he reeled it in... *Very nice.* And he mentioned the universe. That was the first time she had ever heard that from a guy. And a cute one at that.

"Well, that's very nice of the universe, isn't it?" Diana had long ago given thanks to all the gifts the universe could bring when you needed them the most.

"For sure," he said, and gave her a sideways glance with a warm smile.

"Would you like to cast?" He turned his body towards hers and held out the pole as an invitation.

"Sure, thanks. I used to be pretty good at this. But I must confess, I haven't fished for a very long time, let alone surf-casting."

"Well, it's probably like riding a bike." He handed her the rod and explained how to hold the button down to control the line then release it when it felt right. "That's the tricky part."

Diana completely failed at the first attempt, the line taking a 90-degree turn and hooking the nearby cooler instead. She nervously giggled; he patiently unhooked her conquest and took in the reel for her.

"Let's try that again." He handed back the rod and lightly put his left arm around her to help position it correctly. He put his right hand over hers and began moving the rod up and down to give her the right action. He was so close Diana could smell him. Not full of aftershave, he just smelled clean and naturally sweet. Her heart was beating wildly. She almost broke away to try to get some control back, but instead turned her head towards his and looked deep into his eyes. They didn't speak, just looked into each other's eyes for what seemed to be a long time and no time at all.

"Shall we give it another go?"

Diana nodded. "Yes, let's."

THE END

Acknowledgements

I would like to express my heartfelt gratitude for the invaluable feedback from the generous people in my life who patiently read my manuscript with special thanks to Don, Mary, Matt, and Pat.

I would like to thank my instructors and classmates at the Westport Writers Workshop who got me started and the Grub Street Center for Creative Writing who provided the guidance to happily take me to the point of no return.

A special thanks to my developmental editor, Megan Records, who helped me clarify direction when I was stuck and inspired me to revise the story to reach its present state. To the three amazing women at Onion River Press, Rachel Carter, Rachel Fisher, and Riley Earle, I am grateful for your commitment.

Lastly, I thank the readers who will take a chance on this debut novel with special recognition to those who have experienced the pain of betrayal.

Beautiful Jail is the debut novel of **Janet H. Wolfe**. Currently an Associate Professor of Marketing and brand consultant, Ms. Wolfe was compelled to write this novel to champion those who must navigate through the destructive forces of life's betrayals, bringing inspiration to readers as they witness Diana Wall transform from victim to vigilante.